THE LAST FALCON

BOOK 1 OF THE CAEL STONE

— COLLEEN RUTTAN —

First Edition, June 2012

ISBN 978-1477570395

www.colleenruttan.com

To Stan

Map by
Agathe Delange
& Colleen Barnett

CHAPTER 1

'*D*on't let them catch you, Erynn.*"

Erynn had no idea how much time had passed. She sat quietly in the dim light of the cave, her arms folded over her chest and her forehead on her knees; too scared to move in case she made a sound that drew the soldiers. She had climbed up the narrow tunnel as far as she could go, until she was sure they couldn't reach her, but now the rocks pressed in close all around her, their hard coolness making her shiver and their musty dampness filling her lungs until it seemed she couldn't breathe.

She'd heard sounds before nightfall — the footsteps of soldiers searching for her and others arguing somewhere nearby — and a few more when light eventually trickled back up the cave. But then exhaustion had caught up with her and she'd drifted in and out of sleep for what seemed like hours. Something crawling over the back of her head finally woke her and reminded her that she didn't think she could handle another night in the cave. She knew she needed to leave, but still couldn't bring herself to move. It wasn't just the soldiers. She was too afraid of what else might be waiting for her outside.

Then a twig snapped.

"Erynn?" came a man's voice.

Erynn raised her head. At first she thought maybe she was hearing things — her father's voice again — but then she glanced down at the mouth of the cave and saw the shadow of someone standing outside.

"The soldiers are gone," the man said. "It is quite safe to come out."

Erynn remained still, wondering if this was a trick. He didn't sound like one of the men — he actually sounded much older — but they could have heard her father say her name and she wasn't about to be fooled.

"Erynn?" the man repeated a few moments later, this time sounding a little more concerned. "I assure you, I mean you no harm. Just want to help if I can."

Erynn wasn't sure what to do. She still didn't think he sounded like one of the soldiers — in fact, there was something about his voice that almost seemed familiar, like a voice she could trust — but she remained wary. She couldn't let them catch her. Not after what they did. She sat in silence for a while longer, wondering if at some point he would give up and leave, thinking perhaps he'd made an error about someone hiding in the cave. And then something skittered across her foot and she barely stifled a scream. Now she couldn't help it. She had to get out of that cave. She just hoped she was right about what she heard in that voice.

"Who — Who are you?" she called out, her own voice sounding somewhat hollow in the narrow cave.

"Just a friend. Soren, if you would prefer a name. I heard the trouble with the dragon and thought someone might need help. I would have come sooner, but I am not as young as I used to be and needed to wait until the soldiers had gone."

"How do you know my name?"

A hand reached into the cave and set down a thick stack of parchments, all wrapped in an old leather case and bound with a strap.

"I found these in the wagon. I thought they might have been searching for someone, and when I saw this, with the name on it, I took a look myself. I noticed your tracks and they lead me here. You write well, Erynn. Although, I must say if you are still hoping to see elves in Galia, you will probably be disappointed. I have seen more than a few over the years, but they do tend to prefer the warmer climates. You are more likely to see dwarves in these hills, even though we are still some miles from the mountains."

Erynn started down the rocks toward the mouth of the cave, suddenly more annoyed that some stranger had been rifling through her journal than afraid he'd come to harm her. "Are my quill and ink still there?"

"Yes, but those fine-looking horses are gone. They even took the two hitched to the wagon."

Erynn came as close to the cave opening as she dared and snatched up her journal. Then she moved back out of reach in case he tried to grab her. She could see more of his cloak now, and a pair of old and wrinkled hands, but nothing else. She made a quick check of her journal, noticing her name at the top of the first entry, but everything seemed to be in order. "They weren't our horses. They belonged to King Wryden."

"King Wryden? Of Alyria?" The man sounded surprised.

"My father bought them for him in Cold Lake five days ago. For his breeding stock."

"Why would the King of Alyria send someone all the way to Galia to buy horses?"

Erynn remembered asking her father the same question before his last trip to Galia two years ago. Her mother was already starting to show signs of the illness that would eventually take her life and Erynn hadn't wanted him to go. "Because they're the best horses in all of Valentia. And my father has a friend here. He's bought horses from him before."

"Unfortunately, it seems those soldiers must have agreed."

Erynn closed her eyes, remembering the look on their leader's face. The fair-haired man with the limp and the jagged scars — one under his right eye that ran halfway down his cheek and the other on his chin. Her father had pleaded with him to just take the horses and let them be, but the man's eyes were hard and cold. It was when he dismounted and ordered them down from the wagon, slowly drawing his sword as he limped toward them, that her father told her to run. Part of her now wished she had — that she hadn't stopped and turned back.

"Was it just the two of you?" the man asked.

Erynn rubbed a hand across her face, trying to wipe away that last searing image. The one that had haunted her throughout the night: a flash of silver and her father collapsing to the ground — and in the background that horrible scream. "No. My friend's brother came with us. But he's gone. He left us in Cold Lake."

"I see. And do you know where he is now?"

"No. On his way to Ethlon. I don't know."

"Have you traveled with your father before?"

"A few times. But this was the first out of Alyria."

The man was quiet, and then he bent over, bones creaking, and peered inside the cave. He appeared much older than Erynn had imagined from his voice, perhaps in his late sixties, with a dark grey beard and green eyes.

"I am terribly sorry about your father, Erynn," he said.

Erynn felt her throat go tight and she just nodded and looked away.

The old man hesitated. "I wrapped him in one of the blankets from the wagon, but he needs a proper burial. Before the animals come. Do you think you can help me? I would rather not ask, but I doubt I can manage alone. And it would be best if we hurry. In case those soldiers return."

Erynn wasn't sure why they'd bother. It was the horses they wanted and now they had them. But the old man's comment about the animals now had her worried. Going back to that road was the last thing she wanted to do, but she couldn't bear the thought of any animals touching her father. So she clutched the journal to her chest, hoping again that she could trust the old man and wasn't making a mistake, and crawled the rest of the way out of the cave.

It was difficult to stand at first, her entire body stiff and sore, but Soren waited patiently and when she was ready, led her back through the trees. It was earlier than Erynn had expected, and there wasn't a cloud in the sky, but the air was cool.

The walk took longer than she remembered — so much so that she grew amazed she had even found the caves. All she remembered was running through the trees, half-blinded by tears and panic, with an odd buzzing in her ears and the low branches stinging as they slapped her face and snatched at her hair. She scanned the gaps between the trees as they walked, watching for any sign of the soldiers, and even looking up at the sky — half-expecting the dragon to swoop down at them. But all seemed still and quiet.

"Krystalix is gone too," Soren said.

"You saw him?" Erynn asked, not realizing he'd been watching her.

"I did, but only briefly as he flew past."

"Do you live nearby?"

"Not far. I was actually out for a walk when I saw him."

Erynn heard the dragon's scream in her mind again, a sound unlike any she had ever heard before. He had dropped out of the sky like a golden bolt of lightning — at almost the very same instant her father hit the ground — and had snatched one of the soldiers from his saddle and tore him in half right in front of her. Her father used to tell her stories about the dragons — stories that up until yesterday she had always loved — but they were nothing like seeing one for real. "I've never seen him before. Just in some drawings and paintings. A few books."

"Not many do see the dragons these days. Not like they used to. Which is a shame. He tends to stay in Alyria, up in the mountains like most of them do, but I have seen him around here before."

"My father said it was rare for dragons to attack people. Unprovoked, anyway."

"Yes, I would say that is true."

"Then I don't understand why he attacked. Those soldiers weren't bothering him."

"I am sure he had his reasons, difficult as it is to understand them now. Perhaps he was trying to help you."

Erynn wanted to tell him that if the dragon wished to help, he should have arrived a few seconds sooner, but she couldn't bring herself to speak the words. She was finding it hard to keep a handle on herself and was scared of what might happen if she did.

Ahead of her, Soren stopped. They had reached the road.

"How old are you, Erynn?" he asked, his voice quiet.

"Fourteen."

He sighed. "Far too young to have witnessed such violence."

At least a half-dozen men lay dead on the road, their bodies bloodied and ripped apart by the dragon. Among them, looking very much alone, stood her father's wagon, the two old geldings that had pulled it now gone and their clothes and other belongings scattered nearby. Her father still lay in the same spot she saw him collapse, but was now wrapped in a dark blanket. The same dark blanket he had slept under every night of their trip.

Tears rose to Erynn's eyes.

"Can you find a good place while I fetch the spade?" Soren asked. "I noticed one in the wagon."

Erynn nodded, but seconds passed before she finally turned away. She searched along the roadside until she found a suitable spot to bury her father — a fairly open and sunny area between the trees — and when Soren returned they each took turns with the spade. When they were finished, they used the dark blanket to carry her father's body across the road and lower him into the grave. It took several minutes, and was by far the hardest thing Erynn had ever done or — or even imagined she would do — but she knew she had no choice. The alternative was just not something she could bear.

"Rest now, Erynn," the old man said when it was over. "I can finish."

He motioned for the spade, but Erynn shook her head. She wasn't finished yet. She started covering her father's body with dirt, and then she gathered up stones from around the road and arranged them over the grave. When she was satisfied that he was safe from the animals, she went to the wagon to grab her pack and what few things of value were left besides her journal: the quill and ink pot her father had given her years before, some papers on the purchase of the horses, a bit of left-over food, and a couple changes of clothes.

Soren remained seated by the grave the whole time, watching her silently.

"He's not one of them," she said when she finally returned

with her pack and sat down next to him. "The man who killed him."

Soren gazed at the bodies still lying in the road. "You know for sure?"

Erynn nodded. She had checked every one of those bodies while collecting stones and gathering her things. The soldier with the limp and the scars wasn't among them. He had survived.

"Well, I am sure life will catch up with him sooner or later," Soren said. "Always does with men like him."

Erynn wished she could find comfort in that. But she didn't. She wanted her father's killer to pay for what he did, and she wanted him to pay now. Not years from now in some stupid fight or battle somewhere. But he was a nameless soldier in a kingdom with thousands like him and she was just a girl. A servant. Not even from Galia. She would have felt some measure of justice if the dragon had killed him, but he hadn't and now it seemed like she'd never have it.

Soren pulled himself up and brushed the dirt from his cloak. "We should go. If we can make our way through these woods to the Ring Road before dark, there's a chance we can find someone headed to Alyria. Someone who can give you a ride to the castle."

"The castle?" Erynn said, looking up at him.

"You must go see the king, Erynn. Tell him what happened. Those were his horses, after all."

Erynn didn't like the sound of that. King Wryden was bound to be more upset about the loss of his horses than her father. She returned her gaze to the grave. "I think I'd rather stay here. I have nothing to go back there for anyway."

"You have no family left in Alyria?"

Erynn shook her head. "My mother died last summer. She got sick."

"I am sorry to hear that, Erynn. But it is still important you return. What about your friend?"

Erynn looked up again. "My friend?"

"Does she know her brother went to Ethlon?"

For a moment, Erynn was confused, but then she realized she hadn't thought about Adena at all. Her friend was back home in Alyria — all alone now that her parents were gone and completely unaware that Jared had left. Erynn and her father hadn't even known he was leaving until the night before they departed Cold Lake. Jared had come to them late that night, saying he'd heard men down in the bar talking about his father — how he was supposedly living at the castle in Ethlon. Jared was convinced that his mother was there with him and was determined to go find them. Erynn's father had tried talking him out of it, worried that it was too dangerous in Ethlon, and that even though Jared had become quite skilled with a sword, he was still barely seventeen. But Jared wouldn't listen.

Erynn felt an ache inside, wondering what might have happened if he'd stayed. Wondering if it might have made a difference. She hadn't wanted him to leave and had tried to tell him that night. But when it came to Jared — tall Jared with his dark hair and his deep brown eyes — she had always had trouble finding the words. She pushed his face from her mind and reached for her pack. Adena had been her best friend for over five years, even though her father was one of the most senior knights in all of Alyria and Erynn's was merely a servant. She was even there for Erynn when her mother died. She couldn't leave her alone now.

"No, she doesn't know he left," she said, pulling herself to her feet. "I do need to go back."

Soren nodded, and as he turned and headed for the road, Erynn paused to stare one last time at her father's grave. She wondered if she'd ever see it again. If she'd even remember this place. Without thinking, she reached down and picked up a small stone lying near the edge of the grave — smooth and black and almost perfectly oval in shape. She squeezed it tight in her hand for a few moments, then slipped it in her pack and started after the old man.

"How did you end up on this road, by the way?" Soren asked after she caught up to him. "The Ring Road goes through Cold Lake. It would have been the fastest route back to Alyria."

Erynn felt a lump rise in her throat and again found herself unable to speak. She gestured briefly at some treetops down the road. "We were on the Ring Road, but then we saw smoke that way and thought someone might need help. A lot of smoke. That's where we were headed when we ran into those soldiers."

Soren glanced down the road, and a slightly troubled look passed over his face. "Yes, I saw it, too. I was actually headed that way myself when I saw Krystalix. I think it was coming from Berridge, a town just across the border in Brye. Not far from here."

Erynn realized she could still smell the smoke, although it was faint and she couldn't see it anymore. Tears came to her eyes again, but she quickly brushed them away. She was the one who had convinced her father to leave the Ring Road and come this way. She had always had a bit of a sensitive nose for smoke and had often smelled it during their trip a long time before either he or Jared did. But this time the smoke had been almost overpowering, and had brought with it the strangest feeling that someone needed help. A feeling that had nagged at her until finally she couldn't stand it any longer and had pleaded with her father to change direction. To head toward the smoke. He had been worried about the king's horses at first, not wanting to risk putting them in harm's way, but eventually he gave in. It wasn't long after that they ran into the soldiers.

"My birth parents died in a fire in Brye," she said, only just making the connection. "And now I'm orphaned again because of one."

The old man paused to look at her, but then he continued walking, nodding sadly. "Life does work in mysterious ways sometimes."

"Do you think it had something to do with Krystalix? The smoke, I mean? Maybe he attacked someone else?"

"It would be odd behavior for a dragon," Soren said. "But considering what he did to the men who stole your horses …" His voice trailed off and he stopped, his eyes fixed on the ground ahead of him. "And what might this be?"

He bent over to pick something up and when he straightened Erynn noticed a letter tube in his hand. Attached to it was the slightly bloodied leg of a large bird. Another image flashed through her mind, something she hadn't even remembered until now — a falcon with blue-grey wings soaring up into the sky, only to be snapped up by the golden jaws of the dragon. "They had a falcon. One of the soldiers released it after Krystalix attacked, but he ate it."

"Indeed," Soren said, detaching the tube and handing it to her before tossing the leg away. "Strange they would have had a falconer. Might be useful to see what the letter says."

Erynn hesitated, not sure if it was right — or even wise — to read someone else's correspondence — let alone someone so violent — but the old man didn't seem bothered at all and in fact seemed to be waiting for her to read it to him.

"Why do you think it's strange?" she asked, picking off the wax seal.

"Because falconry is still a fairly rare talent. Or, at least, communication-wise, that is. Someone who can make the birds understand where the letter is supposed to go, and get it there quickly. Men — and women — like that can be hard to find, so they are not usually sent out on routine errands or patrols. Too great a chance you might lose one."

"Jared's good at falconry," Erynn said. "He's my friend's brother. The one who went to Ethlon. He wanted to be a falconer, but his father wasn't happy about it. Said he wanted Jared to be a knight like him."

"Yes, it is also not a very appreciated talent. Not until you need to send a letter anyway."

Erynn had removed the seal and now worked at getting the tiny cork out of the tube. "You think those soldiers were up to something?"

"They obviously needed to report back to someone. Most likely someone at the castle here in Galia." A rather ominous tone had crept into his voice.

"Queen Naedra?" Erynn asked.

"Perhaps. And given what trouble she has been up to lately, the contents of that letter might prove useful."

Erynn didn't see how knowing what the Queen of Galia was up to could be of any use to her, but he still seemed to be waiting for her to read him the letter so she pushed that thought aside. She shook the roll of parchment out of the tube and read the few words scratched across it out loud. *"Task accomplished. Did not locate book. Returning to castle. S."*

Soren raised a brow. "Book? I wonder what that means." He appeared to think about this for a few moments, and then motioned to the letter. "What do you suppose we should do with it?"

"Me?" Erynn said. "You found it."

"Seems like it should be yours. Given what happened here, and who it obviously belonged to."

Erynn read the letter again, her gaze lingering on the initial at the bottom — the only clue she now had to the identity of the man who killed her father. "I guess I could give it to King Wryden. When I tell him about the horses. Maybe he could send it to Gareth. That's his son, or the elder one anyway. He's been over in Ridan the last couple of years, helping them in their fight against Galia."

Soren frowned. "I was not aware Alyria had joined the war."

"We haven't," Erynn replied, trying to remember what her father had told her about it. "Or at least not yet. Gareth only went as an advisor or something. That's actually why Jared went to Ethlon. His father was one of the men Gareth took with him, but there were rumors last year that he deserted. His mother left Alyria several months ago and he and my friend haven't heard from her since. They think she went to Ethlon to find him."

"Well, hopefully Gareth finds success in Ridan," Soren said. "And your friend, Jared, in Ethlon, too. It would not be good for Valentia if yet another kingdom fell to Naedra's armies. The west is still relatively safe these days, despite the most unfortunate circumstances you and your father ran into, but if Ridan falls, I fear that will change." He seemed troubled again, but then his face cleared and he turned back to the road. "Enough talk of that now. We need to find that Ring Road and get you back to Alyria."

CHAPTER 2

Erynn moved quickly up the winding tower stairs, her fingers closed tight over the letter tube. Two years had passed since she crawled out of that cave in Galia, but every trip up these stairs was the same — so certain that the cool stone walls were moving in all around her and slowly squeezing the air from her lungs. So certain she could barely breathe. She tried not to think about them, and to just stay focused on what she still needed to do — just as she had tried not to think about them every other time she had to make that long climb up the tallest tower in Caraden Castle — but it was impossible. Within seconds she was back in that cave in the hills, trapped in the musty darkness with the ants and the spiders and terrified of what might be waiting for her outside.

When she reached the top of the tower, she found the falconry quieter than she expected. A dozen short posts stood on the far side of the room, the floor beneath them littered with droppings and enough tiny grey feathers to stuff a small pillow, but instead of a dozen falcons staring back at her, this time there was only one. It was perched by the eastern window, its dark eyes following her the second she entered the room.

"Another letter from the king?" Faris Hatcher asked. The King's Falconer was standing by his desk, a tall, almost gaunt-looking man with long black hair he wore tied back from his face. He glanced at Erynn and the two guards by the stairs before returning his attention to a stack of small letters in his hand.

Erynn walked toward him and held out the tube, well aware that the guards were watching her — just like they always did. "His Grace wants it sent right away."

Faris looked up from his letters somewhat reluctantly, then reached out and plucked the tube from her hand. "Let me guess … to Gareth?"

Erynn simply nodded, amazed he had even bothered to ask. Other than his old friend Lord Brison, Gareth was pretty much the only person with whom King Wryden still corresponded. His younger son, Holden, had gradually taken over his father's letter-writing duties in the past few years, until he now handled virtually everything. Erynn had been helping the king with his letters ever since she returned to Caraden and he had brought both her and Adena to live at the castle — his fingers so stiff with age that he now had trouble holding a quill. She had seemed an unusual choice for such responsibility, especially since she was only fourteen at the time, there were others in Caraden plenty more qualified, and he had also put her to work in the castle kitchen. But she was hardly in a position to refuse.

Faris sat down at his desk, setting the tube in front of him. "This is his third message to Gareth in the last two weeks. His Grace is certainly keeping you busy."

Erynn shrugged. "He's worried the others haven't reached him."

Faris smiled, but didn't seem very pleased. "Well, you can

assure him it's not the falcons. Ours are among the best in western Valentia. And I've been doing this for twenty years now, without a single letter lost." He shifted his attention back to the stack of letters he had been reading when she arrived.

"He's not blaming anyone," Erynn said. "It's just been months since he's heard anything. Even any news of the war." She glanced out one of the windows at the lake and forest west of the castle — both a dizzying distance below thanks to the combined height of the tower and the high outcropping of rock on which Caraden Castle sat — and realized it was later than she'd thought.

"I'm sure there's a reasonable explanation."

Erynn turned back to Faris. "You don't think it's strange?"

"No, I suspect the war is keeping Gareth busy." Faris was still flipping through the stack of letters, appearing to scan each one.

"I think he's worried that Galia has won the war. And that Gareth is dead."

If Faris shared the king's concern, he didn't show it. "If the war was over, we'd have heard. If not from Gareth, then someone else. It would hardly be a secret."

Erynn knew he was right, but still couldn't shake the feeling that something was wrong. Gareth had been in Ridan over four years now, much longer than even he had anticipated, but he had always been regular in his letters and there had been no word now in well over two months. The king was so worried it was affecting his health, and that worried her. Holden didn't seem concerned at all, but it was fairly common knowledge that he and his older brother had never really gotten along so that wasn't totally unexpected.

Erynn walked closer to the desk. She was waiting for Faris to take the tube to the falcon, so he could send the king's letter on its way and she could be on hers, but he was still scanning through that stack of letters and didn't appear to be in a hurry. She could still feel the guards staring at her, but tried her best to ignore them. They had been a fixture there for over six months now, ever since Holden passed his new law banning unauthorized falconry, but for some reason their presence still bothered her.

"Was there something else?" Faris asked, not bothering to look up.

"Something else?" Erynn replied.

"Something more you needed? I do have work to attend to."

His tone reminded Erynn that it wasn't just the guards that bothered her about the falconry lately. Faris had also been acting odd. "His Grace wanted it sent right away."

"Yes, I heard you. And it shall be, Erynn. There is no need to wait."

"He told me not to leave until you'd sent it."

Now Faris looked up. "Why would he ask you to do that?"

Erynn hardly thought it appropriate for him to question the king's orders, but didn't want to argue. She wanted to leave. Mirella was sure to have noticed her absence by now and the headservant never missed a chance to punish her — even when it wasn't her fault. And the last thing Erynn wanted was to be sentenced to the crypt again. Making sure all of the candles in those long and cavernous halls remained lit was her least favorite job in the whole castle. "He's worried about his son. You know how he is. He just wants to know his letter's been sent."

Faris didn't even blink. "I've been his falconer for thirteen years, Erynn. If he had an issue with my work, I'm sure he would have raised it by now."

Erynn caught the bite in his words and wasn't sure why he was getting so upset. She'd seen him send letters before. Not recently, since the king no longer sent very many, but she had. "I'm just following —"

"Aren't you expected in the kitchen? It must be busy this close to meal time and I don't imagine Mirella will be happy if you're late."

Erynn felt the heat rise to her face. "I can't leave. I told you —"

"And I've assured you it will be sent."

Erynn crossed her arms over her chest. "I'm not lying. Why can't you do it now? You have a falcon." She waved a hand at the bird and it immediately rose up on its legs and briefly stretched out and flapped its wings. As if it knew exactly what they were talking about.

"Because I'm the falconer and I'll decide when he leaves. His Grace may have chosen you to write and deliver his letters, Erynn, but he chose me to send them. You've done your job. Now it's time to go."

Erynn was stunned. This time he had the same tone in his voice that she often heard from the other servants around the castle, but it was the first time she'd heard it from him. They didn't understand why the king had chosen her as his scribe and seemed convinced that something else was going on — like maybe she was really his illegitimate daughter and the whole story of her birth parents dying in a fire in Brye was a lie. She heard them whispering about it behind her back all the time, but didn't believe it — because she'd actually gathered up the courage to ask the king one day and he'd said so. Now it just made her mad.

"Shall I tell him you said that?" she asked.

Now the falconer's face grew red. "I have but one falcon, and it just returned from a long flight. It needs to rest before it can go out again. Especially to Ridan."

Erynn blinked. "How long of a rest?"

Faris waved a hand. "A couple of hours. Maybe more."

Erynn gazed over at the falcon, sure she'd never heard of a rest requirement before. "It doesn't look tired."

"And you're not a falconer are you? It's a seven-day flight to Ridan. Well over a thousand miles. If a falcon isn't properly rested, it might not make it there at all. Or in very good time. So I'm sure the king won't mind waiting."

Erynn wasn't a falconer, but she did know a little about falconry and had a feeling he was lying. She wished Jared was around so she could ask him, but no one had seen or heard from him since he had left her and her father in Cold Lake, and she hadn't seen old Sheldon Birch at the market in months. Sheldon had been the King's Falconer before Faris so would definitely know if he was lying. She stared at the falcon, not sure what else she could do but come back later.

"Did it bring any news from Ridan?" she asked, wondering if there was some news she could tell the king, and just interested herself.

"That's not your business."

"But you said it just returned from a long flight. That must mean the east?"

"I have work to do, Erynn."

"Are you expecting any other falcons soon?"

Faris sighed. "Not for a few hours at least."

Erynn suddenly found this odd, and she noticed again how different the room seemed from what she was used to. "Where are the rest of your falcons? You usually have several."

"Out delivering letters. That's what falcons do."

"But if they're out delivering letters, surely that means some have arrived? Haven't any been for the king?"

Faris rubbed at his forehead. "Erynn, I really don't understand the point of all these questions. Aren't you just making yourself more late?"

"But don't you know? Don't you see the letters when they come in?"

Faris slammed a hand down on the desk. "Enough!" He pointed to the stairs. "Leave now or I'll ask one of these gentlemen to escort you."

Both of the guards stepped forward, one actually looking rather pleased at the thought of physically removing her from the falconry.

Erynn reached for the king's letter tube, but Faris blocked her with his arm.

"What are you doing?" he asked.

"I want it back. I'll return later, when the falcon's rested. Or when you have another."

Faris lowered his hand over the tube. "I hardly think it's appropriate for you to be running around the kitchen with the king's letter in your pocket. Besides, it'll get there faster if I just send it when I can."

"But I have to —"

"Leave!" Faris said, pointing with his other hand to the stairs. "Now."

The guards started toward her. Erynn turned to go, unable to believe this was actually happening, but she hadn't gone more than a few steps when she heard someone running up the stairs.

"Faris!" a man's voice cried out. "Faris!"

The falconer rose to his feet, muttering something under his breath, and walked past Erynn to the stairs. Seconds later, his assistant Clay Waverly appeared. The young man's face was red and he seemed winded, as if he'd just run all the way from the main gate.

"Yes, what is it?" Faris snapped.

"They're here," Clay said, gasping for breath. "In the

courtyard."

For a moment, Faris looked speechless. "Now? At the castle?"

Clay nodded. "Do you know what it means? Why they've come?"

Erynn found something in his voice unsettling and suspected the guards had as well because they had also stopped and were now staring at him. She stepped forward. "Who's here? Do we have visitors?"

Clay flinched, not seeing her behind Faris.

The falconer spun around, his eyes flashing, and pointed to the stairs. "Leave!"

The guards started toward her again, but Erynn ducked around them and fled down the stairs. She heard Clay whisper something to Faris, something that sounded like an apology, but didn't hear a response. And didn't care. She'd go find out for herself who had come to the castle and then she'd head to the kitchen. And when the king sent for her later and asked if she'd watched his letter leave — which she knew he would — she'd tell him everything.

She barely noticed the close stone walls on the way down the tower, too preoccupied with thoughts of what she was going to tell the king. When she reached the bottom, she hurried down a long series of corridors and stairs to the main balcony overlooking the courtyard. Two guards were standing outside the king's study across the hall, signaling he was likely still present inside, but they were busy talking to each other and didn't pay her any attention as she ran by.

Three other servants were already out on the balcony, women responsible for cleaning the rooms on the upper floors of the main keep. Their eyes widened when they saw her, and right away they started whispering, but Erynn ignored them and moved past them to the ledge.

The first thing she noticed was the strange silence in the air, followed by the shock and confusion on the faces of those who had gathered all around the inner ward to watch. Alyrian soldiers stood still and expressionless in two long lines three men deep on opposite sides of the courtyard — and what looked like all fifty of Caraden Castle's resident knights in a similar stance around the front stairs. In the two years Erynn had lived at the castle, and even in the previous nine she had lived down in the village, she had never seen such a display of Alyria's military strength. It almost took her breath away.

And then she saw the visitors — and gasped.

Two dozen had arrived in all, their large black horses breathing hard and lathered in sweat. Most still sat in their saddles, but several had dismounted and were now gathering near the stairs. Four wagons stood among them, and at the back, a lone rider holding aloft a staff bearing their banner — the head of a roaring black dragon on a sea of red.

The mark of Galia.

Erynn felt the strength drain from her legs and reached out to steady herself on the ledge. Galians in Alyria? But how? For what seemed a long time she just stood there, unable to move and trying hard to understand what this might mean. And then it hit her: the king's fears had come true. The war in Ridan was over. Gareth was dead.

A numbness came over her and for a brief moment she wasn't sure what to do. Then her gaze passed back over the crowd and she saw a sight that struck her cold.

One of the Galians, a man with light-colored hair, was moving towards the stairs. She could tell right away he was their leader. She could see it in the way he dressed, the way he held his head, the way the other men parted in front of him. But that wasn't what caught her attention. It was the way he walked: with a limp favoring his right leg. And even from the balcony she could make out the scars: the one that ran halfway down his right cheek, and the other on his chin.

He was the man who killed her father.

CHAPTER 3

Erynn remained still, watching as the man who killed her father walked to the foot of the stairs. The man she had thought about every day for the last two years but had never really believed she would see again — even if she had wanted to find him. And especially not here at the castle in Alyria. Part of her wanted to run, to flee before he could look up and see her, but the other part felt no fear.

She caught movement at the top of the stairs and saw Holden Salinger step outside. Even from this distance, the king's younger son looked as polished as he usually did — dressed in his finest clothes with his dark hair freshly clipped and his sword at his side. A taller man with a slightly leaner build and short brown hair stood next to him. Marik Fayne was Holden's closest friend and the man he had officially named Commander of the Alyrian Army less than a year before — having unofficially held the role for another year before that. A man whose name had become well known throughout Alyria in the years since Gareth left and not in a good way. The sort of man people didn't even like to talk about. His promotion had angered the king, who didn't trust Marik and thought him far too volatile for such a command, but like most things over the last few years, he didn't do anything to stop it. He seemed reluctant to quarrel with Holden and to think Gareth would straighten everything out when he came home. But as the years passed, it started to become less and less certain when that might be.

Holden smiled as he gazed down at the Galian soldiers, looking oddly relaxed given their history, but Marik stood straight and tall, his eyes scanning every inch of the courtyard, and taking in not only the visitors but also the long rows of Alyrian knights and soldiers and everyone else who had gathered around the inner ward to watch. When Holden proceeded down the stairs to greet her father's killer, Marik followed, but other than a short nod to the Galian, he didn't appear to say much.

Erynn looked over at the balcony outside the king's study, half-expecting to see him there, his face pale. But all she saw was a section of deep blue drape, pulled out of the open doors by the wind. Had anyone even told him? It was clear the Galians were expected. She didn't need to see the large turn-out of the army, or hear Faris and Clay talking about them in the falconry to know that. There were only two bridges across the Delorin River — the river that marked the boundary between Alyria and her closest neighbor, Brye, to the east. One was at North Falls, the other at South Crossing, and falconers were posted at each. Falconers that would have sent word to the castle the second the Galians crossed. But she knew the king wasn't aware they were coming. If he was, he would have mentioned it in his letter to Gareth.

The king's guards appeared at the ledge next to her, obviously abandoning their post for a better look at the scene below. Wondering if she might have a chance to catch the king alone — and enough time to tell him who was here — Erynn left the balcony and went across the hall to the study doors. She didn't bother to knock, just opened the door and slipped inside.

King Wryden was seated at his large oak desk in front of the fireplace, the same place she had left him not that long ago. The sounds of men and horses drifted up from the courtyard, but he didn't appear to have noticed anything unusual. He sat slightly hunched in his high-backed chair, his eyes focused on a letter in his hand; the other hand absent-mindedly stroking his thin grey beard. What looked like a dozen more letters lay on the desk in front of him, on top of an old map of Valentia. A map that Erynn knew was one of his most prized possessions and which she often caught him gazing at these days — as if the mere sight of Ridan somehow made him feel closer to his son even though they were so far apart. A map she herself could easily sit and stare at for hours if only she was given the chance.

As Erynn crossed the room, her eyes were drawn to a large painting above the mantle. The dragon Krystalix seemed frozen in time, his golden body surrounded by flames and his jaws wide in a furious attack. Brought before the king the day she returned to Caraden, she hadn't been able to take her eyes off it. The king told her that few had ever seen a dragon, let alone witnessed an attack — and survived — and that she was probably the only one still alive in Alyria who had. Word of her experience had spread throughout the kingdom and even after two years people still whispered about it. But she knew all of that had changed now. Her father's killer had also seen the golden dragon attack — and survived.

"Erynn?" the king said, looking up as she reached the desk. "I didn't hear a knock."

"Your Grace, something's happened," Erynn said. "I came to —"

"Did you watch Faris send the letter?"

Erynn hesitated, distracted by the concern in his eyes. Minutes ago she had been eager to tell him about her trouble with Faris in the falconry. Now it no longer seemed to matter. Gareth was dead. He had to be. Why else were the Galians here? And she didn't have time to explain anyway. "Yes, Your Grace."

The king seemed relieved, but then he noticed her continued distress and sat forward, lowering the letter to the desk. "What is it? Is there news from the east? From Gareth?"

"Your Grace, there are Galian soldiers in the courtyard."

He recoiled slightly. "Did you say Galian?"

"Yes, Your Grace." Erynn pointed to the balcony. "At least two dozen. With wagons. They just arrived."

At first he just stared at her. Then he was up and heading for the balcony, faster than she'd ever seen him move before. She followed him outside.

He gasped as he reached the ledge and saw the sight below. "No, this can't be!"

By now, all of the Galians had dismounted and Alyrian stablehands were running through the crowd, tending to the horses and leading them off to the stables behind the main keep. A handful of soldiers stood by the stairs, but Holden, Marik and her father's killer were gone.

Erynn was gripped by a sudden panic, wondering if Holden would ask her father's killer to wait in the throne room, or bring him up to the study to meet the king. She trembled at the thought of coming face-to-face with him again, but forced herself to remain calm. "I saw Prince Holden greet their leader, Your Grace. They must have gone inside."

The king's jaw tightened. "Holden would have known they were coming. Obviously he chose not to tell me."

"Your Grace … their leader's the man who killed my

father."

The king turned, looking far more unsettled by this news than she had expected. "You're sure it's him?"

"Yes, Your Grace. He's dressed different. Nicer. But it's him. I know it's him."

The king grabbed her arm. Not hard, but enough to startle her. "Did he see you?"

"No, Your Grace. I was on the balcony." She motioned to the main balcony over the courtyard, noticing the king's two guards quickly slipping back inside, and he blinked briefly at the three servant women still standing there before releasing her arm and returning his attention to the Galians.

Erynn waited for him to say something. Waited for him to tell her what he was going to do. But the seconds passed and finally she couldn't wait any longer. "Will you arrest him, Your Grace? Make him pay for what he did?"

He remained still, her questions almost seeming to hang in the warm summer air between them, and when he finally turned she saw fear and indecision in his eyes and something else she couldn't identify but which looked a lot like guilt. He seemed about to speak, but then he clenched his jaw and started for the door. "Come, Erynn. First we must send word of this to Gareth."

Erynn simply stood there. Stunned. He wanted to write Gareth? Now?

"Quickly, Erynn," the king called from the doorway.

Erynn felt her throat go tight, unable to believe he hadn't answered and not sure what to do. But then she knew she had no choice. She had to obey. So she followed him inside and just hoped he'd do something once the letter was written.

He motioned to the desk, but seemed to avoid her eyes. "Fetch some parchment."

Erynn sat down in his chair, where he usually allowed her

to sit while he dictated his letters, and reached into the top drawer for the quill and ink pot, as well as a piece of blank letter parchment. She tried to stay focused on what she was doing, so she could follow his instructions about what to write, but she still felt distracted and stung. Surely he would do something?

"We have little time, so I will trust you to choose the words," the king said, starting to pace back and forth in front of the fireplace. "Just tell him Galian soldiers are here and that he must start home immediately. Tell him I am no longer asking him as a father. This is now an order from his king."

Erynn pushed the map and old letters aside to make room to write, but still wasn't seeing the point. "But, Your Grace. Surely, their arrival ... I mean ... you think he's still alive?"

The king paused his pacing. "I doubt Naedra would send so few men if the war was indeed over. And until I know for sure that it is, and that my son is dead, I will hold out hope that he is not. But if he is alive, I need him to know the Galians are here. I need him to come home. You must help me, Erynn. Help me get him this message."

"Yes, Your Grace," Erynn said. She turned back to the parchment, dipped the quill in the ink, and started to write. "Should I tell him who their leader is?"

The king was pacing again. "Just tell him the Galians are here. And that his king orders him home."

Erynn had barely finished her first sentence when there was a sharp knock at the door. She jumped — her heart in her throat — and behind her the king stopped and turned to the door. But before he could say a word, it opened and Holden walked in. Alone.

Erynn couldn't move. Was her father's killer out in the hall? Waiting a call in to meet the king? She stared at Holden, but his dark eyes were on his father as he crossed the room, one hand resting lightly on the hilt of his sword. Then they shifted to her, and down to the quill in her hand. A muscle around his left eye twitched, and he smiled.

Erynn went cold. Holden had never smiled at her before. Not once in the two years she'd lived at the castle. He barely even knew she existed. She started to rise, assuming he'd want to speak to his father in private, but the king placed a firm hand on her shoulder.

"Finish the letter," he whispered. "And you will remain quiet, Erynn."

Erynn heard the warning and sat back down. "Yes, Your Grace."

Holden stopped a few feet from the desk. "Another letter to Gareth, father?"

The king walked around the desk and past his son to the window. "I see we have visitors. Why was I not informed the second they crossed the bridge?"

Erynn kept her eyes on the letter, but she could feel Holden watching her. Then he turned to face his father and walked slowly back across the room towards him.

"You've not seemed well lately," he said. "I didn't see the need to bother you until they arrived."

"These are Galians, Holden! You should have told me at once. Not waited until after you had welcomed them inside the castle walls."

"Lord Caden doesn't bring tidings of war. He's simply come for a short visit."

Erynn raised her head. Her father's killer was a lord?

The king seemed almost as surprised as she was. "Lord Caden?"

Holden smiled. "Lord Silas Caden. The Dragonslayer himself."

The king's mouth dropped open. "The knight who slew

Melaryx? He commands these men?"

"Yes, I thought you might like to meet him. Given your interest in the dragons."

Erynn just about dropped her quill. Her father had told her about the knight who had battled and killed the green dragon Melaryx and delivered her two eggs to Queen Naedra, but she had never heard his name. Naedra had raised those dragons herself and now they fought alongside her armies in Ridan. Gareth had written of them several times in his letters. But that was eight or more years before her father was killed. How could a man do something so brave and end up killing her father some years later over a bunch of broodmares?

"And what of the war?" the king asked. "Naedra has no need of such a man in Ridan?"

"That's why it's a short visit," Holden replied. "Just a couple of days."

"Long way to come for a couple of days. Barely gives them time to rest their horses."

Holden shrugged. "They seemed to think it was important."

"Do they bring word of your brother? Naedra must know he is in Ridan."

"I did not feel it wise to ask," Holden replied, a noticeable coolness slipping into his voice. "But I do suspect that's why they're here. I think Naedra would like to make peace with us. We are their neighbors after all."

The king snorted. "Do not be a fool, Holden. Naedra has no interest in peace. Just ask the people of Ethlon. Or Tallon. She will come west for the rest of us if she gets what she wants in Ridan. Mark my words. Gareth saw it. That is why he went there. To stop her."

Erynn was having trouble staying focused on the letter. The king was obviously not buying Holden's story and neither was she. He was lying. She could feel it. Suddenly he turned and looked at her again — and then down at the half-written letter in front of her.

"You're writing to tell him they're here, aren't you?" he asked.

Erynn flushed and returned her attention to the letter. She started another word, realized the tip of the quill was dry and dipped it back in the ink.

The king was silent for several long moments. Then he cleared his throat. "My letters are not your business."

Erynn paused, certain she'd heard a trace of fear in his voice. Fear and something else. Suspicion? But why would it be a secret who he was writing to?

"You're right, of course," Holden said, and then he laughed. "In fact, maybe that's why the Galians have come. Maybe Naedra wants you to write to Gareth and tell him the news. To get him to leave Ridan. After all, he was the one who talked Parigon into joining the war."

The king was quiet. Erynn risked another peek and saw he was staring at his son, his eyes full of disbelief, anger, and suspicion. But Holden didn't even look fazed.

"And speaking of letters," he continued. "I've written your lords of Alyria, requesting they attend a special banquet in honor of this visit. Two nights from now. I do hope I can count on your attendance?"

The king slammed a fist down on the window ledge, his face red. "I do not wish to honor Galia with a banquet! How dare you do this to me, Holden? Am I not still the king in Alyria?"

"Father, if we don't show Lord Caden our hospitality, he may decide we're unwilling to be friends. Do you really want him taking that message home? You know we cannot count on Brye should Naedra grow weary of Gareth's interference in

Ridan and choose to march against us."

The king looked like he might explode again, but then he turned away and his shoulders dropped. "How I wish your brother was here. I know he would not have disappointed me like this."

Holden stiffened. Erynn could see the tension in his jaw and the way his hand now clenched the hilt of his sword, but for what seemed a very long time he didn't say a word. She sat still, quill poised over the parchment, afraid to make a sound.

"Well, he isn't here, father," Holden said finally. "And I will not keep our guests waiting. Will you come greet Lord Caden, or shall I tell him you're not well? I can handle our relations with Galia if you'd prefer."

The king sighed and slowly ran a hand over his face. "Tell him I will be down shortly."

Erynn was wondering what the king planned to say to her father's killer — and if there was still a chance he might arrest him — when she felt Holden watching her again. Her eyes shifted and met his and it was in that moment she knew the truth: there was nothing the king could do about Lord Caden. Even if he wanted to arrest him for the theft of his horses and the murder of her father, Holden would never allow it. The King of Alyria was powerless.

She looked back down at the letter. Tears came to her eyes and a familiar ache rose up in her chest, but she pushed them away. Seconds later, Holden was gone. She finished the last few words of the letter and held it out to the king as he walked back to the desk, but he waved it off and continued past her to the mantle.

"I trust the letter says what it needs to. Prepare it for me to seal."

"Yes, Your Grace."

Erynn reached into the drawer for an empty letter tube,

but her eyes caught sight of a large key sticking out from beneath a pile of Gareth's old letters and she paused. She had asked the king about it once, intrigued by the elaborately carved design of the bow, but he hadn't really given her an answer. And then, a few months later, she was looking through one of his old books on the history of Alyria — books he had occasionally allowed her read when she wasn't busy in the kitchen or helping him with a letter — and she'd come across a drawing of it. According to the book, it was the key to a tunnel beneath the castle. A tunnel built as an escape route for the Royal Family during times of siege. She had heard rumors when she was young of a secret entrance to the castle, but never anything more than that, and when she saw the drawing she realized that must be it. She was so worried afterward that the king would find out she'd learned the castle's secret and never let her read his books again that she hadn't even told Adena. Now she wondered if the sudden arrival of the Galians meant the king might one day need to use that tunnel. "Do you think the Galians mean to invade, Your Grace?"

The king had fetched another key — this one much smaller — from a red vase on the mantle and was now walking toward a large cabinet on the back wall. "No. Or at least not yet. Naedra has invested far too much effort in conquering Ridan to split her forces now."

"Then why are they here? It can't just be for a friendly visit?"

The king unlocked the cabinet and opened the doors. A dozen or more finely decorated jewelry cases, all of varying sizes and shapes, sat in neat stacks on the lower two shelves. A large and rather old-looking book occupied half of the top shelf, with the usual storage place for the king's prized map sitting bare next to it. "Is the letter ready for me to seal?"

Erynn grabbed a letter tube and shut the drawer. "Almost, Your Grace." She started to roll the letter up, but then she paused. The king had removed his crown from one of the jewelry cases and was holding it in his hands. Staring at it. Without giving it much thought, Erynn reached for the quill, dipped it in the ink, and quickly added five more words to the bottom of the letter.

Silas Caden killed Davy Taylor.

She fanned the ink to help it dry, and had the letter rolled up and in the tube by the time the king returned to the desk, crown on his head. She stuffed the end with a wooden plug and watched as he sealed it with hot wax from a candle on the mantle.

"Make sure Faris sends it right away," he said as he handed it back. "And you are not to leave the falconry until it is sent. Is that understood?"

"Yes, Your Grace," Erynn said. She wondered if Faris had sent the other letter yet, or if it was still sitting on his desk. At least now she knew why he only had one falcon: the others were probably out delivering banquet invitations. And he had likely made up the excuse about the falcon needing to rest because he needed to keep one around in case of last minute requests. He just couldn't tell her that because the banquet was still a secret. She knew one thing for sure: she didn't care what he threatened this time. She wasn't leaving the falconry until this letter was out the window and headed east.

The king started for the door.

Erynn put the quill and ink away and ran after him. "Your Grace? What about Lord Caden?" She already knew the question was pointless — she had seen that much in Holden's eyes — but she knew she had to ask again. She needed to be sure.

The king paused, but didn't turn around. "There is nothing

to be done, Erynn. He is a lord of Galia now. We would have Naedra and the rest of them here on our doorstep if we did anything. I think you know that."

"But he killed my father. He can't just get away with that."

The king turned and looked at her sharply — sharp enough to bite back the tears that were already threatening to surface again. "I want you to stay away from him, Erynn. If he recognized you it might be dangerous. And say nothing of what he did, either. I doubt Holden would take kindly to you spreading unpleasant rumors about his guest, especially with this banquet coming up, and there is no telling what he might do. Is that clear?"

Erynn couldn't believe he actually wanted her to keep it a secret. After what this man did? After her father had died during a special trip to Galia for him? She wanted to refuse, to tell him she'd do no such thing, and that she'd find some way to get justice with or without his help, but he was the king and she knew there was only one thing she could say. She lowered her eyes to the floor.

"Yes, Your Grace."

CHAPTER 4

Erynn found the falconry much the same as she left it. The same lone falcon was perched on the same post by the window. The same two guards were standing by the stairs. Clay was on his knees on the far side of the room, scrubbing the droppings and feathers from the floor. The only difference was Faris was gone.

"Where's Faris?" Erynn asked, trying hard not to scream. Nothing seemed to be going right for her today and here was another delay. Mirella would give her the crypt for sure.

Clay put down his rag and rose to his feet, looking almost uneasy to see her again. "Another letter?"

"Yes, and it's urgent."

"He went down to the throne room to see the Galians, but I can give it to him when he comes back." He walked toward her and held out a hand.

Erynn tightened her grip on the tube, not about to give the letter to anyone but Faris — and even then not until she absolutely had to. "I have to watch it leave."

An annoyed look crossed Clay's face and he dropped his hand. "Then you'll have to come back later when Faris is here." He turned and went back to his work, lowering himself down to the floor and picking up his rag.

"Do you know if he'll be back soon?"

"He didn't say."

Erynn rubbed her free hand through her hair. She'd have to go find Faris and tell him to come back. She didn't have any other choice. If she came back later, he might still be gone and she needed to get this letter sent. The only problem was not getting caught. She had just promised the king she'd stay away from Lord Caden and they'd both be down in the throne room. And Mirella was sure to be lurking about, too. Not being hard at work in the kitchen was one thing — getting caught spectating in the throne room quite another.

She turned for the stairs, deciding she had to take that risk, but then her eyes passed over the falconer's desk and she paused. The letters Faris had been reading earlier were still there, stacked in a neat pile in the center of the desk, but the letter tube she had delivered was gone. "Where's the king's letter?"

"What letter?" Clay asked, still scrubbing the floor.

"The one I delivered earlier."

For a moment, Clay was silent. "Must have taken it with him."

Erynn frowned. "Why would he do that?"

"You'll have to ask him."

Erynn had the distinct feeling Clay wanted her to leave. She could hear it in his voice, and it reminded her of Faris and just how much the falconry had changed in the last few months. Ever since Holden passed that new falconry law and those guards arrived.

One of the guards shifted his feet and crossed his arms over his chest. Erynn wasn't sure why, but she suddenly feared he might try to take the letter and quickly fled the tower.

She reached the main floor a few minutes later, and after pausing at the foot of the rear stairs outside the kitchen to watch for any sign of Mirella, she continued down the hall toward the front of the keep. Holden had clearly given little notice that the Galians were coming and the kitchen and rear hallways by the pantry and storage rooms were busier than she'd ever seen them before. Some of the other servants noticed her as she passed by and cast her rather nasty looks — obviously wondering why she wasn't busy working like the rest of them — but she ignored them. She'd be back at work soon enough. Right now she had something more important to take care of.

Erynn slipped in the back entrance to the throne room and made her way past several of the army's more senior soldiers who had gathered along the side wall. She had never seen the room so full. The king sat on his throne up on the dais, looking rather pale; the chair next to him empty. Gareth's young wife, Lianne, stood to his right, dressed in a deep blue gown lined with gold cord and her long blonde hair pinned back from a face that looked almost as pale. Holden was at the foot of the dais, facing the Galians, Marik a few feet to his left, and on each side of the room, flanking the visitors, was a long row of Alyrian knights.

The king was saying something, but Erynn was too busy scanning the room for Mirella and her father's killer to hear his words. She couldn't see the Galians very well due to all the soldiers in front of her and by the time she returned her attention to the king, he was on his feet and making his way toward the back entrance — Lianne following a short distance behind. As the men stepped back to let them both pass, Erynn slipped further away along the wall, grateful she hadn't arrived a minute later. When he was gone, the men relaxed and some stepped forward to talk to the Galians.

And that was when she saw him.

Her father's killer stood a few feet in front of his men, smiling as Holden walked toward him.

Erynn knew she needed to find Faris and get to the kitchen, but she couldn't take her eyes off him. His hair was a little longer and his face a little fuller, but other than that he seemed the same as she remembered. Tears rose to her eyes as her mind flashed back to that lonely road in Galia, and how she had stood there, helpless, as her father collapsed to the ground in front of him. Part of her wanted to push her way through the crowd right now to confront him, not caring one bit about the king's orders — or Holden — but the other was too scared to move.

Then she noticed an odd sound, sort of like rushing water. At first it was faint and she ignored it, but soon it grew louder. She glanced around, but couldn't identify a source of the noise and no one else even seemed to have heard it. Then a dull ache broke out across her brow and she felt an almost overwhelming urge to flee. And not just the castle — Alyria.

"Quinn," came a voice nearby. "Thought you would have been here for the king's welcome."

Erynn recognized the speaker as one of Marik's more senior soldiers, although she didn't know his name. Another man was moving towards him through the crowd from the direction of the main doors — a man dressed all in black, with dark stringy hair flecked with grey and several days growth of beard. He had a slight scowl on his face, like he didn't want to be there at all, and although a few of the other men nodded at him as he passed by, he didn't pay them much attention. Erynn did know his name: Quinn Dunigan — once a fairly high-ranking soldier in the Alyrian Army and now a hired-sword. She'd heard rumors that he and Gareth had once been friends, but that he'd betrayed him. She also knew the king didn't trust him, and would be furious to learn he was even inside the keep.

"Sorry I missed it," Quinn said, not looking particularly sorry at all. He stopped a few feet in front of Erynn, not appearing to notice her, and turned toward the Galians, his eyes slowly scanning the crowd.

"Well, you didn't miss much. Word is he didn't have much time to prepare."

Quinn made a small snorting sound, which Erynn barely heard over the rushing in her ears. "How does one prepare for Galians?"

The soldier smiled and gave Quinn a glance over. "Where'd Marik send you this time? You look like you've been on the road for days."

"Farglen."

The soldier laughed. "Let me guess. He's got you looking for thieves again? I heard he's had reports out that way. Not exactly the kind of excitement you're used to?"

Quinn didn't take his eyes off the crowd. "You haven't seen Marik when we catch them."

The soldier smiled again, but then he returned his attention to the Galians and his face grew serious. "Any idea what's going on?"

"Marik only tells me what he needs me to know."

"They say their leader's the one that killed Melaryx. That's where he got the scars — and the limp."

"Never a good idea to go messing with dragons."

"Think Gareth will come home when he hears of this?"

Quinn was quiet a moment, but his jaw had tightened. "The man will if he's smart."

"What will you do if he does?"

Quinn turned to the soldier, his eyes hard, but before he

could respond he noticed Erynn standing behind them. He knew who she was and who she reported to — like most of the people around Caraden thanks to all the whisperings — and his eyes narrowed, clearly not pleased that she'd been listening.

Erynn looked away and continued on down the length of the room, the ache across her brow pounding now and the rushing sound loud in her ears. All she wanted to do was find Faris and leave. To get out of that room and away from Lord Caden. She scanned the crowd, standing up on her toes to peer over the men in front of her, and finally she saw the falconer, standing alone near the main doors. She started toward him, but hadn't gone more than a few feet when Marik suddenly appeared next to him and leaned in close to say something. Faris seemed uneasy at first and cast quick glances around the room, but then he reached into his pocket and pulled something out — something small — and quickly handed it to him.

Erynn's breath caught. She was too far away and the object far too small to know for sure what it was, but there was no doubt in her mind that it was a letter tube. And not just any letter tube — the same one she had delivered to the falconry earlier. The rushing in her ears grew louder and the ache across her brow stronger, but she ignored them. Marik was saying something to Faris, his eyes fixed on the falconer. Faris shook his head, but then finally he nodded and Marik turned and walked away.

A murmur rose on the far side of the room, near the tall windows overlooking the courtyard. Everyone turned that way, talking rather excitedly, but Erynn barely noticed. She was too busy watching Marik move through the crowd, craning her neck to see over the men in front of her again. He paused a couple of times to talk to someone, and then continued on. Finally he came to a stop next to Holden. He leaned close to speak to the king's son and as he did he casually handed him something. Holden didn't even look at it, just slipped the object in his pocket.

Everyone was leaving the room now, brushing past her toward the main doors, but Erynn paid them no attention. A rage was rising up inside her, fueled by the pounding in her head. Faris had given Marik the king's letter. The one to Gareth. And now Holden had it. She was sure of it. But why? It didn't make any sense. There was nothing secret in the letter. The king was simply asking his son to come home. Unless Holden thought it contained something else? And then another thought occurred to her — did this have something to do with why Faris and Clay had been acting so unusual lately? Was Holden reading all of his father's letters? Not just this one?

Erynn whirled around, looking for Faris, and saw him disappearing through the main doors. She started after him, but then caught herself. The Galians were leaving the room with everyone else, heading that way, and Lord Caden and Holden were slowly moving with them. She turned to go out the back door instead, planning to catch up with Faris by the stairs — but then she froze.

Mirella was standing in front of her, hands on her hips.

"What are you doing in here?" the headservant demanded. She was dressed in her usual black robes, her steel colored hair pulled back in a tight bun. "You are supposed to be in the kitchen. Working."

Erynn swallowed. "I – I was looking for Faris." She pointed towards the main doors, but the falconer was gone. "The king wants a letter sent right away."

"Did you deliver it to the falconry?"

Erynn hesitated, afraid the headservant might take the

letter if she told her she still had it. She squeezed her hand tight over the tube and pulled it behind her. "Yes, but I just wanted —"

"Then I'm sure Faris will take care of it when he returns." Mirella glanced over at a handful of men still standing near the foot of the dais — men responsible for the care of the castle and certain affairs of the kingdom and which she herself reported to. "I have something to attend to, but I expect to see you in the kitchen when I return. Is that understood?"

"Yes, ma'am," Erynn said.

The headservant glared at her for a few seconds longer, then she stepped aside and waited for her to pass.

Erynn didn't say a word, just lowered her head and left the room. She knew she was in trouble — even more so than before — but right now all she could think about was Faris. She started for the main staircase to the upper floors, searching for him. People bumped into her as they headed for the front doors, appearing in some rush to leave, but she ignored them. Finally she spotted the falconer, one of the only people not interested in leaving, and ran after him.

She caught up to him by the stairs, but he didn't turn around until she had called his name twice.

"Erynn?" he said, looking rather surprised to see her. "Shouldn't you be in the kitchen?"

Erynn's heart was pounding. "Where's the letter?"

"The letter?"

"The king's letter to Gareth. The one I delivered to you earlier."

The falconer glanced around at the people heading for the doors. Then he turned and continued toward the stairs. "I have work to do, Erynn. If you'll excuse —"

"I was just up there," Erynn said, following him. "I know it's not there."

"Aren't you needed in the kitchen? There must be a lot to do now that we have guests."

"You gave it to Marik, didn't you? I saw you."

Faris paused, but then continued on, starting up the stairs. "I don't know what you're talking about, Erynn."

"I'll tell the king."

Faris turned and came back down the stairs so fast that Erynn took a step back. He grabbed her arm and pulled her close, his mouth tight. "If you care one bit about the king, you won't say a word to him or anyone else about what you saw."

"Why not?" Erynn said, wrenching her arm away. His words had shaken her, but she was trying hard not to let him see it. "He has the right to know his letters are being read."

"Because I don't think Holden will tolerate him interfering with his plans."

Erynn stared at him. "What plans?"

"I don't know, but it probably has something to do with this." Faris waved a hand toward the throne room and the Galian soldiers still making their way to the front doors.

"Holden says they've just come for a visit."

"Galians don't come for visits, Erynn. They're here for something."

"What?"

For a moment she didn't think Faris was going to say another word. Then he exhaled. "I don't know. But whatever it is, it's important. Important to Holden."

"But he's the king. If I tell him, maybe he can —"

"He can do nothing, Erynn. Not anymore. And I think you're smart enough to see that. Most of the men are loyal to Marik now and those that aren't are too afraid to speak against him. Holden leaves his father alone because the king lets him do what he wants, but I worry what might happen if that changed."

Erynn swallowed, realizing what he was saying. "You don't think he'd hurt him?" But almost as soon as she said it, she could see the answer in his eyes. Faris was worried about the king.

"I really don't know what Holden would do."

Erynn didn't know what to say. A minute ago she was furious with Faris and now she didn't know what to think. Finally she shook her head. "Then someone has to do something."

"There's only one person who could and he's a very long way from here."

Erynn's breath caught, suddenly realizing the full extent of what was very likely going on. "Holden's keeping letters from his father, isn't he? Not just reading those he sends out. That's why the king hasn't heard from Gareth in months. Gareth has written."

Faris straightened, not looking comfortable at all. "I think you've asked enough questions. Marik tells me you've another letter?"

Erynn took a step back, pulling her hand behind her. "The king wants it sent right away. That's why I was looking for you."

Faris held out his hand. "And now you found me."

Erynn didn't move. "Are you going to send it or give it to Marik?"

"I don't have a choice, Erynn. You've seen the guards."

Erynn took another step back. "But we need to tell Gareth the Galians are here. You have to help me."

Faris shook his head, looking frustrated now. "Impossible. The falcons are guarded day and night. It's better you give me the letter."

"Why?"

"Because Marik wants it, that's why. You really want him

paying you a visit in the middle of the night?"

Erynn shuddered at the thought, but still couldn't bring herself to give Faris the letter. She didn't understand why Holden was so threatened by Gareth finding out about the Galians, but had a very bad feeling about what was going on and knew he needed to come home. She also knew that Gareth was probably the only hope she had to get justice for her father. "Then I'll have to find another way."

"It's too dangerous, Erynn. Falconry is illegal now. Marik's killing people he catches doing it. People once close to me. Women. I doubt the king even knows half of what that man's been up to in the last few years. There's no way you can get Gareth that letter."

Erynn gripped the tube even tighter. "I have to try."

CHAPTER 5

The first thing Erynn noticed when she reached the kitchen wasn't the heat and smoke of the many fires, the humidity, or the thick smell of roasted pork and spices. It was the tension. Everyone in the large room seemed to be talking about the Galians; about why they were here and what their visit meant for Alyria. The whole room was buzzing.

The second thing she noticed was her friend, Adena, who appeared to be the only person not engaged in conversation. She was busy peeling potatoes at Erynn's usual table on the far side of the room, her long brown hair framing a none-too-pleased face. Erynn wasn't surprised. She knew how much her friend hated the kitchen. The king had brought her to the castle with Erynn, after hearing about Jared's departure in Cold Lake, but she soon demonstrated that the kitchen was not the place for her and after numerous mishaps was sent to the stables instead. Now she didn't appear in the kitchen unless she was being punished — which happened fairly regularly since she was the only girl in the stables and wasn't the kind to take teasing from the other men lightly. Especially when she probably knew more about horses than the rest of them.

Erynn started across the room, wanting nothing more than to talk to her friend and tell her everything that had happened. As she made her way around the other servants and tables and baskets of food stacked in the aisles, she noticed the rushing in her ears had stopped and the ache across her brow was receding. She was rubbing her forehead and thinking how curious this was, when one of the cooks reached out and grabbed her arm.

"Wryden favors you," he said, his voice urgent. "Did he tell you why they're here?"

Erynn twisted herself loose of his grasp. He was a big man, with receding brown hair, and had given her trouble before. The two women standing next to him had as well. "His Grace told me to get to work."

She tried to go around him, but he stepped further out into the aisle, blocking her path. "But you were with him, weren't you? When the Galians arrived?"

Erynn realized the room had gone quiet. Everyone had paused what they were doing to watch. Even Adena had stopped peeling. Erynn felt heat rise to her face, always hating their stares. "He didn't tell me anything."

The cook narrowed his eyes, as if not sure whether to believe her.

"They're here because Gareth's dead," said one of the women standing next to him.

A whisper went around the room, but the cook just shook his head. "We'd have heard if he was dead. I don't believe it."

"But they say the king hasn't had word from him in months," said another woman nearby. "Why else would they be here? Why come all this way?"

"What if the war's over?" came another voice. "What if we're next?"

Now everyone started talking, their voices growing louder

as they argued over whether this might be true. Erynn could barely watch. She wondered who had leaked the news about the lack of word from Gareth. She doubted it was Faris. More likely Clay or the guards.

"If it was over, we'd have heard about that, too," the cook said.

"I want to know about the dragon," said the other woman standing next to him. She was older, with thick grey hair, and hadn't taken her eyes off Erynn.

The room went quiet again.

"Krystalix?" Erynn said. "What about him?"

"He flew over the castle," the cook said. "Numerous times. Low enough they thought he might attack."

Erynn gasped. Krystalix flew over the castle? Her eyes went to Adena, who nodded her head silently, and then she remembered the commotion in the throne room and the way everyone had headed for the doors.

"What do you make of that?" the grey-haired woman asked. "I've never heard of him doing such a thing. And so soon after the Galians arrived?"

Erynn felt strange. As far as she knew, Krystalix hadn't even been seen since the day her father died, and she couldn't recall any stories of him ever being spotted around the castle. So it couldn't just be a coincidence. "I – I don't know. I don't know why he'd do that."

"Maybe he doesn't like Galians," Adena said.

Everyone turned to look at her, but Adena simply shifted her eyes back down to her potato and continued peeling. For several long moments no one said a word, and then the whispers started again, a few at first and spreading fast.

"What is going on in here?" came Mirella's loud voice from the front of the kitchen.

A flurry of activity erupted around the room as all of the

servants quickly went back to work. The headservant's eyes darted around and finally landed on Erynn and the cook.

"We were just talking about the dragon," the cook said, stepping casually out of Erynn's path and back to his table. "We heard he flew over the castle."

"Dragons aren't for you to worry about," Mirella said. "You're here to work. We have guests to feed and judging by what I see already there's still much to be done."

The cook turned and went back to his work. Erynn continued on her way, finally reaching Adena and sitting down on a stool next to her. She grabbed a small knife and potato from the pile on the table and began peeling. She could feel Mirella watching her, but then the headservant turned away and started her inspection, marching up and down the aisles, tasting the food, and barking out orders.

"King keep you late again?" Adena asked, using her foot to slide over two wooden buckets on the floor. One was half full of peel, the other almost full of peeled potatoes.

"Sort of," Erynn muttered. "She also caught me in the throne room."

Adena raised a brow. "What were you doing in there?"

Erynn was trying to keep an eye on Mirella, who was still making her way across the kitchen and leaving a seemingly endless stream of complaints in her wake: the meat was too tough, the stew too runny, the bread too stale. Erynn knew she was headed in her direction. She was just taking her time about it. "I was looking for Faris. It's a long story."

"Another letter?"

"The second today."

"Second?"

Erynn finished her potato and dropped it in the bucket. She wasn't sure it was safe to say anything with Mirella around, not wanting to get into even more trouble for gossiping when she should be working, but she felt she might burst if she didn't say something. So as she reached for another potato, she leaned close to Adena and told her about Lord Caden. Her friend's eyes grew wide and she appeared about to say something, but Erynn shook her head and motioned to Mirella. "I'll tell you the rest later."

Adena looked disappointed that she had to wait, but eventually she nodded and went back to her work.

Several strips of peel missed the bucket, but Erynn didn't bother to pick them up. She kept her head down, peeling two more potatoes and starting on a third, when she finally sensed the headservant's presence.

"How long were you in the throne room before I found you?" Mirella asked.

Erynn flushed, instantly aware of both the letter tube she had slipped into her apron pocket before entering the kitchen and the fact that everyone in the room was watching her again. "A couple of minutes."

"I was going to sentence you to a week in the crypt," Mirella said. "But since we need all the help in the kitchen we can get right now, you'll do the dishes instead. All of them. On your own. For the rest of the week. Until every last one is cleaned and dried and put away. Is that understood?"

"Yes, ma'am," Erynn replied right away — because she knew there was nothing else she could say. Part of her was relieved that she wouldn't be stuck working in the crypt, but the other wasn't exactly looking forward to a week's worth of dishes. Especially with the extra guests. And the upcoming banquet.

Adena looked up at Mirella, but Erynn shot her a warning glance.

"You have something to add, Adena?" Mirella asked. "Perhaps you'd like to stay and help your friend? Or have you already caused enough trouble for one day?"

"No, ma'am," Adena said. She sat up straighter and shifted her attention back to her peeling.

When Mirella was gone, heading off toward other side of the room to continue her inspection, Erynn dropped her shoulders and sighed.

"One of these days you need to tell her where to go," Adena whispered.

Erynn knew that would only make things worse, and right now Mirella was the least of her worries. What was she going to do about the letter — and her father's killer — if she was stuck in the kitchen the entire time he was here?

She finished her potato and tossed it in the bucket. As she reached for another, she raised her head and noticed Marik standing in one of the doorways to the great hall. He appeared surprisingly casual, a mug of ale in his hand, but didn't seem at all interested in dinner preparations. He was staring at her. And just as she realized it, he winked.

Erynn looked down at her hands. Had he talked to Faris? For a second she couldn't move, wondering if he was going to come over and ask her for the letter — the same one she'd already told Mirella she'd given to Faris. Then she tried to continue peeling, but her fingers wouldn't cooperate.

"He's watching me," she whispered.

"Who?" Adena said, glancing up.

Erynn cringed, not really wanting her to do that. "Marik. Over by the door to the hall."

"I don't see him."

Erynn raised her head. Adena was right. Marik was gone.

"Why's he watching you?" Adena asked. "Because of Lord Caden?"

"Not exactly," Erynn said. She started peeling again, but still felt rattled. She wanted to tell Adena everything, especially about the letter and what was going on in the falconry, but Mirella was still in the room. "Wait until she's gone. Tell me why you're here instead."

Adena was quiet, sending more long strips of peel into the bucket. Then she shrugged. "I got into a fight."

Erynn wasn't surprised, but thought she noticed something different in her friend's voice. "What did they do this time?"

Adena sent a few more strips of peel into the bucket. "One of them called Jared a traitor. Said he was probably working for the Galians, just like my father."

Erynn paused and looked over at her friend, but her head was down and her long hair hid her face. She shifted her eyes back to her potato, but couldn't bring herself to resume peeling. Jared's desertion in Galia was still a bit of a sore issue for her, one that she and Adena had argued about before, but she also knew how much her friend missed her brother and was worried about him. "It's not true, Adena. About Jared anyway. I don't think he'd do that."

"I've heard the rumors about my father, Erynn."

"And that's all they are. Rumors."

"But those men in Cold Lake said my father was living at the castle in Ethlon, right? That is what Jared said he heard? Where he said he was going?"

Erynn started peeling again. "Still doesn't mean Jared's working for them."

Adena said nothing more and Erynn couldn't think of anything else to say that might make her feel better. So they peeled in silence for a while and when Mirella finally left, Erynn leaned in close again and told her friend everything. From her first visit to the falconry, to her conversation with Faris by the stairs. When she was finished, Adena looked stunned.

"You have to tell the king," she said. "Let him worry about sending the letter."

Erynn wasn't so sure. "I'm worried about what Faris said. That Holden might hurt him."

"It's not your problem, Erynn."

"Yes, it is. If it wasn't for the king, we'd both be on the streets. Mirella would kick me out of here for sure if something happened to him." Erynn paused. "Your father's not the only one they whisper about, you know. Why else do you think she picks on me so much?"

"Because she thinks you're his daughter?"

"Well, I was adopted," Erynn said, well aware that her circumstances could easily be viewed as proof of that ridiculous rumor. "And he did bring me to the castle after my father died. Did choose me to write his letters. I'm barely sixteen. Doesn't that strike you as strange?"

"Yes, but I know you don't believe it. The king even told you it wasn't true."

Erynn sent another thick strip of peel flying. "Doesn't matter. Mirella believes it. She was close to Queen Sera. She'd kick me out the first chance she got."

Adena dropped her potato into the bucket. "Queen Sera died before you were born."

"Not long before I was born. And that doesn't help, Adena."

Adena sighed and rubbed her forehead. "Who's to say Holden will do anything?"

"You don't know him the way I do. He's up to something with the Galians. I'm sure of it."

"Still not your problem."

Erynn didn't even want to talk about that any more. "What about Lord Caden? I need you to help me figure out what to do."

Adena thought about this. Then she smiled and motioned to the cauldrons bubbling with hot stew along the far wall. "Maybe we could slip something in his stew."

Erynn stared at her. "You're not serious?"

"You want him dead, don't you?"

Erynn hesitated. She had wished death upon the man who killed her father from the very moment he struck him down, but had never really thought about doing it herself. She had never even thought she'd see him again. "I guess. I just don't know if I could do something like that."

"But surely you've thought about it?"

"I'm not like him, Adena. And neither are you. Besides, he's a Lord of Galia now. The Dragonslayer. If we did something like that and they caught us … they'd kill us, too."

Adena shrugged. "Just let me know if you change your mind."

Erynn continued peeling, but her thoughts remained on Lord Caden for a while and what Adena had suggested. Finally she swept them both from her mind and returned her thoughts to the letter and how she was going to get it to Gareth. And then all of a sudden she had the answer. "What about Sheldon Birch?"

"The old guy from the market? What about him?"

"He always has falcons with him. And he used to be the King's Falconer. Maybe he could send the letter."

"Have you seen him with a falcon since that new law was passed?"

Erynn's shoulders dropped, a sinking feeling in her stomach. "I'm not sure I've seen him at all actually. Not since last winter."

"Faris did say Marik was killing people for practicing falconry."

Erynn felt horrible. She had always enjoyed her visits with

Sheldon, whenever she was down in the market and he happened to be around, especially since he had once been a close friend of her father's. Holden's new falconry law had sounded absurd when she first heard of it, but the reality of it was now staggering. Still, Sheldon Birch might be the only chance she had. "One of us would have to go down to the village. See if he's around."

Adena laughed. "Not with the banquet in two days."

Erynn sighed. She doubted she could get away either, especially after what happened today, but this was important. "Maybe if I left early. Right when the gate's up. I'm not usually expected until breakfast is over."

"If Mirella catches you she will sentence you to the crypt. As well as the dishes."

Erynn knew she was right, but didn't see any other choice. A short time later, someone came over to fetch the peeled potatoes and they worked in silence for a while, waiting for the bucket to be returned.

"Any idea what Holden's up to?" Adena asked when the bucket was back and they were alone again.

"Wish I knew. Maybe it would help me figure out what to do about Lord Caden."

"You mean spoil their plans?"

"Maybe."

"Doesn't really sound like justice to me."

"Depends on what those plans are. Faris seems to think it's important, whatever it is. And besides, short of poisoning Lord Caden's stew or somehow getting Gareth back here in two days, there isn't much else we can do."

Adena was quiet a moment. "You think it's odd that Krystalix shows up the same day Lord Caden does? Just happens to fly over the castle?"

Erynn glanced at her. "Definitely."

CHAPTER 6

Erynn had to abandon her plan to sneak down to the village the next morning when another servant woke her before dawn and put her to work in the kitchen. She was tired, barely able to sleep after everything that had happened, and was up so late doing dishes that she was the last one to return to the large room over the first stable that she shared with Adena and a dozen other women. But she went about her chores as diligently as she could, refusing to give Mirella any excuse to increase her sentence, and by the time she was finally allowed a short break, around mid-morning, she was eager to find Adena. She had found out something interesting while listening in on the gossip around the kitchen and was dying to tell her. She was also starving, so stopped just long enough to throw together a small sandwich out of breakfast leftovers before heading out the door into the rear ward.

She hadn't gone more than a few steps when she heard dogs barking.

Erynn froze — her sandwich halfway to her mouth. She had heard those dogs before and knew exactly what they meant: Holden was going hunting.

The thought had barely entered her mind when four

Alyrian soldiers rode out from the second of the three stables behind the keep, six large black dogs at their feet. They were followed by Holden, Lord Caden, and four Galians.

Erynn quickly shrank back into the shadows near the door, afraid Lord Caden might turn his head and see her, but the dogs were jumping and barking at almost everyone and everything they passed and he was having trouble keeping a rein on his horse. Larger and blacker than those of his men, the stallion had its ears laid back and shied every time one of the dogs came close. Erynn had seen the horse before. It was the same one Lord Caden was riding when she and her father encountered him in Galia.

Erynn crept along the edge of the keep as the men rode toward the inner gatehouse, peering around the corner just as they passed under the portcullis and on to the outer ward. It wasn't until they were completely gone from sight that she breathed a small sigh of relief, glad she had stopped for something to eat and hadn't left the kitchen a few minutes sooner. Then she took a bite of her sandwich and turned for the first stable — and once more she froze.

Marik was standing in the doorway of the same stable the men had just left. Another soldier stood next to him, and appeared to be saying something, but the Army Commander's eyes were on her.

Erynn swallowed. This was the second time she had seen him this morning. He had entered the kitchen not long after she started her chores, stepping in through the rear door and walking right past her to the great hall — giving her just the hint of a smile. The other servants had noticed and immediately started whispering, and now here he was again. She felt an urge to reach down to her pocket and touch the small letter tube, to make sure it was still there, but she resisted. Instead, she raised herself up, took another bite of her sandwich, and walked as calmly as she could across the ward to the first stable.

She found Adena mucking out one of the stalls at the far end of the corridor, a bay mare standing patiently along the back wall and a wooden cart half-full of manure and soiled straw parked outside the open door.

"He's definitely watching me," Erynn said as she stepped inside.

Adena looked up. "Who? Marik?"

Erynn nodded, taking a quick glance up and down the corridor to make sure they were alone. "I saw him in the kitchen this morning, and then again just now. Outside."

"Think he talked to Faris?"

Erynn could still see the look on Marik's face in the kitchen. The smile. "He must have. Faris probably told him I refused to give him the letter and now he thinks I still have it."

"And do you?"

Erynn reached into her pocket and pulled out the letter tube, showing it to her friend.

Adena took one look at it and turned back to her work, scooping up a clump of soiled straw with her pitchfork and adding it to the growing pile in the cart. "Well, he knows you can't send it without Faris. I think he's just toying with you. I've heard he's like that."

Erynn snorted. "You'd think the Commander of the Alyrian Army would have better things to do. Especially with Galian soldiers at the castle." She took another bite of her sandwich and started pacing back and forth across the stall. The bay mare raised her head and stared at her, clearly wishing the two of them would finish their business in her home and move on.

"I'm surprised he didn't go hunting," Adena said. "Holden

and Lord Caden just left."

"I know. I saw them." Erynn felt a chill thinking about how close she had come to being seen by Lord Caden. She didn't know if he would recognize her after all this time, but wasn't in a rush to find out.

"I still don't understand why you don't just tell the king what's going on. If Marik wants the letter so bad, let him get it from him."

"I told you, Adena. I can't."

"What about Lianne?"

"What about her?"

"Why not tell her? She is Gareth's wife. Maybe she can do something."

Erynn shook her head. "She'd just go to the king. Or confront Holden." She took another bite of her sandwich and remembered what she'd learned in the kitchen and had been so eager to tell Adena. "I heard Krystalix didn't just fly over the castle yesterday. He attacked the Galians right after they crossed the bridge. Killed two of their men. And he followed them all the way here, too."

Adena paused what she was doing and straightened up, a frown on her face. "That's odd, isn't it?"

"Yes," Erynn replied, still pacing. "The day my father died is the only time I've ever heard of him attacking someone unprovoked."

"The only time?"

"As far as I know. I did hear that a few of the old kings sent out men to try and kill him, and that most of them never came back alive. But that was different. They went after him."

"You think maybe it has something to do with what happened in Galia? To your father?"

That was exactly what Erynn was thinking. Ever since she first heard the news. The only problem was it didn't make sense. "I don't know. I can't think of anything else that would explain it." She paused. "I know the king has a book on Krystalix. Sort of a history book. He keeps it locked up in a cabinet in his study, along with his crown and the Queen's jewels. It's apparently been used for hundreds of years to record sightings of Krystalix. Encounters. Stuff like that. If he has done something like this before, it would be in there."

"Think the king would let you look at it?"

Erynn knew he wouldn't. The history of Krystalix was the one book in the king's whole study she had most wanted to read, ever since she'd first laid eyes on it, and the only one he had ever forbidden her from touching. "I've asked. He says its too old or something."

Adena shrugged and went back to her work. "Well, maybe it's nothing. Maybe Krystalix doesn't like Galians. Or maybe he's after Lord Caden because of that other dragon."

"Melaryx? If that was it, why hasn't Krystalix killed him already? I mean, I've seen him rip men apart, Adena. Easily. I know what he can do."

Footsteps came down the corridor. Erynn finished the last of her sandwich as a young man with blonde hair and a very black eye walked by. Adena straightened and fixed him with a hard stare, but he didn't say a word. Seconds later he was gone.

"Let me guess, the one who called Jared a traitor?" Erynn asked.

Adena didn't respond, just started flattening the pile of soiled straw in the cart with the edge of her pitchfork.

Erynn headed for the stall door, thinking maybe it was time to leave.

"What are you going to do about the letter?" Adena asked.

Erynn paused. "I don't know. There's no way I can get down to the village now. And tomorrow's going to be even busier."

"Do you really think Gareth's written? And that Holden's keeping the letters?"

Erynn remembered the look in the falconer's eyes when she asked him about the letters. "Yes."

Adena stopped her flattening. "Think he'd keep them?"

Erynn stared at her friend, recognizing something in her voice — something she knew likely meant trouble. "Maybe. Why?"

Adena motioned in the general direction of the inner gatehouse. "They have gone hunting. Probably won't be back for hours."

Erynn realized what she was suggesting. She peered up and down the corridor again, and then took a step closer. "Do you know how dangerous that is? Searching his solar? What might happen if we got caught?"

Adena laughed and shook her head. "Not me. I'm stuck here. You're the one who spends time with the king. And has access to the upper floors of the keep."

Erynn rubbed a hand across her face, not sure she could do it — and especially if she had to do it alone. She was intrigued at the thought of finding Gareth's letters, if they did exist, but was also terrified of getting caught. Holden was not Mirella. If he found out she'd been snooping around in his solar, he would definitely see her punished — and not with dishes. "I don't know, Adena."

"Unless you don't think he'd keep them in his solar?"

"He wouldn't keep them in the falconry. I don't think he trusts Faris. That's why he had Marik post the guards."

For a few moments, neither of them said a word. Then Adena stepped even closer.

"You have been in there before?" she asked, her voice almost a whisper. "Haven't you? I remember you telling me."

Erynn could feel her heart pounding already. "Yes, but this is different, Adena."

"How? Just pretend you're cleaning or something."

Erynn turned away and started pacing across the stall again, still not sure she wanted to risk getting caught, but then suddenly she remembered something and her eyes widened and she spun back around. "If Holden was expecting the Galians, maybe they exchanged letters before they crossed the bridge. Letters that could tell us why they're really here."

Adena smiled. "Exactly."

CHAPTER 7

Erynn kept watch for Marik as she headed back across the inner ward, but saw no sign of him. Still, she couldn't shake the feeling that at any moment she might turn around and find him watching her — and that made her even more nervous about what she was about to do. But if Holden had letters that would explain why the Galians were here, she definitely wanted to get her hands on them.

When she reached the kitchen, she found Mirella lecturing two of the other servants over by one of the cauldrons and almost everyone else watching them. No one even seemed to notice her enter the room, let alone grab three pitchers from a shelf near the back door and slip down the hall to the cistern. She filled the pitchers with water, and took one final look around before heading up the rear stairs.

The pitchers were heavy and awkward to carry, but Erynn made her way to the king's solar without much trouble and was glad to find her path deserted. The last thing she needed was to run into one of the other servants, who might realize what she was doing and tell Mirella. The headservant usually chose someone different to freshen the Royal Family's drinking water every day, and while she had picked Erynn three times in the past, Erynn had accidentally dropped and shattered a pitcher in the king's solar the last time and she was sure Mirella would never ask her again.

Erynn knocked on the king's door, and within seconds it was opened by his chamberlain, an older man with thinning white hair. He took one look at her and the pitchers in her arms and let her in without a word, but she caught the annoyance in his eyes. The king had fortunately not been present when she dropped the pitcher, but his chamberlain had and he wasn't at all pleased with the mess. Erynn hoped he wouldn't complain to Mirella, and took extra care as she set one of the pitchers down on the table by the king's bed. Then she grabbed the pitcher another servant had left there the day before, still half full of water, and quietly left the room.

Lianne was present in her solar, but was busy with two of her maids as they fitted what appeared to be a new green gown for the banquet. None of them paid any attention to Erynn as she replaced the empty pitcher of water on a side table and left the room.

Erynn's heart beat faster as she headed down the hall toward Holden's solar, and she wondered again if she was making the right choice. If she was caught, she didn't even know if the king would understand — or be able to save her from Holden. But still she kept moving. She glanced back several times, afraid she might see Marik following along behind her, but saw nothing. The halls were quiet.

When she finally reached Holden's door, she knocked and held her breath, almost hoping his chamberlain would be there so it would give her an excuse not to go through with this, but when seconds passed without a response, she took one last glance up and down the hall and quickly slipped inside.

Holden's solar was on the north side of the main keep and

therefore cooler than the others. A silver goblet half-full of wine sat on a desk in front of the balcony doors, right next to an empty pitcher of water. On the other side sat an unlit candle, burned almost to the base, and a shallow silver tray containing a small pile of ashes.

Erynn set the pitchers down and took a closer look at the ashes. Tiny pieces of parchment were scattered throughout the pile — enough to prove Holden had been burning letters, but no way to tell who they were from. She closed her eyes, fearing she was too late and that he'd already burned all of the letters she had hoped to find, but then she pushed those thoughts from her mind and went around the desk to search the drawers. Refusing to give up just yet.

She found several letters, but none were from Gareth or the Galians. Three were from the king's lords, addressed to the king and expressing concern over Holden's new falconry law, including one from Lord Brison, the king's closest friend. Erynn had met Lord Brison once. He lived in the south, but had visited the castle not long after she returned from Galia and had even called her to the king's study so he could tell her how sorry he was about her father. He said her father used to manage his stables, before the king sent for him to come work at Caraden, and that he had always been one of his most trusted servants. He even claimed that her father used to bring her to his house quite often. Erynn had thought something about him seemed familiar, but couldn't remember any specific memories.

Erynn doubted the king had seen Lord Brison's letter, or any of the others, and was tempted to take them as proof of what Holden was up to. But then she remembered her conversation with Faris and put them back. If Holden discovered the letters missing, he'd know someone had been in his desk and would most likely suspect his father.

A cabinet stood on the far side of the bed, similar to the one in the king's study except smaller. The doors were locked and Erynn was immediately curious about what might be inside, but she wasn't able to find a key and knew she didn't have time to look. She searched around the bed, in case a letter had slipped off one of the side tables, and then she turned to the wardrobe.

She found a letter in the pocket of one of Holden's coats, folded twice in half. She recognized the handwriting the second she opened it and her hands trembled: it was the same as the handwriting in the letter old Soren had found near her father's grave in Galia. She had mentioned the contents of that letter to the king the day she was first brought to see him, but had no idea whether he'd ever sent the information to Gareth. She still had the letter in the pack she kept under her cot, along with that small black stone she had taken from her father's grave. Two reminders of that horrible day.

She switched her attention back to the letter in her hand, reminding herself that what she was doing was far too dangerous for distractions. It was dated three days before the Galians arrived.

Holden, Dragon attacked after crossing bridge. Lost two men. Seems intent on driving us out but will press on. Expect delay. Naedra warned this might happen so we were prepared. Will explain everything when we arrive. Again, it would be best if your father was not advised we are coming. Silas

Erynn was confused. Naedra knew Krystalix might attack? But how was that possible? And why would he want to drive the Galians out of Alyria? She read the letter over several times, trying to commit it to memory. Trying to understand it. But other than a vague confirmation that the Galians had indeed come for something, and were possibly worried about the king's interference, it had only left her with more questions.

She had a feeling it was time to leave, so she folded the letter and put it back where she found it. Then she went to the desk, grabbed the pitchers, and headed for the doors.

"Erynn!" came a sharp voice the second she stepped out into the hall.

Erynn froze.

The grey-haired woman from the kitchen, the one that had questioned her the day before about Krystalix, was walking down the hall towards her and not looking at all pleased. She gazed down at the pitchers in her arms, and then at the door to Holden's solar. "What were you doing in there?"

"Just replacing the water," Erynn replied.

The woman snatched the pitchers one-by-one from her arms. "Mirella already tasked someone to do that."

Erynn shrugged. "I was just trying to help. You know, to make up for being late yesterday."

"Maybe you should just do what you're told. That way when His Grace sends for you, we don't have to go searching the entire castle to find you."

Erynn felt a sudden rush of anxiety, even though she had known this would happen sooner or later. "The king asked for me?"

"Right away," the woman said, giving Erynn one last glare before storming off down the hall.

Erynn slipped a hand down to her pocket and touched the letter tube. He was going to ask her about it. If she'd sent it. What was she going to tell him? She took a deep breath. She knew only one thing: she couldn't possibly tell him the truth.

The king was on his feet the second she entered the study. He looked tired, his grey hair slightly unkempt, and there were dark circles under his eyes. "Did you send the letter?"

"Yes, Your Grace," Erynn said as she reached the desk. She kept her hands folded in front of her, over her pocket, fearing he might notice the outline of the tube through the fabric.

"You watched Faris send it?"

"Yes, Your Grace."

"Good." The king sank back down in his chair and ran a hand over his face. "He should have it in seven days. Or eight perhaps, depending on the falcon. The journey will take weeks of course, but at least he will be on his way."

Erynn felt horrible and could barely bring herself to look at him. She gazed up at the painting of Krystalix, but was bothered by the way the dragon seemed to be staring at her, and shifted her attention back down to the desk instead. She noticed he had his map out and found her eyes drawn to Ridan in the east. Had she made the right choice in lying to him? The capital city of Stonehaven seemed so far away and she knew she needed to get Gareth this letter. If she couldn't figure out some way to get down to the village so she could look for Sheldon, she didn't know what she was going to do.

She spotted the quill first, out of the corner of her eye. And then the ink pot and the old book lying open in front of him. But seconds passed before she realized what it was: the history book on Krystalix. "Were you writing about the dragon, Your Grace?"

At first the king didn't seem to understand the question, his mind clearly elsewhere, but then he followed her gaze and noticed the book. He reached out a hand and closed it, clearing his throat. "Yes, I was just making note of his appearance here yesterday. It has certainly been a while since anyone saw him. Or reported it anyway."

"Since I saw him."

"That is correct. Since you saw him."

Erynn wondered what he'd written, and why he seemed so concerned that she might read it. "I heard he attacked the Galians after they crossed the bridge. Even killed two of their men."

The king leaned back slightly in his chair, but still kept his hand on the book. "Yes, Lord Caden went on about that for some length at dinner last night. The man seems to think he has a way with dragons. To keep walking away from them without getting himself killed."

There was anger in his voice and Erynn knew she needed to tread carefully. Sometimes the king was accommodating of her questions, and sometimes he was not. But she knew she couldn't stop now. She had to know more. "Do you know why Krystalix attacked them, Your Grace? I wondered if it was because of my father. If Krystalix remembers Lord Caden. Or if it was maybe because of Melaryx."

The king was quiet, staring at her in a way that suddenly made her a little uncomfortable. But then he gave a slight shrug. "I do not know why Krystalix did what he did, but it is certainly possible he remembers Lord Caden. Whether he would know about Lord Caden's responsibility for Melaryx is hard to say. It would seem unlikely, but dragons certainly are intelligent creatures. More so than some of us like to think anyway."

"Krystalix doesn't want the Galians here though, does he, Your Grace?"

"No, Erynn, I do not believe he does."

Erynn thought she detected something in his voice. Something that told her he knew more about the dragon's unusual behavior and what was going on with the Galians, but for some reason was not willing to say. She wondered if he'd written everything he knew in the book. "Did you need help with the writing, Your Grace?"

The king shook his head. "I can manage this time, Erynn."

"But don't you find it difficult?"

A bit of a stern look crossed his face and she knew right away that she'd gone too far. He motioned to the door. "That will be all, Erynn. I will send for you later. I slept very poorly last night and want you to bring me a cup of that tea before I retire."

"Yes, Your Grace," Erynn said. She didn't want to leave. She wanted to know what he had written in that book. But she knew she had no other choice but to obey, so she took one last look at the book and quietly left the room.

Perhaps it was her success in Holden's solar that did it, finding that letter from Lord Caden without getting caught, because by the time she returned to the kitchen she had already come up with a new plan — one that she hoped would give her some answers. She would bring the king his tea later, the same tea her mother had given her as a child whenever she had trouble sleeping, and then, when she had finished the dishes — and was sure he and everyone else in the castle was asleep — she would return to the study. She was going to read that old history book for herself and find out just what was going on with the dragon. It didn't matter that he kept the book locked up in his cabinet. She knew where he kept the key.

CHAPTER 8

Erynn received a very public scolding from Mirella for going out of her way to freshen the Royal Family's drinking water — as well a two-day extension to her dish sentence — but she barely heard a word. She had known searching Holden's solar would be dangerous and was just glad she hadn't been caught. She spent the rest of the day trying to stay out of Mirella's way and concentrating on her plan to read the history book on Krystalix later. She also thought a lot about what sort of answers she might find inside and as the day she passed grew even more eager to return to the study.

It was late when the king finally sent for his tea and she had already started the dishes. But she stopped what she was doing and heated some water over the fire, and when it was ready she poured some in a mug and made her way up the rear stairs. She found him standing by the window in his solar, gazing down at the stables.

"I brought the hot water, Your Grace," she said as she crossed to the table by the bed.

"Better make it a strong one," he replied. "I think I will need it tonight."

Erynn was already planning to make it strong. The last thing she needed was him still awake when she went to the study. "Yes, Your Grace."

The pitcher of water was on the table where she'd left it earlier and she set the mug down next to it and took a small parchment-wrapped package from the drawer. Inside were the dried leaves of a blackish-green plant. She dropped several pieces into the water, and as she gave them a stir she studied what was left and figured there was probably enough for two more cups. Then she'd have to get some more.

Her breath caught. Those dried leaves had just given her an idea.

She glanced at the king, but his attention was still outside. Erynn assumed he was watching the Galians. Most were staying in the barracks on the upper floor of the second stable and she had noticed a few talking out in the rear ward while she was heating the water. She turned back to the package of dried leaves and moved quickly, dumping the rest down her apron pocket. As she pushed the leaves down against the letter tube, they crumbled and several bits stuck to her hand and fell to the floor. Fortunately the stone was dark enough that she didn't think the king would notice, but she still used her foot to slide as many of the bits under the bed as she could. Then she picked up the spoon and continued stirring. "This is the last of it, Your Grace. I'll have to fetch you some more."

"The last?" the king said, turning his head.

"You asked for it strong."

The king thought about this a moment. "Yes, I suppose I did."

Erynn wiped at the front of her dress with her other hand, hoping none of the tea leaves were clinging to the fabric. "Will you want some after the banquet?"

The king snorted and started towards the bed. "I doubt I will ever sleep with Galians inside these walls."

Erynn waited, not wanting to appear too eager. "I could go early, Your Grace. As soon as the gate's up. Before Mirella needs me."

The king seemed about to respond, but then he paused and a strange look passed over his face. "Yes, that is a fine idea, Erynn. Do it first thing, but be quick. Mirella will no doubt need your help tomorrow." He eased himself down on the edge of the bed. "In fact, I want you to tell her when you return. Right away. Then she will know where you are in the morning and can plan for your absence."

Erynn hadn't planned to say anything to Mirella at all, afraid she would only insist on adding the tea to the list of food and other supplies she sent a wagon down to the village for every morning. But she didn't want the headservant asking about her either and the king finding out she'd disobeyed. "I will, Your Grace."

"Do you need my seal?"

"No, Your Grace," Erynn said, removing the spoon and carefully handing him the mug. "The herbalist knows who I am. And that it's for you. My mother used to buy herbs from him all the time. She said he was probably the best herbalist in all of Alyria."

The king said nothing, his eyes on the tea.

Erynn waited for him to dismiss her. "Will that be all, Your Grace?"

"Actually, there is one more thing," the king said. "Should Mirella or anyone else give you any trouble tomorrow, maybe try to stop you, I want you to let me know. Is that clear?"

Erynn thought it an odd request. "Why would anyone give me trouble, Your Grace?"

"Because of the banquet, I suppose. I know Mirella will

need all the help she can get tomorrow, but I want that tea before I retire, and I want you to get it for me. Not her driver." He looked up and smiled. "You know the type to buy."

He had a bit of a pained look in his eyes, but Erynn just assumed he was tired and thought nothing more about it as she headed back down to the kitchen. She had the excuse she needed to go look for Sheldon and that was all that mattered. She just hoped the old falconer was around.

The stack of dishes waiting for her was twice as high as when she left, but Erynn was so pleased with herself and her new plans that she didn't mind the work. She told Mirella about the king's request and when the headservant complained and insisted on sending her driver, Erynn simply told her the king had been specific that she go — and why — and eventually, after much eye-rolling, she relented. But she warned Erynn to be quick and said that if she heard she'd been seen dawdling, she'd add more time to her dish sentence.

Erynn agreed and went back to work, and after a while the kitchen grew quiet, and only a few servants still remained there working. Laughter drifted in from the great hall now and then, but she didn't give it much thought. She was far too focused on her plan to read the history book later, and what she was going to say to Sheldon if she did find him in the morning. Falconry was illegal after all, so what she wanted to ask him wasn't exactly a small favor.

She had just grabbed another one of the meal trays off the pile and plunged it into the water when she heard footsteps enter the room.

"Where can a man get more ale?" came a loud voice from the front of the kitchen.

Erynn froze. She knew that voice without even needing to turn around. It was Marik.

Somewhere behind her, two of the remaining male servants started whispering.

"We'll have to fetch another keg, sir," one of them said, and then it sounded like both promptly left the room.

Erynn stood very still, staring down at the soapy water and the tray in her hand. Waiting for Marik's footsteps to head back to the great hall. Seconds passed before she heard them again, but instead of leaving the kitchen they were coming towards her, his boots ringing out on the stone floor. Her heart pounded in her chest, but she gripped the tray and somehow managed to resume her scrubbing.

Marik came right over to the wash basin, standing so close that his arm brushed hers and she could smell the ale on his breath. She tried to step aside, but was blocked by the table stacked with dirty dishes to her right.

"Does Mirella have you doing all of these yourself?" he asked.

Erynn finished the tray and reached past him to put it on another table to her left. "Yes, sir."

"Are you being punished? Or is this something you do every day?"

He seemed amused, but Erynn knew he wasn't there to ask about her chores. She grabbed another tray and pushed it down into the water. "I was late."

"I find that hard to believe. It was the king's fault, wasn't it? Keeping you late with his letters again?"

Erynn could feel the tube in her pocket, pressed between her, all of the mashed tea leaves, and the wash basin. "I was late."

For several moments, Marik remained quiet. Erynn was trying hard to concentrate on what she was doing, but it was awkward with him standing so close. She wished he would leave. Instead, he leaned closer.

"Are you loyal to His Grace, Erynn?"

The words came as a warm whisper against her cheek, giving her a chill, but Erynn continued scrubbing, rinsing the tray and reaching past him to put it on the other table. "Of course. He's the king."

"You do what he tells you? Even if it makes you late and Mirella punishes you?"

"Yes."

"Then why haven't you given the letter to Faris?"

Erynn kept her eyes down, hesitating for a second before grabbing another tray.

"Tell me the truth, Erynn. I know you still have it."

Erynn stopped and raised her head. His cheeks were lightly flushed, the whites of his brown eyes a little red. He'd clearly been drinking — she could still smell the ale on his breath — but not much. That wasn't his style. He had a smile on his face, but it wasn't one that made her feel any better. In fact, she had a feeling it was the same smile many Alyrians had seen right before they died. "Because I know the guards won't let Faris send it."

Marik laughed. "Smart girl. That must be why His Grace chose you to write his letters. Personally, I never really believed the rumors."

Erynn saw something in his eyes then, something very similar to what she had seen in Holden's the day before. Up in the king's study. Something that troubled her and at the same time left her a little annoyed. "What do you want?"

"What do you think I want?"

Erynn returned her attention to the tray and continued scrubbing. He was toying with her. Just like Adena said. "There's nothing secret in it. His Grace just wants Gareth to come home."

"And I would rather our brave prince stayed in Ridan."

Erynn tried not to look bothered by the comment, but from the tone of his voice it almost sounded like a threat. She kept scrubbing. She still wasn't going to give him the letter. Not after what she wrote on it. Not when she finally had an excuse to go to the village to find Sheldon. She rinsed the tray and reached past him to put it on the table, wondering what was taking the other servants so long with the ale.

Marik leaned back against the table, arms crossed over his chest. "Did His Grace tell you why he fears the Galians?"

Erynn gave a slight shrug and grabbed another tray, wishing again that he would just go away. "He fears for Alyria. And for his son."

"Everyone fears those things, Erynn. Naedra can be rather unstoppable when she sets her mind to something. What I want to know is if the king told you why else he fears them?"

Erynn paused and looked up at him again, curious now what he was talking about. But before she could respond, footsteps approached.

"Marik?" Mirella asked, concern in her voice. "Is there something you need?"

Erynn had never imagined the headservant's presence could make her feel so relieved, but a small part of her wished she hadn't shown up just yet. She wanted to know what Marik meant. Why else would the king fear the Galians?

Marik smiled. "Yes, Mirella. Ale. We seem to have run out. And I thought I would have a word with Erynn while I waited for your men to fetch more. Are you really making her do all these dishes by herself?"

For a moment, Mirella looked speechless. But then she fixed Erynn with a glare — a glare that told her she knew from Marik's presence that Erynn had been up to something and that she would somehow figure out what it was and make her pay for it. "Erynn continues to disrespect the rules of this kitchen."

"Seems to me such a smart young lady could be put to better use. She is the king's scribe, after all. At least let us see her pretty face in the hall? Serving meals perhaps?"

Mirella seemed a little flustered, obviously not caring for Marik making a suggestion about something she considered her domain, but she quickly gathered control of herself. "Is there anything else you need, Marik?"

Erynn waited for him to ask her for the letter. The letter she had already told Mirella she'd given to Faris. But he simply pushed himself away from the table and headed back across the kitchen toward the great hall.

"Just the ale, Mirella," he said. "Just the ale."

CHAPTER 9

Erynn remained unsettled for some time after Marik left, tensing every time someone entered the kitchen and glancing over her shoulder to see if it was him. She thought about the dragon book, wondering if it was still wise to go up to the king's study to read it, but the thought of abandoning her plan only made her angry. Whatever the king knew about Krystalix and his odd behavior was in that book and right now she wanted answers. She just needed to be careful.

The evening passed quickly, and eventually Mirella and the other servants left and she was alone. Voices still drifted in occasionally from the great hall, but no one came in to bother her, and when she was finally finished she went to one of the doorways and peeked inside. Quinn and two of his men sat at one of several long tables around the large room, talking quietly, with four rather drunk Alyrian knights at another, but she saw no sign of Marik.

It was time. Erynn grabbed a candle and headed for the stairs.

The hallways on the second floor were dark, the light from only a few candles still flickering in the sconces on the walls. As she approached the study, she felt a warm breeze and heard the sound of distant laughter and realized the doors to the balcony across the hall were open. She paused to listen at the study door, and when she was convinced the room was empty and it was safe, she quietly slipped inside.

The study was pitch black; the heavy drapes pulled shut. The walls were close and cave-like in the light of the candle, but Erynn tried not to think about that — or to even look up at the painting of Krystalix. His eyes seemed strangely aglow in the dim light; his teeth sharp and threatening. She set the candle on the desk, shook the key from the red vase on the mantle, and went to the cabinet.

The history book was in its usual place on the top shelf, right next to the king's rolled-up map. Erynn glanced at the jewelry boxes on the lower shelves, well aware that if someone came in right now, they'd think those were what she was after. That she'd come to steal a ring, or maybe one of the late queen's necklaces. Not to simply read a book. She didn't even want to imagine the punishment she would face if she was caught, so she refused to let herself think about that and reached up instead to grab the book. She returned to the desk and sat down, pulled the candle closer, and opened the book to the first page.

It was dated 1437. Four hundred and fifty-six years ago. The pages were yellowed and the ink faded, but most of the words were still legible and Erynn immediately began to read. She knew King Wryden's last entry was at the back of the book, and that she should probably go there first and read that, but the sight of the old book and the feel of it under her fingers brought up such a strong need inside her to know everything she could about the dragon — all four hundred and fifty-six years — that she couldn't bring herself to stop.

Krystalix was first sighted along the edge of the northern mountains. As dragons had become a fairly rare sight in

Valentia over the years, a report of the sighting soon made its way to King Arrellian, who recorded it with interest, along with several others that trickled in over the next few years. Curious to see the dragon for himself, the king eventually traveled to the mountains but searched for days with no luck. Then he encountered a young man walking alone through the woods who suggested he climb a certain peak and told him that a woman in the area could talk to the dragon and had said his name was Krystalix. King Arrellian was stunned, for he knew of only one line of women known for their ability to talk to the dragons, the descendants of a woman named Maegan, but he thought they no longer existed. He searched for the woman for some time, but found no trace of her, and when he went back to try and clarify the directions, couldn't find the young man, either. He assumed the directions he was given for finding the dragon would also turn out to be false, but after climbing up the suggested peak, he soon saw Krystalix sail past overhead.

As Erynn read King Arrellian's entries, she thought back on everything she knew about Maegan — which was mostly from stories she had heard from her father. Maegan had lived almost two thousand years ago, during the reign of the last One King, Terren Rothguard, and although she was eventually executed for treason against him — up at the old mountain castle of the One King in Hale — she was said to have been quite influential in the politics of the time, helping the One King mediate disputes with the elves and the dwarves and even with his own lords — lords that rose up against him not long after and eventually resulted in both his death and that of his young son, and the complete disintegration of the One Kingdom itself. But mostly Maegan was known for her gifts of fire and healing and her ability to talk to the dragons — gifts she attributed to the brilliant black stone she wore on a silver chain around her neck and claimed had been given to her by the dragons.

Queen Naedra had claimed many years ago to be a Daughter of Maegan, as Maegan's female descendants came to be called, as had her older sister Sasha, the late Queen of Tallon, and it was this ability of Maegan's descendants to talk to the dragons that many believed was the reason behind her success in rearing those two dragons from Melaryx's eggs. Erynn had once asked her father how many Daughters there were in Valentia — other than Naedra — but he said they were rumored to have been almost wiped out over the years and that only the Order of the Cael, a group dedicated to their protection, really knew for sure.

Erynn continued to turn the pages, devouring the words. As the years passed, so did the kings, but most continued King Arrellian's tradition of recording all sightings and encounters with the dragon. She learned that Krystalix was most commonly seen in the north, near the mountains, but that he had also been seen in other areas of Alyria, as well as Brye and Galia. She also found most of the reports the same: simple sightings of him flying by overhead, or complaints about missing livestock. Not a single report said he had ever threatened anyone.

And then, in 1664, she came across a different story. Two merchants traveling through the south spotted a young woman with long dark hair walking alone by the side of a river. Soon after, they saw Krystalix fly by, heading in her direction. Fearing the young woman might be in danger, the men returned to the river to warn her, but found her gone. They noticed the dragon on a plateau above the river, inside a ring of tall stones, and when they climbed up the hill for a closer look, saw the woman standing next to him, his head down and her hand on his nose. He seemed to sense their presence, because he suddenly raised his head and flew toward them. The men scattered, terrified, and when they finally found the courage to return, both Krystalix and the woman were gone.

Although there was no mention in the report, Erynn wondered if the dark-haired woman was a Daughter of Maegan and a descendant of the woman King Arrellian had gone searching for in the northern mountains over two hundred years earlier. She also wondered if the plateau with the ring of tall stones was one of the three temples built in the years after Maegan's death to honor her memory. Erynn hadn't even known such places existed until she saw the king's map and asked about the three small "M" symbols marked on it — each surrounded by a circle. One of the symbols was in central Alyria, and the other two in Brye and Cardel. She had been especially surprised to learn there was a temple in Alyria, and couldn't recall her father ever mentioning it before. That seemed strange to her, because he had traveled all over Alyria so surely would have known it was there, and it sounded like just the sort of place he would have liked to visit.

Erynn scanned the pages faster, knowing she didn't have all night, and then, twelve years after the incident by the river, she came across an entry that made her sit up straight. Krystalix was reported to have attacked a group of men after they crossed the bridge at North Falls. A few of the men were killed, but the rest continued on into Alyria. Several reports followed, each describing Krystalix as either following or attacking the group, but when the king sent out men to find them, they were unsuccessful, and no one was ever able to determine who the men were or where they were from. And then it seemed all reports of the dragon stopped, and nothing more was written about him for almost eighty years.

Erynn wondered if something had happened to Krystalix,

or if the current king simply hadn't recorded his sightings, but when the entries resumed she noticed a distinct change in how he was discussed. Years may have passed, but the incident with the unknown group of men was obviously not forgotten and Krystalix was now seen as a threat to Alyrians. A couple of kings even sent out men to hunt him down — most never returning alive — but other than these few isolated incidents, there were no more reports of him ever threatening or attacking people, or even being seen anywhere near Caraden.

Eventually Erynn reached the first report written by King Wryden. Halfway through it she heard a noise out in the hall, but she was so focused on the words that she didn't pay it any attention. Then the noise grew louder and she looked up. Someone out in the hall was laughing.

Erynn froze. It was Holden.

There was no time to think. Erynn grabbed the book and ran around the desk to the balcony, slipping in behind the heavy blue drapes just as the door opened. She clutched the book to her chest and pressed further back, until she could feel the cool glass of the balcony doors. Then she gasped — she hadn't extinguished the candle or properly closed the cabinet!

"My father must have been in here before he retired," Holden said.

The drapes were thick and full of dust, but Erynn could make out two shapes moving across the room toward the desk. One was carrying a candle, the other had a noticeable pattern to his walk — a limp. Her mouth went dry. She thought about slipping out the balcony door, but feared they might notice the movement of the drapes or the candles might catch the draft, and she knew there was nowhere to go once she was out on the balcony anyway. She was trapped.

Someone set an object on the desk. Then the chair scraped

against the floor and one of the shapes sat down. A drawer opened. The other shape limped toward the fireplace.

"Nice painting."

Erynn felt a chill pass through her and hugged the history book tighter. Two years might have passed since she last heard that voice, but it wasn't one she'd forgotten.

"I hope you have a strategy for getting home," Holden said.

"We'll manage."

The drawer closed. The chair creaked and something light scraped against the desk.

Erynn's heart was pounding so loud she could hear it in her ears. She was finding it increasingly difficult to breathe with all the dust and the fabric was itchy against her skin. She closed her eyes and tried to remain calm, hoping the men would get whatever it was they'd come for and leave.

"So, you're sure Naedra can do this?" Holden asked.

"As long as we still have our agreement and you give her what she wants."

Holden laughed. "Of course. You have no idea how long I've wanted this."

"Then I'm sure Naedra will be pleased."

Erynn opened her eyes. She didn't know what they were talking about, but something in Holden's voice had just given her a really bad feeling in her stomach. Something that told her he probably wouldn't be happy to find out she'd been listening.

"You still haven't given me any details," Holden said, a slight amusement in his voice. "You must know, of course, that I'm not sleeping."

"That's only because Naedra doesn't want all of her plan known. It's obviously in your best interest that she succeed."

"And hers?"

"Yes, and hers. Your brother certainly has influence."

"Surely you can tell me something?"

Lord Caden limped back toward the desk. "King Riel is hosting a banquet in Sarda in twenty-seven days — to honor the life of his recently departed father and celebrate his own coronation. Everyone will be there of course — including your brother. From what we've gathered, Gareth is hoping to use the occasion to get Riel's support for the war. Just like he did with Parigon. He seems to think if he gets it, the war will be over."

"And will it?"

"With both Parigon and Sarda backing Ridan? Let's just say it's something Naedra would rather avoid. We'd have won long ago if he hadn't interfered with Parigon."

"I'll wait eagerly for the news then," Holden said. "And you can assure Naedra I'll tell no one of her plan."

"Not even Marik?"

"Marik knows about our agreement, but I see no reason for him to know all the details."

"And you trust him?"

"I know he doesn't want Gareth returning to Alyria any more than I do."

"Good, but I would prefer we keep those details between us. Naedra will not be happy if her plan fails. Gareth won't be as accessible to us once he's back in Ridan."

Erynn's breath caught as she suddenly realized what they were talking about. Naedra was planning to kill Gareth! She had to do something!

"Well, you can tell her I'm pleased," Holden said, and then he laughed. "Together, we'll have old King Agar and the rest of Brye on their knees!"

"Just make sure you keep her pleased," Lord Caden replied, warning in his voice. "Give her what she wants."

"You have my word. She'll be ready when you leave."

Erynn was still grappling with the news about Gareth, but now realized there was more. She? Were they talking about a person? Was that why the Galians had come to Alyria? They wanted someone?

"What about your father?" Lord Caden asked.

Holden was quiet for a moment. "I think he suspects."

The shape that Erynn knew was Lord Caden now moved even closer to the desk. "You said you had everything under control. That we could wait." Tension had crept into his voice.

"I do. And we can. You've seen my father. He's a feeble old man with no one left to trust. Even if he does suspect, there's nothing he can do. And by the time he does find out it will be too late. Believe me, I won't let him interfere."

Erynn could hear the hatred in Holden's voice and she realized Faris was right. If she had told the king the truth about the falconry he would have only questioned Holden. And if Holden could so easily discuss plans to kill his own brother, she didn't even want to think about what he might do to his father.

"I hope you're right," Lord Caden said. "For both of our sakes."

"I am," Holden said, his voice firm and full of confidence. "You worry too much, Silas."

Lord Caden laughed, but it didn't seem like he thought Holden was being funny. "That's only because I know what Naedra will do if she doesn't get what she wants. To both of us."

There was a brief silence, and then the chair scraped against the floor and the shape that Erynn knew to be Holden stood. "Shall we go find more wine?"

One of the candles was extinguished; the other moved

with the men to the door.

The second it closed, Erynn pushed back the drapes and let out a breath it seemed she'd been holding a lifetime. She felt ill, disoriented in the darkness, her knees weak and her arms sore from clutching the heavy book tight. For several moments she just leaned back against the balcony doors and tried to catch her breath. Now she knew the truth about why the Galians were here, but she still couldn't believe it. They were going to kill Gareth. She had to warn him!

Unable to see even a hand in front of her, Erynn pulled back the drapes to let in some moonlight and brushed the dust from her hair, face, and clothes while she waited for her eyes to adjust. Then she carefully made her way to the cabinet, using her free hand to guide her, and set the history book on the top shelf. As she stepped back, her hand knocked one of the jewelry boxes on the lower shelf and it fell with a crash to the floor, the lid popping off and an assortment of rings and other baubles scattering out at her feet. A few precious stones twinkled up at her in the faint moonlight.

Erynn froze, half-expecting the door to open and Holden to step back inside, alerted by the noise. But she heard nothing and soon fell to her knees and quickly gathered up the pieces, terrified that if she missed even one, the king would see it in the morning and know someone had been in his cabinet — someone who knew where he kept the key.

When she had picked up all the pieces she could find and returned them to the box, she set it back on the shelf and locked the cabinet. Then she returned the key to the vase, grabbed the candle, and made her way to the door.

She had just slipped outside and turned for the stairs when she caught movement across the hall.

Someone was standing out on the balcony. A tall, dark shape moved toward the doors and stepped quietly over the threshold.

"A little late for you to be up here alone."

The voice was quiet, but had a distinct rough edge and Erynn knew right away who it was — even before he stepped closer and the dim light from the candles on the wall slowly revealed his face.

Quinn Dunigan.

"What were you doing in there?" the mercenary asked.

Erynn could barely breathe let alone speak, her feet like two slabs of stone. What was he doing up here on the second floor? "What — What do you mean?"

His eyes were dark — and questioning. "Holden was just in there with our new Galian friend, the Dragonslayer. I don't recall them mentioning you. Were you hiding?"

Erynn tried to swallow, but her mouth was dry. Her eyes darted to the main staircase across the hall, and then down toward the back of the keep and the rear stairs, wondering which might offer her the fastest means of escape.

"I didn't see them," she said, trying to sound like she didn't know what he was talking about. "I only went in there a moment ago."

Quinn stepped even closer. "If you'd gone in there a moment ago, I would have seen you."

Erynn reached into her pocket and pulled out the letter tube. "I came for this. A minute ago. The king asked me to send it, but I got busy in the kitchen and forgot."

Quinn smiled as he glanced down at the tube, and then he reached up a hand and scratched at his chin. "Kind of late for deliveries to the falconry, don't you think?"

"I was going to send it in the morning."

Quinn shook his head. "You were hiding. You knew you'd be in trouble if Holden caught you in the king's study alone."

Erynn closed her fingers over the tube and lowered her

hand, not wanting him to see she was trembling. She wanted to run, to get away from him, but feared if she did it would only prove her guilt. It took everything she had to pull herself up a little taller. "You must be mistaken. You were probably looking down at the courtyard and didn't see me."

She turned to leave, intending to walk as calmly as she could down the hall to the rear stairs, but he reached out his hand to the wall and blocked her path. He leaned close, and she caught a waft of smoke and ale and noticed an inch-long scar near the brow above his left eye.

"I want you to tell me what you heard," he whispered. "Or I might just tell Holden and his friend what I saw."

Erynn swallowed. "I – I didn't hear anything." Then she ducked under his arm and ran.

CHAPTER 10

Erynn half-expected Quinn to chase after her, or demand she stop, but he did neither. Still, she raced from the main keep and across the ward to the stables, not stopping until she had reached the servants' quarters. By now, all of the other women were asleep, so she moved quietly down the moonlit aisle to her cot and crawled in, not even bothering to change her clothes.

Somewhere outside, likely up on the thick wall that divided the inner and outer wards, a man laughed.

Erynn pulled her blanket up to her chin and lay still, staring back down the aisle at the door and listening for heavy footsteps on the stairs. She knew one thing for sure: if Quinn did tell Holden what he saw and he sent Marik to arrest her, she wasn't going to go quietly. She'd wake everyone up. Make sure they all knew what Holden was up to with the Galians. And since it might be her last chance, she'd tell them about Lord Caden, too.

She closed her eyes as an image came to mind, of the one and only time she'd ever met Gareth. It was the day before his wedding to Lianne, and only a few days before he left with Adena's father and a small host of men for Ridan. She was in the market, shopping for her mother, when she saw her father step into one of the shops across the street. She had wandered in after him, but found the store empty and his voice coming from the back room. Not bothering to knock, she walked in and saw him talking to Gareth and a bald man with a red beard she'd never seen before. Her father had seemed oddly upset at the interruption, and the red-bearded man had quickly slipped out the door, but Gareth didn't seem annoyed at all and had even talked to her for a few minutes. She knew he was leaving for Ridan and had asked if he was scared to be going off to a war, but instead of answering he had kneeled down in front of her and asked if she thought she could fight to protect those she loved. She said she was just a girl, not a knight with a sword, but he said that didn't matter and that if she loved someone, or something, enough she could do things she never thought possible. She had believed him for a while, but then her mother's illness worsened and no matter how hard Erynn worked to take care of her, it made no difference. She had been powerless to save her father, too.

Erynn opened her eyes. Was she powerless still? Gareth had written her not long after she returned from Galia, to tell her how sad he was to hear of her father's death. It was a letter she had been absolutely stunned to receive and which she still kept, safely stowed away in its letter tube, in the pack under her cot — along with the black stone and the letter old Soren had found. That the future King of Alyria would take time away from the war to write her had touched her in a way nothing else had at the time. More than anything the king himself, Lord Brison, or anyone else had said. How could she let them kill him now? Telling the king was out of the question. And Faris wasn't likely to be of any help, either. The guards weren't just watching the falcons and she wasn't sure she could trust him anyway. Her only hope was Sheldon

Birch. If she could find him and convince him to send a letter to Gareth, warning him about the banquet, maybe she could do something this time. Maybe she could save him.

Erynn hadn't expected to sleep, but before she knew it light was creeping into the room and the other women were up and getting ready for the day. For a second she wondered if it had all been a bad dream, and that Holden wasn't really conspiring with the Galians to kill his brother, but then she realized she was still dressed and knew every moment of it was real.

Adena glanced over at her from the next cot and seemed to pick up right away that something was wrong, but Erynn motioned for her to say nothing. She rose and changed her clothes, discovering with some alarm that she had forgotten all about the dried tea leaves in her pocket and they had spilled out into her cot during the night. She discreetly swept up as much of them as she could and tucked them back into her pocket, reminding herself to get rid of them on the way down to the village.

Erynn waited until she and Adena had left the servants' quarters and were down in the stables, alone, before finally telling her everything — from the plan she had come up with to go down to the village, to her overhearing the plot against Gareth and her encounter with Quinn. But it wasn't until she had finished her story and Adena was still trying to absorb everything, that Erynn realized who it was the Galians might be after.

"Lianne?" Adena said with a frown. "Why her?"

"Because she was originally supposed to marry Naedra's son," Erynn said. "Her father called off the engagement after Galia invaded Ridan."

"Her father's the King of Verdan, right?"

"Right," Erynn said, remembering that Adena had never

95

cared much for history or politics.

"But why would they want her now? That was four years ago."

"I don't know. The king told me once that Galia and Verdan haven't gotten along since she married Gareth. Maybe this has something to do with that. Maybe Naedra wants Lianne because she thinks it will give her some control over her father."

"Or control over Gareth?"

"Lord Caden seemed pretty sure they could get to him at that banquet."

"Well, you have to tell the king what you heard. Or at least Lianne."

But Erynn had already made up her mind. "I can't. Now I know Holden will do something if his father tries to interfere. And I already told you I can't tell her. She'd probably just go to the king. Or confront Holden. Maybe even tell him where she learned of his little plan."

"Well, you can't handle this yourself," Adena said, whispering as a couple of stablehands walked by. "It's too dangerous."

"I don't have any other choice, Adena. I can't let them kill him. Besides, Lord Caden said Naedra will be upset if her plan fails. Maybe she'll blame him and kill him herself."

Adena still didn't look like she agreed, but she finally sighed and at least seemed resigned not to bother her about it anymore. "Well, I still can't believe you didn't read the king's last entry. That's why you went up to the study in the first place."

Erynn hadn't even remembered that fact until she had almost finished her story. She knew why the Galians were here now — or at least she was certain she did — and how Holden was conspiring with them to kill his brother, but she still didn't understand why Krystalix cared so much. What would make him go against his usual behavior and kill two of the Galians? She rubbed a hand over her eyes, still able to smell the dust from the drapes amid the faintly sweet scent of dried tea leaves. An image came to mind of the dark-haired woman she had read about in the history book, standing next to Krystalix with her hand on his nose, but then another stablehand walked by and she pushed the thought away. "I need to go before someone sees me and tells Mirella I'm dawdling. I'll try to see the king when I get back. If he does suspect the Galians have come for Lianne, maybe I can find out more."

"They want me to help with the Galian horses today," Adena said. "Who knows, maybe I can learn something useful, too."

After wishing each other luck, Erynn headed out the stable doors and turned south toward the inner gatehouse. She was hungry and wanted nothing more than to go to the kitchen and grab something to eat, but didn't want to risk running into Mirella.

Halfway across the ward, she saw a sight that stopped her cold.

Marik was standing near the gatehouse, talking with two men she'd never seen before. The men seemed agitated about something and had horses waiting nearby, as if they'd just arrived at the castle, but Marik seemed calm. Standing next to him was Quinn.

Erynn stopped and glanced around, feeling a sudden urge to hide but too far from the stables or the keep to duck out of sight. She couldn't believe her luck. Why did they both have to be at the gate now? Right when she wanted to leave?

A wagon rolled past and she realized it was the one Mirella sent down to the market every morning for supplies. The same one the headservant had insisted on sending for the tea. Without giving it much thought, Erynn stepped in behind the wagon and moved to the side opposite Marik and Quinn. She knew she couldn't hide from them completely, but hoped they'd be too busy talking to notice her pass by.

The wagon rumbled forward toward the gatehouse. People passed by on foot and on horses, but Erynn kept her eyes down and simply focused on putting one foot ahead of the other. Soon the shadow of the inner gatehouse loomed in front of her and then she was through it and into the outer ward. And then finally, several minutes later, she was through the main gatehouse and out on the road, making her way down the long winding hill towards Caraden Village.

The road was thick with horses and wagons, so she kept close to the side to avoid being hit. As she walked, she dropped bits of dried tea leaves onto the road and tried to figure out what she was going to say to Sheldon. She just hoped he felt as strongly about saving Gareth as she did.

She hadn't been gone long when a group of horses rode up quickly from behind. She tensed and glanced back.

It was Quinn. He and all five of his men were galloping down the hill towards her.

For a moment Erynn was sure he had come to arrest her, but he didn't slow down and simply caught her eye and gave her a brief nod as he thundered past. The two men she had spotted talking with Marik were also with him, and as she continued walking and watched them disappear around the corner at the bottom of the hill and then reappear a short time later on the road west, she wondered where they were off to in such a hurry and if he had said anything to Holden. The not knowing was starting to drive her crazy.

The market was busier than Erynn had ever seen it before. News of the Galians — and the banquet — had clearly drawn people from all over Alyria and they filled the aisles and seemed far more interested in talking about what was going on than buying or selling anything. She wandered around for a while, watching for Sheldon and listening in on bits of conversation to see if she could find out anything new about the war, but she heard nothing of interest. Just some talk of recent thefts in the northern towns around Caraden. Eventually she made her way toward the back of the market, where Sheldon usually kept his stand, but instead of the old falconer, she found a younger man selling a variety of kitchen goods — plates, mugs and utensils.

"Anything interest you, miss?" he asked as she approached. "Some new plates perhaps?"

The last thing Erynn was interested in was plates, but she smiled politely. "I'm actually looking for Sheldon Birch. Do you know him? This is usually his stand."

The man shook his head. "No, but then I'm new around here. I did hear he might not be back for a while though. Some sort of tragedy in his family, I believe."

Erynn's heart sank. "Who told you that?"

He gestured toward a rather large woman selling baskets on the other side of the market, a woman Erynn had seen before and knew was one of the organizers. She thanked him and headed down the aisles toward the woman, hoping with all her heart he was mistaken.

"I'm looking for Sheldon Birch," Erynn asked when she reached the woman, interrupting a conversation she appeared to be having with a shorter woman in the aisle. "The man at his stand said he wasn't expected back soon and that something had happened to his family. Is that true?"

The woman exchanged looks with the other in the aisle, and then a sad look came over her face. "I'm afraid so. We heard the news a couple months ago. His son was killed. And his daughter-in-law. Awful, awful news."

"Killed?" Erynn asked. "What happened?"

A slight look of unease crossed the woman's face, as if she didn't feel comfortable saying anything more. She looked again at the other woman before finally glancing around and leaning her great weight forward across the table, between two baskets. "They said it was soldiers from the castle. Marik Fayne."

Erynn closed her eyes, suddenly not sure she wanted to hear the rest.

"I can't imagine what Sheldon must be going through," the woman in the aisle said, shaking her head sadly. "He taught his son everything he knew about those birds and it was falconry that got them both killed."

"Falconry?" Erynn gasped, and as both women nodded she remembered what Faris had said about Marik killing people who weren't obeying Holden's new law. And how dangerous he said it would be for her to try sending the letter herself. She felt ill, like she needed to sit down, but at the same time she knew she couldn't leave yet, that there was still one more question she needed to ask. The only problem was, she no longer wanted to ask it. "Do you know where he lives? It's really important that I find him."

"Only that it's in the south somewhere," the woman behind the stand said. "He never said much about himself, or his family. Just liked talking about those falcons."

Erynn thanked the women and headed back across the market, wandering rather aimlessly for a while. Her thoughts went to Adena's brother, Jared, and how Sheldon had given him lessons in falconry. Secret lessons, so his father wouldn't find out. If Marik could so easily kill Sheldon's son and daughter-in-law, he could easily kill Jared, too. She knew how much her friend missed her brother, but now she wondered if maybe it was better he wasn't in Alyria.

She stopped several times to ask other vendors she knew had been around for a while if they knew where Sheldon lived, but they all seemed somewhat uncomfortable discussing the old falconer and simply told her the same thing: that he lived down south somewhere and no one expected him back soon. Eventually she gave up and headed across the market towards the herbalist. She still wasn't sure what she was going to do about the letter in her pocket, but knew she didn't have any more time for that now. She needed to pick up the tea and get back to the castle before she landed in even more trouble with Mirella.

The herbalist recognized her at once and immediately set to work preparing a package of the same blackish-green leaves. An old woman sat next to him on a stool and hadn't stopped staring at Erynn the entire time they talked. Erynn knew she was his mother, but had had a few odd encounters with her in the past and wasn't in the mood for one now. So she turned away as she waited and let her eyes pass back over the market.

Her attention landed on two men at one of the stands a few aisles over. They had a rather rough and menacing look, and were both wearing long dark cloaks and swords — unusual for the market. The taller man was thin, with a slightly pointed chin and black hair. He had a tool of some kind in his hand, which Erynn wasn't able to see very well through the crowd, and he appeared to be trying to sell it to one of the vendors. The other man had a barrel chest and a receding brown hairline and kept casting glances around the market. The vendor was shaking his head, not looking interested in buying the item let alone even talking to the men, but the taller man didn't appear willing to take no for an answer.

The herbalist handed Erynn a small parchment-wrapped

package of tea, and she forgot all about the two strange men with the swords and turned for the road. But she hadn't gone more than a few steps when she felt a tug on her arm.

It was the old woman.

Before Erynn could speak, the old woman leaned close and pressed something into her palm — a package similar in size and shape to the one the herbalist had just given her.

"Put it in their drinks, dear," she whispered.

Erynn frowned. "What is this?"

The old woman's eyes darted around. "Do it during the evening meal and no one will know."

For a moment, Erynn was speechless. "I don't understand. Who —"

"The Galians, dear. Do it for your father."

Something in the old woman's eyes and the tone of her voice set the hairs on the back of Erynn's neck on end. What had the old woman given her? She raised the bundle to her nose and noticed it had a slightly nutty smell. "Is this ... poison?"

"Sshhh!" the old woman said, waving a hand to silence her. A heavy-set man brushed by in the aisle and she waited for him to pass before leaning close again. "No one will know, dear. They'll go to sleep but won't wake up."

Erynn felt a chill run down her spine — suddenly very aware of all of the people moving around them in the market. It was poison! She could see it in the old woman's eyes. She wanted her to kill the Galians! As she glanced back down at the package, her mind reeling, she remembered Adena's comments the day the Galians arrived. About slipping something in Lord Caden's stew. The old woman had just given her exactly what she needed to do it. To give her the justice she wanted. But could she?

She shuddered. Was this how Naedra planned to kill

Gareth? To slip something in his meal at the banquet in Sarda? She could feel the old woman watching her, nodding silently and waiting for her to head back up to the castle with the poison clutched in her hand. A wave of nausea rose inside and she clenched her teeth. She wanted justice, but couldn't bring herself to do it this way. She thrust the package back. "Take it. I don't want it."

The woman seemed disappointed — and refused to take it. "Do it for your father, dear. They deserve it. All of them. Once they have Ridan, they'll come for us!"

"No," Erynn said, shaking her head. "Take it!" But still the woman refused.

People turned their heads, but Erynn ignored them. She was going to drop the package on the ground if the old woman refused her again.

"Mother?" the herbalist said, obviously noting the commotion and coming around the stand. "What are you doing?" He looked at Erynn and saw the package on her outstretched palm.

"Tell her to take it," Erynn said. "I told her I don't want it."

Before he could speak, the old woman snatched the package and tried to slip it in her pocket, but he grabbed her arm and wrenched it from her hand. He raised it to his nose and a split-second later his eyes went wide.

"You gave this to her?" he asked, disbelief in his voice.

The old woman shrugged, as if she didn't think she had done anything wrong. "She works in the kitchen. Those Galians deserve to die for what they've done. Every one of them. One day she'll wish she had."

The herbalist looked at Erynn, shock and apology and even a touch of fear in his eyes, but she just turned away and started for the road, wiping the palm of her hand against her dress. People crowded the aisles, the market getting even busier as the day wore on, but she pushed her way through, causing more than a few to remark on her rudeness. She only glanced back at the herbalist and his mother once — and that was when she walked right into him.

A hand grabbed her arm — tight — and she whirled around, her mouth automatically opening to apologize for not watching where she was going. But then she froze.

It was Marik.

"Why, Erynn, what are you doing here?" he said with a smile. "I would have thought you'd be busy in the kitchen."

Erynn pulled back and he immediately released her arm, but for a moment she was so stunned to see him that she couldn't speak. Had he followed her all the way from the castle? And more importantly — had he overheard her conversation with the old woman? "I – I was just picking up some tea for the king."

"Tea?" Marik said with a frown. "Surely we have enough at the castle?"

"It's a special kind. It helps him sleep."

He raised a brow, a slight grin on his face. "Not sleeping with the Galians around, is he?"

Erynn said nothing. A couple of soldiers were standing out on the road, looking like they were waiting for him with his horse, but other than that she didn't see any more of his men around. Several people had stopped and were staring at them and whispering.

Marik watched her a moment longer. Then his face turned serious and he motioned toward the road. "You better get going. It's a long walk back to the castle and I'm sure Mirella's expecting you."

CHAPTER 11

Erynn didn't glance behind her once the entire walk back to the castle, too afraid she'd spot Marik. She wondered if Quinn had told Holden about seeing her outside the study, and that's why Marik had followed her, or if this was still about the letter in her pocket. If so, she didn't understand why he didn't just take it. Even if she refused to hand it over, there wasn't much she could do to stop him from taking it. And surely someone in his position had better things to do than follow her around all day?

She was tempted to go find Adena when she returned to the castle, but she knew she needed to get back to the kitchen and headed up to the study instead. She just hoped she had enough time to deliver the king his tea and ask about Lianne before she started her chores.

When she arrived, she found two men she didn't recognize standing across the hall, talking quietly, and learned the king was with someone and she would have to wait. She turned to leave, figuring she'd just have to come back later, but then the door opened and a well-dressed young man stepped outside. He appeared to be in his early twenties, solidly built with brown hair, but he had a look on his face that suggested he wasn't at all pleased. He started toward the men across the hall, but then he noticed Erynn and frowned, as if he thought she looked familiar. Still, he didn't pause and soon he and the other men were gone and the guards were ushering Erynn inside to see the king.

Her mouth went dry the second she stepped into the study and the door closed behind her. The room seemed different to her now. Sinister. A reminder of everything she had heard there only hours before and how she still needed to find a way to warn Gareth. The balcony doors stood open in the sun, the heavy blue drapes pulled back, but she could still smell the dust and feel the itch of the fabric on her skin. On the other side of the room, the cabinet doors stood slightly ajar, the history book visible on the top shelf. Her eyes searched the floor, looking for any pieces of jewelry she might have missed, but she saw none.

The king sat at his desk, gazing down at a letter in his hand. The dark circles under his eyes had faded, but he still looked tired. He had the map out in front of him, but the rest of the desk was bare.

"I have just learned Lord Brison is ill," he said as she approached. "I had hoped he would be here for the banquet tonight. That was his son, Jeth." He folded up the letter and slipped it inside the top drawer.

Erynn was sad to hear the king's friend wasn't well, and even more curious why his son seemed so displeased. At least now she understood the recognition on his face. Lord Brison did say her father had brought her to his house when she was younger. Perhaps Jeth had seen her when she was there. Not sure what to say, she just pulled the parchment-wrapped package from her pocket and set it on the desk. "I picked up more tea, Your Grace."

The king reached across the desk and picked it up. "Good.

Did you have any trouble leaving the castle?"

Erynn thought about Marik, but she knew if she said a word the king would only ask questions. "No, Your Grace."

He seemed surprised. "None at all?"

"Mirella did want to send her driver, but I told her what you said."

The king stared at her, until Erynn started to wonder if he somehow knew she was lying, but then he looked away, toward the window.

"Perhaps I was mistaken," he said, his voice quiet. He slipped the tea in the drawer.

"Your Grace?"

The king smiled and motioned to the door. "That will be all, Erynn. I will send for some tea later, after the banquet." He shifted his attention to the map and pulled it closer.

Erynn hesitated, not wanting to leave until she'd asked about Lianne. She wasn't sure how best to bring it up, so finally just blurted it out. "Your Grace? Do you think Princess Lianne's in danger from the Galians?"

The king's head jerked up. "Lianne? What would make you ask that?"

Erynn flushed, not quite expecting the sudden intensity of his gaze. "I – I was just trying to figure out why they're here, Your Grace. You said once that they didn't get on with her father, after he broke off her engagement to Prince Thade. I thought she might be of some use to them. Perhaps to control her father."

The king glanced back down at the map and the kingdom of Verdan up in the northeast corner. "Naedra certainly wasn't happy that she married Gareth, even though it was her own fault, but I doubt there's still enough conflict to send men all the way here for her. And I'm sure Lianne's father would have sent word if he had concerns."

Erynn wondered if Lianne was still receiving letters from home, or if Holden was now screening those letters, too.

The king raised his head, and this time his eyes were slightly narrowed. "It is an odd question to ask, Erynn. An odd conclusion to have made. Have you heard something? Perhaps some gossip around the castle? It is very important that you tell me if you have."

"No, Your Grace," Erynn said, shaking her head. "I was just wondering. I saw her after they arrived and she didn't seem very happy. I guess it started me thinking."

"Lianne understands the danger the Galians pose. As does her husband, which is why he went to Ridan. Unfortunately, my other son does not." The king paused. "Erynn, if you should hear anything like that about Lianne — or any other reasons why the Galians might be here — I want you to tell me right away. Is that clear?"

"Yes, Your Grace."

The king sat back in his chair, his eyes returning to the map.

Erynn waited for him to dismiss her again, but soon she noticed a rushing sound — the exact same one she had heard in the throne room the day the Galians arrived — and a dull ache broke out across her brow. She blinked and shook her head, but neither went away.

"Have you seen my son today?" the king asked.

Erynn almost didn't hear him. The rushing sound was growing louder and a rush of anxiety was building inside. She rubbed her temples, thinking maybe she should have risked going to the kitchen for something to eat before she headed down to the village. "No, Your Grace."

"So he has not tasked you with anything?"

The question sounded casual, but Erynn found something about it strange. Holden had never once asked her to do anything. Ever. Other than leave the room when he wanted to speak to his father. But before she could answer, a sudden commotion rose outside — men were shouting all around the inner ward.

A blanket of darkness swept over the room and a bone-chilling scream ripped through the air. The entire castle seemed to shudder.

Erynn's eyes flew to the painting of Krystalix. She had heard that scream before.

"Not again!" the king said, looking up. Then he was on his feet and heading for the balcony.

Erynn clamped her hands over her ears, the rushing sound growing even louder. Once again she felt an almost overwhelming urge to run — a feeling that she wasn't safe in the castle — but she resisted. She had to. She had nowhere else to go.

Darkness passed over the room again — and then it was gone.

Erynn lowered her hands. And before she knew it she was outside on the balcony, next to the king. Gazing up at the dragon.

She had forgotten how big he was.

Krystalix sailed low over the castle, his golden wings outstretched and his head turned to watch the people below. He passed over the outer walls, banked slowly, and flew high over the forest and lake west of the castle as he came back around.

Erynn squeezed her eyes closed. She could still see her father lying motionless on the road. See the terror on the faces of the Galian soldiers as the dragon swooped down and snatched them from their saddles. See the falcon soar up into the air and be snapped up in those massive jaws.

Krystalix screamed again and this time, when she opened

her eyes, she saw him descend toward the outer walls, passing over the soldiers patrolling the walkways and disappearing out of sight behind the keep. She searched the sky, waiting for him to reappear, and seconds later he flew over the castle — right above them — and so low she could see the light colored scales of his belly and feel the rush of heat in his wake.

Men were still shouting down in the courtyard and running around the side of the keep toward the stables. Krystalix banked over the forest and came back around, and this time it wasn't long after he disappeared behind the keep that Erynn smelled smoke.

"He's attacking the stables," she said, barely aware she'd spoken the thought out loud.

The king didn't turn his head. "He wants the Galians to leave."

Erynn was about to ask him why — to even insist this time that he tell her what he knew about the dragon and his strange behavior — when another thought entered her head.

Adena!

Erynn turned and fled back inside.

"Wait, Erynn!" the king cried after her. "It's too dangerous!"

But Erynn didn't listen. She raced out of the study and down the hall towards the stairs.

Out in the rear ward, the middle stable was on fire. Flames were already reaching for the sky from the roof and upper windows, and slowly creeping down to the main level, but so far the other two buildings remained untouched. A crowd had gathered behind the main keep, many of them servants who had come out to see what was going on, and almost all were staring up at the dragon as he circled overhead. Soldiers were scrambling to put together a line of men from the well tower at the back of the ward, stablehands were leading terrified horses from the stables and taking them around to the courtyard, and at least two dozen archers were arranging themselves out in front of the crowd.

Erynn could still hear the rushing in her ears and feel the dull ache in her brow, but she ignored them as she made her way through the crowd. She saw familiar faces everywhere, women from the kitchen, men who worked in the stables and around the ward, but she saw no sign of her friend.

Marik stood in front of the crowd, shouting orders to the archers as they lined up and raised their arrows towards the dragon. Waiting for him to descend for another attack.

Erynn stopped and glanced up — suddenly afraid Krystalix might be hurt.

The dragon dropped down for another pass, unleashing a massive ball of fire on the stable roof and sending the flames even higher.

"Fire!" Marik yelled.

Dozens of arrows sailed up into the sky, but Krystalix saw them coming and easily flew up out of reach. He circled high overhead, his head turned to watch the scene below.

Erynn continued her search through the crowd, looking for her friend and eventually retracing her steps when she failed to find her. She was getting anxious now. The middle stable was where both the Galian soldiers and their horses were staying during their visit, and Adena did say she was supposed to work there today. So where was she?

Minutes later Erynn still hadn't found her and now it seemed most of the horses had been evacuated from the stables and cleared from the rear yard, the last few still being lead by stablehands around to the front of the keep.

Erynn paused near the front of the crowd, and as she gazed back along the line of archers to Marik, she saw he was staring at her. He had the strangest look on his face — like he was furious with her — but then one of his men shouted something and he turned away. Another man was running toward him across the ward, his face red and streaked with sweat. Behind him, the upper floor of the middle stable was now completely engulfed in flames and the fire spreading quickly through the lower level.

"Did they get all the horses out?" Marik yelled.

The man had a grave look on his face. "All but one, sir. Lord Caden's horse. He went crazy when the dragon attacked. No one could get near him."

Marik cursed, but before he could say anything further, Krystalix screamed and dove towards the stables again. "Fire!"

Another volley of arrows tore through the air, reaching for the dragon, but he changed his path and flew higher.

Erynn scanned the crowd once more, fear gnawing at her stomach. Then shouts rang out and people started pointing to the middle stable.

A large black horse had emerged from the building, passing through a gap in the flames. He galloped straight for the crowd, wild-eyed, and then veered sharply right as half a dozen Galians ran forward to intercept him. As he passed alongside the crowd, a rider became visible on his back — pressed down low against his neck.

It was Adena!

The stallion skirted the crowd and headed for the courtyard.

Erynn felt a surge of relief and ran after them.

By the time she reached the courtyard, the stallion had slowed and was pacing back and forth beneath the inner wall on the far side of the ward. Adena was talking to him and rubbing his neck, trying to calm him down. He stopped briefly and she slipped down, one hand still gripping a rope fixed to his halter. Several of the Galians advanced, causing the stallion to shy — his nostrils flared and his ears flat back — but she managed to hold on.

"Stay back!" she yelled.

The Galians paid no attention. One lunged toward her and snatched the rope from her hands, knocking her to the ground. The stallion reared, kicking at the man and trying to bolt, but he held on and another darted in and grabbed his halter. Together, they slowly lead the stallion toward the stairs, where the rest of the horses from the second stable were waiting.

Erynn ran to her friend. "You alright?"

"Fine," Adena muttered, glaring at the Galians as she picked herself up and brushed the dirt from her clothes. Her face was red and glistening with sweat, her hair singed, but otherwise she appeared unharmed.

"You know that was crazy, right? You could have been killed."

"I couldn't leave him in there. No matter who his master is." Adena seemed unable to tear her eyes away from the Galians, but finally she glanced up. "Is he gone?"

Erynn realized it was quiet. She could still hear the shouts of the men battling the fire on the other side of the main keep and see the smoke rising up into the sky — for her, the air seemed almost overwhelmingly thick with it — but she saw no sign of Krystalix. Just the king up on his balcony, watching her. She looked away, hoping she wasn't in trouble for disobeying his orders. "I guess so."

"Why did he attack like that?"

"The king thinks he wants the Galians to leave."

"Well he certainly destroyed the stable. But I don't think he got any of them." Adena paused, her eyes on the Galians again. "I saw something interesting before he attacked, though. Marik almost got into a fight with some guy in the stables. A young guy, dressed like a lord's kid. He seemed pretty upset about something."

Erynn frowned. "Brown hair?"

"You know who he is?"

"Jeth Brison. Lord Brison's son. He was talking to the king when I got back from the village, but didn't look very pleased when he left. The king said his father was sick and couldn't make it to the banquet."

"Well, I couldn't hear what they were talking about, but he didn't seem very pleased to see Marik, either. I don't think I've ever seen anyone stand up to him like that."

Erynn remembered the smile on Marik's face when she saw him in the village; the way he acted like running into her was just a coincidence. "He was probably in the stables looking for me. Thinking I'd come to see you. He followed me to the village."

"Followed you?" Adena said, looking surprised.

"Holden has to be worried I might try to send this letter to Gareth myself. Maybe Quinn did tell him what he saw last night."

"But why doesn't Marik just take it? Or lock you up?"

"I don't know. Maybe they still will."

"Did you find Sheldon?"

"No," Erynn said, and then she rather reluctantly told her friend what she had learned in the village — leaving out the part about the herbalist's mother.

When she was done, Adena raised her hands to her head. "See? I told you it's too dangerous to do this yourself. And now Marik probably knows you've been asking about Sheldon."

Erynn crossed her arms over her chest. Part of her knew her friend was right, but the other didn't see what else she could do. "Well, they can't arrest me for simply asking about a falconer."

"I wouldn't be too sure," Adena said. She sighed and ran a hand through her hair, seeming like she wanted to say something more but knowing it was pointless. She eyed the Galians again. "So what are you going to do?"

Erynn was about to say she still didn't know, but her friend stiffened and she turned to follow her gaze.

Holden and Lord Caden had emerged through the main doors of the keep and were walking down the stairs. They paused to check on Lord Caden's horse, who seemed to have finally settled down, and then talk to the other Galians. One of the men pointed towards Adena.

"Great," Adena muttered.

Holden smiled, spoke a few words to Lord Caden, and then they both started across the courtyard.

Erynn gasped and turned back toward her friend, trying to hide her face and wishing with all her heart that she could disappear. She had half a mind to leave Adena and run, to get as far away from Lord Caden as she could, but Holden was clearly walking toward them and there was no time. And deep down inside she knew she would have to face her father's killer sooner or later.

"Adena," Holden said as they approached. "Lord Caden wanted to come and thank you personally for saving his horse. That wasn't just a spectacular ride; it was also very courageous."

Adena gave a slight nod, seeming uncomfortable with the attention. "Your Grace."

Lord Caden cleared his throat. "Yes, we saw the whole thing from the balcony. Very brave indeed. That horse can be a handful at times, but I've had him for years. And I'm glad I still will."

Adena gave another short nod. "My Lord."

Erynn's heart was pounding. She had her head down, her eyes on the ground, but she could feel Holden's gaze. And Lord Caden's.

"What did you think, Erynn?" Holden asked. "Is your friend a hero?"

Erynn slowly raised her head. Holden was smiling, and as he turned to glance at Lord Caden, her own eyes shifted and met those of her father's killer. She expected a frown, or a sudden flash of recognition, but she saw neither. The recognition was already there. He knew exactly who she was and how they had met before, and didn't seem at all bothered or surprised to see her again. One corner of his mouth raised up in a smile and she looked away, back at Holden. "Yes, Your Grace. But then I always knew she was good with horses."

Holden laughed. "Yes. I'm sure Keegan would be so proud if he were here."

Lord Caden turned to Adena. "Holden tells me you're Keegan Fields' daughter?"

Adena nodded again, although somewhat stiffer this time. "Yes, my Lord."

"I've heard of him, but can't say I've had the pleasure. If I ever do, I'll be sure to mention what I saw here today."

Erynn immediately had the sense he was lying. Something in his voice.

"Well, I think such a feat deserves a reward," Holden said. "And I have a fine idea. Why don't the two of you join us in the hall for breakfast tomorrow? I was planning to send a letter to Queen Naedra and King Krone, thanking them for the visit, and since Erynn is my father's official scribe, it seems only appropriate that she write it. Bring a quill and some parchment, Erynn. I'll have Mirella set a couple of places at one of the tables."

Erynn thought her jaw might hit the ground. Holden was inviting them to breakfast? Something about the request unsettled her, but she simply swallowed and nodded her head. "Yes, Your Grace."

Seconds later, the men turned and headed back to the keep.

Erynn watched them go, unable to move.

"That was odd," Adena said when they were out of earshot. "Has Holden ever asked you to write a letter for him before?"

"Adena, he just invited us to breakfast."

"So it's beyond odd. Why do you think he did it?"

"I don't know, but it can't be about you saving that horse. I doubt he cares."

"Are you going to go?"

"Do I have a choice?"

"But I thought the king told you to stay away from Lord Caden?"

Erynn kept her eyes down but had a strong feeling the king was still watching from the balcony — and that he had seen the entire exchange. "He did. But that was because he didn't want Lord Caden to recognize me." She paused, remembering the look on the Galian's face. "I could see it in his eyes, Adena. He already knew. He must have seen me earlier."

Adena shrugged. "I doubt he'll do anything. He probably doesn't want anyone to know what he did."

Erynn wished she had her friend's confidence, but her only reassurance was that at least this visit by the Galians was almost over. This time tomorrow Lord Caden and his men would be gone. She just wished she'd found a way to get justice for her father. And to safely warn both Gareth and

Lianne, if that was who they'd come for. "I think he was lying about your father. He has met him."

"Why would he lie about that?"

"Might be awkward. Especially if the rumors are true and your father is working for them." It was difficult for Erynn to say, but she had a feeling her friend had already accepted those rumors as true. Even if she couldn't admit it.

"Well, he doesn't strike me as someone who'd have trouble with awkward," Adena muttered. She started toward the stables, but hadn't gone more than a few feet when she gasped and whirled back around. "Wait — you don't suppose that has something to do with it?"

Erynn didn't understand. "Do with what?"

"What if my father's done something? If he is working for the Galians. What if ..." Adena went pale. "What if it's me?"

Erynn still wasn't following. "You what?"

"What if it's me Naedra wants? What if it's not Lianne at all?"

CHAPTER 12

Despite the short notice, the surprise attack by Krystalix, and all of the efforts afterward to put out the fire, the banquet went ahead without any further problems and seemed to be a success. Or at least that's what Erynn picked up from Mirella and the gossip around the kitchen as her own work kept her so far away from the great hall that she didn't know what was going on. But she didn't mind and barely noticed, too busy thinking about Holden's request and Adena's worry that the Galians had come for her. A growing sense of unease had also been building inside of her, ever since coming face-to-face with Lord Caden, and she wasn't looking forward to working in the kitchen alone.

Erynn hoped Adena might be sent to the kitchen to help out again, but she saw no sign of her, and eventually it grew late and the number of servants still working began to dwindle. She waited for the king to send for his tea, wanting to tell him about Holden's request and find out if he approved, but the hours passed without word and she started to wonder if maybe he really was upset with her. And then finally she was alone.

Erynn worked as fast as she ever had before, eager to

119

finish up the dishes and leave. Occasionally she heard noises coming from the great hall, but no one came to bother her or request more food or drink, and she saw no sign of Marik or Lord Caden. When she was finally finished and had put everything away, she started for the door, but noticed a basket of onions under one of the tables and stopped. She knew Mirella would likely blame her for leaving it out if she saw it in the morning, so she picked it up and headed for the pantry.

Only a few candles remained lit in the rear hallway, leaving the corner by the stairs draped in shadows. Erynn went to the pantry door and stepped inside. Two candles still burned low on a nearby shelf, but the others were out. Baskets filled with vegetables from the castle garden were stacked along the side wall and she set the onions down next to them and left the room.

She had just turned for the rear door when a figure stepped out of the shadows by the stairs and grabbed her arm.

Erynn gasped. It was the king.

He forced her back into the pantry with a strength that surprised her and quickly closed the door.

"What did Lord Caden say to you?" he asked, his grip tight on her arm.

Erynn was so stunned that at first she couldn't speak. "N – Nothing, Your Grace. He thanked Adena for saving his horse."

"Did he recognize you?"

Erynn remembered the look in Lord Caden's eyes. "I – I think so."

"What about Holden? What did he say?"

Erynn didn't understand what was going on, and the grave look on his face was scaring her. How long had he been waiting by the stairs? "Your Grace?"

The king squeezed her arm tighter. "Erynn, what did

Holden say to you?"

"He asked me what I thought of Adena. What she did."

"Is that all?"

Erynn hesitated. Something in the way he was looking at her had just set off a cold gnawing in the pit of her stomach. "He asked us to come to the hall for breakfast in the morning. He said he wants to send a letter to Queen Naedra and King Krone and that he wants me to write it. He told me to bring a quill and some parchment."

The king's eyes grew dark and he finally stepped back and released her arm. "Then it is as I feared. I am such a fool!"

Erynn didn't understand. "Did I do something wrong, Your Grace?"

The king shook his head, his anger suddenly seeming to have lessened. "No. You did nothing wrong, Erynn. I did. I suspected, yet did nothing. I thought Holden would have acted sooner if he knew, and then when you went to the village I assumed I was wrong. But perhaps he just wanted to avoid talk at the banquet. To wait until the very last second. When it would be too late for me to help you."

The gnawing in her stomach grew stronger. "Your Grace?"

The king took a deep breath. "Erynn, I have something I must tell you. Something that will no doubt trouble you to hear, but hear you must. I regret not telling you sooner and only hope it is not too late. You are in great danger."

Erynn stepped back. Danger? She opened her mouth to speak, but voices passed by in the corridor outside and he raised his hand. He waited until they were gone before speaking again.

"You were not adopted from an orphanage in Brye," he said. "And your real parents did not die in a fire. A friend of mine brought you here as an infant and asked me to take care of you. I agreed and, with Lord Brison's help, we found two people we trusted to raise you. They did a tremendous job, but unfortunately life was not so kind in return. I brought you to the castle after your father died so I could continue to watch over you. To fulfill my promise."

It was like the wind had been knocked right out of her, and for several long moments Erynn could barely breathe let alone speak. "Are – Are you saying they're still alive? My real parents are still alive?"

"Possibly, although I do not know who they are or where they are. All I know is your mother was being hunted by Naedra, and her fear for you was so great that she felt she must part with you to keep you safe. I was told she would come for you — or send someone in her place — when she felt the time was right."

Erynn couldn't believe she was actually hearing this. And then suddenly it hit her — so hard it almost knocked her off her feet. She was the one the Galians had come for! Not Lianne. Not Adena. That was why Holden had asked her to come to the hall in the morning. Not because he wanted her to write some stupid letter! And that had to be why Marik kept following her around. And why he had never actually demanded she give him the letter. The letter was an excuse!

"I – I don't understand," she said, voice trembling now. "Why was Naedra hunting my mother? And why do they want me?"

The king tried to smile, but his eyes were tired and full of concern. "You are a Daughter of Maegan, Erynn. As is your mother and her mother before her. Naedra's been after the Daughters for years. Not much is spoken of it, but many know."

Erynn could hardly believe what she was hearing. A Daughter of Maegan? An image flashed in her mind of a dark-haired young woman standing next to Krystalix amid a ring of tall stones. And then all of a sudden she understood why the dragon had been acting so strange lately. Why he had attacked the Galians and the castle. And why the king had always been so secretive about that history book. "I'm the reason Krystalix attacked the Galians. And the castle. Why he's been following them."

The king sighed. "I have never understood the relationship between dragons and Daughters — or with Maegan for that matter — but I do know there is one. Krystalix must be aware they have come for you and is trying to protect you. Just like he did the day your father died. Although it does seem odd that Lord Caden has somehow played a part in both events."

Erynn felt dizzy, her legs weak, but there was nowhere to sit down. And then another image popped into her mind — one she had not thought of in a long, long time. An image of a woman she had encountered in the woods behind their house when she was young, back when they still lived in the south. A woman with fair skin and golden hair, riding a dapple-grey horse. Fair skin and golden hair very much like her own. She no longer remembered what the woman said, or even if she said her name, but she had always remembered the warmth and compassion in her eyes and the feeling that she knew the woman somehow. She shivered. Could that have been her mother? Erynn raised a hand to her head. "But I still don't understand. I thought Naedra was a Daughter of Maegan? Why would she be hunting her own kin?"

"You are aware of the Prophecy? The last words Maegan spoke to her three advisors before she was arrested?"

Erynn nodded. Her father had told her the story when she was young. "She promised that a daughter of hers would one day return with the stone to Hale, and bring peace to Valentia."

"Yes, Maegan's stone. The one reportedly given to her by the king of the dragons himself — Cael. Naedra's been after that stone most of her life. From what I have heard, she seems to think she is the Promised Daughter and that she is destined to bring peace to Valentia — under her rule, of course. And raising those dragons only seems to have fueled that belief. That is why she invaded Ridan. She thinks the stone is there. And that is why she hunts the Daughters. She wants to prevent anyone else — even one of her own kin — from getting their hands on it first."

"But I don't care about the stone. Or being the Promised Daughter. I —"

The king raised a hand, silencing her. "There is another reason Naedra is after you, Erynn. A much more personal reason. She believes you mean to destroy her."

"Destroy her? I don't even know her. Why would she believe that?"

"I do not know exactly. Only that she has apparently had some vision of this and believes it."

"But why me?"

"That I do not know."

Erynn couldn't believe this was happening. Now she really needed to sit down. "So she wants to kill me?"

"Yes."

"What – What are you going to do?"

The king sighed. "Erynn, if Holden has made some agreement with her for you, which I now suspect he has, I will be powerless to stop it. Most of the men are loyal to him now — or fear Marik. You must leave the castle — and Alyria — right away."

"Leave?" Erynn said. "But, Your Grace, can't you do something?"

"If I knew of someone in this castle I could trust, I would

gladly send them with you. But there is no one and I am mostly to blame for that. I had hoped Lord Brison would come to the banquet, so he might help, but then I heard he was ill and was not sure Jeth was up to the responsibility. I looked for him at the banquet, after I saw you with Lord Caden and decided I had no other choice. But I saw no sign of him. I fear he may have gone home."

Erynn remembered Adena's comment out in the courtyard. "I heard he almost got into a fight with Marik in the stables."

The king seemed troubled by this news at first, but then he sighed. "Yes, I would say he most likely went home."

Erynn couldn't believe that after telling her that Queen Naedra wanted to kill her, and that he wished he had said something sooner, he was now telling her there was nothing he could do. And no one who could help. She wondered what would have happened if she had told him the truth about the falconry — and about what she learned in the study. If he would have told her sooner. She thought of mentioning it now, but as angry and hurt and terrified as she was, she could see the guilt and disappointment in his eyes and couldn't bring herself to hurt him. If he couldn't help her now, there was nothing he could do to help Gareth, either, and maybe it was better he didn't know. "Where am I supposed to go?"

"You must find a man named Paddon Morell. He is the one who brought you here. He was close to your mother and should know where she is. Hopefully she and her friends can protect you."

"Her friends?"

"The Order of the Cael. They are dedicated to protecting the bloodline of Maegan."

Erynn had heard the name before, but other than some association to the Daughters of Maegan, she didn't know anything about them. "I don't understand. If the Order is dedicated to protecting the bloodline of Maegan, how did I end up here? Why couldn't they protect me?"

"A question I asked Paddon myself when he brought you here," the king replied. "But, unfortunately, he would not say. Only that he needed my help." The king looked away. "And I could not refuse."

"Where do I find him?"

When the king turned to her again, Erynn was surprised to see tears in his eyes. "It has been some time since I heard from him, but you can most likely find him in Highcastle. His family has lived there for generations."

Erynn's jaw just about hit the floor. Highcastle? That was in southern Brye! He expected her to go all that way on her own? By foot?

The king pulled a red velvet pouch from the pocket of his robes and handed it to her. It was tied shut but clearly full of gold coins. "This should help you get there. It was all I could manage without drawing Holden's attention. Perhaps you can buy a horse in one of the towns. And some food, of course."

Erynn glanced down at the pouch, realizing that she was holding more gold than she'd ever seen in her life, and yet that somehow only made her feel even worse.

The king pulled a silver chain from around his neck and slipped it over his head. On the end dangled a small silver key. He handed it to her. "I have no idea what this is for, but Paddon said it was very valuable and not to lose it. And that it was to be given to you when you were ready."

Erynn stared at the key, too stunned by everything she had learned to even be curious what it might open. Somehow she got it over her head and safely tucked out of sight under her dress.

"Leave the second the gate is up," the king said. "Do not

wait any longer. And if anyone asks, just tell them I have sent you to the market."

"Yes, Your Grace."

"And I would not advise telling anyone who you are or where you are going. The road can be dangerous, as you well know, and Naedra will no doubt pay highly for you. You must not trust anyone, Erynn."

Erynn thought of Marik and how she'd seen him at the gate. Was he there because he was watching for her? Or was it just a coincidence? If he did follow her to the village, he must have noticed her leave. What if he was there again tomorrow? "Yes, Your Grace."

"And I would take the bridge at South Crossing. It is not as closely guarded or as busy as the one at North Falls."

"Yes, Your Grace."

The king hesitated, as if he wanted to say something more but couldn't find the words. Then he turned for the door. "We best go. My guards think I have gone to my study but may come looking for me if I am not back soon. And it would not surprise me if everything I do eventually gets reported to Marik."

"Do you know how Naedra found out, Your Grace? About me being here?"

The king paused. "If Holden does know who you are, which I am now certain he does, he did not hear it from me. I can only assume Naedra found out somehow and contacted him."

Holden knew, of that Erynn was sure. She could see it now in the way he had looked at her in the study the day the Galians arrived. And then she remembered something else. The way another prince of Alyria had once looked at her, that one and only time they had ever met. "Does Prince Gareth know?"

"Yes, it was necessary to tell him in case something happened to me. Davy and Jenna did, too. I needed them aware of the possible dangers."

Tears rose to Erynn's eyes. Her parents knew? And never said a word?

A look of concern passed over the king's face, and he reached out a hand and gently squeezed her shoulder. "You have done well, Erynn. If your birth parents are still alive, I am sure you will find them."

Her throat went tight. She had a feeling this might be the last time she ever saw the king, but somehow couldn't think of a single thing to say. Thank you for taking care of me all these years? For keeping your promise? It had all been a lie. "I'll try, Your Grace."

He tried to smile, but soon turned away. "Wait a few seconds before you leave. It is best no one sees us together."

And then he was gone.

CHAPTER 13

Although the king had told her not to tell anyone who she was or where she was going, Erynn knew she couldn't leave without saying good-bye to Adena. She woke her friend as soon as she returned to the servants' quarters and led her down to a storeroom on the main floor of the stable. And then, still overwhelmed by all she had learned, she told her everything.

Adena was stunned to find out that Erynn was the one the Galians were after — and why — but even more shocked that the king had claimed he couldn't do anything to help.

"Leave?" she said. "He just gave you a sack of gold and told you to leave?"

Erynn sank down on a crate by the window. "He doesn't trust anyone. He even thinks his own guards are reporting on him to Marik. Which I'm sure they are. At least now I know why Marik came to see me in the kitchen yesterday. He must have heard I'd seen the king and was trying to find out if he'd warned me."

Adena just stared at her. "But he's the king, Erynn. Surely he can do something?"

Erynn just lowered her head to her hands. Adena remained

still for a few moments, then turned and started pacing back and forth across the small room.

"Maybe if Gareth was here it would be different," Erynn said finally.

Adena snorted. "If Gareth was here, things would be a lot different." She shook her head. "First it was my father. Then my mother. Then Jared. And now you. Everyone I care about leaves."

"Adena, I don't have a choice. Naedra wants to kill me, remember?"

Adena stopped pacing. "Then I'll just have to come with you. That's what I'll do."

"Come with me?" Erynn said, sitting up now. "But what about your family? Jared promised —"

"Jared could be dead for all I know. Your father said Ethlon was dangerous." Adena crossed her arms over her chest. "My mother's been gone almost three years, Erynn. My father four. They're not coming back and you know that." She paused. "They can't."

Erynn realized she had known this for a while. She didn't know what had happened to Jared, whether he'd been hurt or there was some other reason why he hadn't returned by now, but there was no doubt in her mind about their parents. After all, how could they come back after what Keegan Fields had done? He had deserted, and that was a crime punishable by death. "If Jared does come back —"

"I'm not going to wait here forever, Erynn. Not by myself."

Erynn had to admit that the thought of having her friend along made her feel much better, like maybe she could make it to Highcastle after all, but she didn't want her to regret the decision later — or see her get hurt. "You've never been outside Caraden. It could be dangerous."

"Then you'll be safer if you have someone with you, so don't try to talk me out of it. Besides, you're my friend. I can't let you do this alone. And my mother always wanted me to see more of Valentia. Now's my chance."

Erynn was touched that her friend wanted to help her and said nothing more to try and change her mind. They remained in the storage room for a while longer, figuring out their plan for leaving the castle in the morning, and when the first rays of light finally did appear through the small windows of the servants' quarters a few hours later, they were both up and preparing for their journey. Most of the other women were also up and heading off to the keep to start their day, so they moved quietly, stowing what little they had to take with them in the packs they each kept under their cots.

Erynn knew she couldn't take her journal, that it was far too big and bulky and would only slow her down, but she was determined to take the quill and ink pot her father had given her and made sure the ink was well wrapped in an extra under-tunic to prevent it from spilling. Other than the sack of coins and an extra dress, the only other things she made sure to pack were the three letters she now possessed, still in their tubes — the one old Soren had found in Galia, the one she had received from Gareth after her father died, and the one she had been trying to send him about the Galians — as well as the black stone she had taken from her father's grave. Then they grabbed their cloaks and headed back down to the storeroom, where they waited out of sight until they heard the rumble and clank of heavy chains that signaled the rising of the inner gate.

They stepped out of the stable and walked quickly toward the inner gate. But they hadn't gone far when horses rode out of the third stable and approached from behind.

Erynn felt her heart leap up into her throat. She glanced

back.

Quinn and all five of his men were riding toward the gate.

She turned away, hoping he wouldn't notice her, and seconds later the men rode past them and around the crowd already waiting by the gate. As soon as the portcullis was high enough, they continued on into the outer ward. The rest of the crowd also started forward — but then stopped.

"What's going on?" Adena asked a short time later, when the crowd still hadn't moved. "Why isn't anyone leaving?"

It was then that Erynn noticed the guards. At least a dozen were lined up on either side of the gatehouse, more than she'd ever seen there before, and two more were standing out in front of the crowd, blocking everyone's path. The older of the two appeared to be arguing with one of the men at the front of the crowd, a man Erynn recognized as one of the castle blacksmiths.

"But we have work to attend to in the village," the man said. "Things we need. We have to leave."

The guard shook his head. "No one leaves until after the Galians have departed."

"But what about those men?" a woman said, waving a hand toward the gate. "The ones that just left?"

"They have permission," the guard replied. "Everyone else has to stay. At least for now."

The blacksmith turned to another man, shaking his head, and the woman stormed off toward the stables. The rest just stood there, looking like they didn't know what to do.

Erynn knew what this was about. Holden was obviously worried she might try to flee and was trying to make sure she couldn't escape. She stepped forward. "We have orders from the king to go to the market."

The guards appeared surprised at first, but obviously weren't persuaded enough to move.

"No one leaves the castle," the older one repeated.

"But these are orders from the king," Adena said, stepping forward, too. "How can you stop us?"

The guard laughed. "Easily. We have our own orders and unless His Grace comes down here to tell us otherwise, we're following them and you're staying."

Erynn knew there wasn't much hope of that happening. She stared at the guard, and then past him through the gatehouse to the main gate and the road beyond. She felt trapped; so close to escape and yet unable to get there. She heard Adena say her name, but couldn't bring herself to move. Then her friend grabbed her arm and pulled her back toward the stables.

"Now what?" Adena whispered. "Try to hide? Wait and see if we can figure out something else?"

"There isn't anywhere to hide," Erynn said, her eyes scanning the inner ward and the guards up on the wall and finding it all seemed so much smaller now. "At least nowhere they wouldn't find us sooner or later."

"Well, we have to do something. Find some other way out of here."

An image flashed through Erynn's mind. An image of an old key in one of the books in the king's study. She stopped, but for a moment couldn't speak — a cold feeling trickling down her spine and gripping her tight. "There is another way. A tunnel under the castle."

Adena looked surprised. "The secret entrance? You know about that?"

"I heard about it a long time ago. When we lived down in the village."

"You know where it is?"

Erynn nodded. "I read about it in one of the king's books once."

Adena almost looked offended. "You never told me that."

"I was worried you might want to go see it."

"Well, where is it? How do we get there?"

Erynn hesitated, still not sure she should have even brought it up. She had never seen the tunnel before, but she could imagine it. Narrow and dark and cold. Just like that cave in Galia. Not a place she wanted to visit at all. "Through the crypt."

The expression on Adena's face changed. She knew how much Erynn hated that place. "It might be our only chance, Erynn. The only other way out."

"I know." Erynn wished she could think of something else. Anything else. But her mind was blank. "We need a key. The king keeps it in his study."

Adena grabbed her arm and pulled her towards the keep. "Then we have to go get it. If he's there we'll just tell him you need it. He owes you that much. Unless he does want to come down to the gate and help us get out of here."

A wagon was parked out behind the kitchen, the two horses hitched to the front munching on some hay on the ground.

Erynn paused to look in the back, wondering if maybe they could smuggle themselves out through the gate and she wouldn't have to face the tunnel at all.

Adena seemed to realize what she was thinking because she tugged on her arm. "It's too risky, Erynn."

Erynn knew she was probably right, but before she could turn away, Mirella appeared in the kitchen doorway on the opposite side of the wagon.

"Erynn!" she said. "Why are you in your cloak?"

Erynn hesitated, trying to casually hide her pack behind the wagon. "The king wants me to go to the market. Adena was going to come with me."

"You went to the market yesterday."

"I – I know, but he forgot something. He told me to go after the Galians have left."

Mirella rolled her eyes, not looking pleased but at the same time not looking like she was in the mood to argue, either. "Well you better get to the hall. Holden told me he's expecting you and I don't want you to keep him waiting. They should be gathering soon."

Erynn pointed to the rear door, near the back stairs. "I was just going to get a quill and some parchment. Like he asked."

"Then I suggest you hurry."

As soon as the headservant headed back inside, Erynn and Adena both bolted for the door. Erynn knew she had no choice now. Like it or not, she needed to find the key to the tunnel and use it to escape the castle. It was her only hope.

The hallway outside the study was deserted. Erynn was relieved, not really sure she wanted to see the king right now, and she went ahead and entered the room without knocking.

She went to the desk and opened the drawer, lifting the king's old letters from Gareth and searching around the quill, ink pot, and empty letter tubes for the key. But she saw no sign of it. Confused, she took a closer look, pulling the letters out and flipping through them in case it had slipped in between. But still no key. She checked the other drawers, starting to panic now, but still found nothing. "It's not here."

Adena was staring up at the painting of Krystalix. This was the first time she had ever seen it, let alone the upper floors of the keep or the king's study. She walked back to the desk, looking concerned. "What do you mean it's not here?"

Erynn collapsed into the king's chair. "I mean, it's not here." She gazed around, certain she had seen it the day the Galians arrived, and then her eyes stopped on the balcony doors. A memory came back — something she had heard that night while hiding behind those heavy blue drapes. "Holden took it. He was doing something in the desk when he was in here the other night."

"You're sure? There isn't somewhere else it could be?"

"No. I've only ever seen it here. In this drawer. Maybe he thought the king would warn me."

"Is that the only one?"

"It's the only one I've ever seen," Erynn said. But as soon as she said it, she remembered something else she had read about the key in that old book. She flew out of the chair and went to the mantle, shaking the cabinet key out of the small red vase.

"What?" Adena asked. "Did you think of something?"

Erynn went to the cabinet and unlocked the doors. "The tunnel was built in case of siege, as a way for the Royal Family to escape. It was custom for the king and queen to both carry a key. In case they were separated."

Adena peered in at all of the jewelry boxes stacked on the lower shelves, and then up at the history book on Krystalix and the rolled-up map on the upper shelf. "And you think maybe it's in here?"

"He keeps the queen's jewels in here."

"It's a key, Erynn, not a necklace."

"Yes, but it could have been worn on a chain around the neck. Like the one he gave me." She grabbed one of the boxes, avoiding the largest one that she already knew contained the king's crown, and when she opened it turned toward the light so she could see better. Queen Sera's crown, gold and encrusted with precious stones, sat inside on a bed of red velvet. She felt carefully around the crown and in the corners and even lifted it up to check the lining, but she found no key.

"Is that the book you read the other night?" Adena asked,

still gazing up at the top shelf. "And that map you said the king's always looking at?"

"Yes," Erynn said as she grabbed another box, her mind solely focused on finding that key. Inside was an assortment of rings, earrings, and brooches.

"Do you want to read his last entry?" Adena asked. "Or what he wrote about the day your father died?"

"Not really," Erynn said, rifling carefully through the pieces inside the box. "I think I have a pretty good idea what he wrote now. Besides, we don't have time." Not finding the key, she put the box back and reached for another. She wondered for a brief moment where she might be if she hadn't been interrupted that night. If she had read the entry about her father's death and somehow figured out she was a Daughter of Maegan. Would she have realized she was the one the Galians came for? Perhaps she would have been halfway to North Falls by now.

"Is Highcastle on that map?"

"Of course," Erynn said, wishing a little that her friend would stop asking so many questions. "It's one of the largest cities in western Alyria." The box held two diamond-studded tiaras, but no key. She put it back and reached for another — her panic building.

"Nothing?" Adena asked.

Erynn sighed and shook her head. She wondered if Holden was in the great hall and how long he'd wait before sending Marik and his men to find her.

The next box was filled with necklaces, some quite tangled, but as she turned back to the light and rifled through them, she noticed a large key at the bottom, strung on a silver chain — and recognized the intricate design of the bow.

"This is it," she said, relieved.

"You're sure?"

"I'm sure." Erynn. slipped the chain over her head and tucked the key under her dress, next to the one the king had given her.

"Then let's get out of here."

Adena was at the door by the time Erynn locked the cabinet, returned the key to its hiding place on the mantle, and grabbed her pack. She reached for the knob, but suddenly the door opened.

Standing in the doorway, and looking very angry, was Mirella.

CHAPTER 14

Adena quickly slipped behind the door, out of sight.

"Why aren't you in the hall?" Mirella demanded as she stepped into the room. "Holden is down there waiting for you."

Erynn motioned to her pack, trying hard not to look at Adena. "I – I just came for a quill and —"

"Yes, I know what you came for. What I want to know is what's taking you so long?"

"I was looking for a good piece of parchment."

Mirella took a few more steps into the study and glanced around. "Where's your friend? I thought she was joining you for breakfast?"

"She had to go back to the stables for something."

Mirella narrowed her eyes, as if not quite sure she believed her, but then she stepped aside and motioned with her head towards the door. "Let's go."

Erynn didn't move. She wasn't sure how she was going to get out of this, but did know one thing for sure: she wasn't going to the great hall. At least she wasn't going willingly.

"Now, Erynn. Or shall I add more time to your dish sentence?"

If Erynn wasn't so scared of Marik or Holden appearing at any moment, she thought she might have laughed. Instead, she swallowed, knowing she was about to make the headservant very, very angry, and calmly folded her arms across her chest. "I'm not going."

Mirella looked stunned — and even more angry. "Holden's given you an order, Erynn. Disobey it and I guarantee you his punishment will be much worse than mine."

"I know why they want me there. And I'm still not going."

"Why they want you there?" Mirella said, sounding a little confused. Then she shook her head. "I really don't know why Holden would want you there, or why the king ever chose you to write his letters, but you have been given an order and I will not let you disobey."

Erynn still didn't move.

The headservant's face was quickly growing red. "This is ridiculous. You're coming with me. Now."

Before Erynn could react, Mirella stepped forward and grabbed her arm. Erynn struggled with her for a few seconds, but finally wrenched herself away and moved further back into the room.

"I'm still not going with you, Mirella," she said.

Behind the door, Adena slowly inched away from the wall.

Mirella continued toward her again, her jaw clenched and hate in her eyes, but then she seemed to change her mind and stopped. "You will pay for this, Erynn. I guarantee it. Even the king won't be able to help you this time."

Erynn felt a rage boiling up inside her — no longer scared of her threats. "You've never liked me, have you Mirella? Ever since I set foot in the castle you've treated me worse than everyone else. Punishing me all the time. I know you're behind the rumor about me. About me and the king. But it isn't true. It's a lie."

Mirella smirked. "And why else would a king take in a fourteen-year-old servant girl and choose her to be his scribe?"

Erynn wished the king was in the study to hear her say that. To hear the disgust in her voice. But he wasn't. "There is a reason, one that actually makes a lot of sense once you've heard it, but I'm not even going to tell you."

A flicker of confusion crossed Mirella's face, but then it was gone. "I've had enough of this. Let's see you try and refuse the guards." She turned for the door, but it suddenly swung shut in front of her. Then Adena leapt out like a cat, barreling into the headservant's mid-section like a bull and sending her flying across the room. She landed in a heap by the balcony doors, clutching her stomach and gasping for air — and staring up at both of them in shock.

"Let's go!" Adena said, and she ran for the door.

Erynn raced after her, pausing only long enough to shut the door behind her — so she could at least delay Mirella calling the guards. Adena started back the way they came, but Erynn grabbed her arm and lead her another way, down a series of corridors to the west side of the keep. They had to duck into a shadowy corner twice to avoid being seen by passing guards, but otherwise the upper halls of the keep were deserted.

Soon they reached the winding staircase leading down to the deepest, darkest parts of Caraden Castle. Erynn descended quickly, only slowing when she neared the bottom and heard voices.

Two corridors branched off at the foot of the stairs, candles burning in sconces along the walls. The voices were coming from the left, the direction of the castle dungeon. Two men were talking about the banquet, although it was clear from their conversation that neither had actually attended.

Erynn pointed to the right, the direction they needed to go, and then stepped quietly to the edge of the stair, peeked around the corner to see if the guards were watching, and slipped down the hall. A second later, Adena followed.

The men continued talking, not noticing the two girls slip by.

Erynn ran down the corridor, holding on tight to her pack to prevent the coins from clinking. Her heart was pounding, but she knew it wasn't just her fear that Marik or his men might appear behind them any minute. She could see two massive doors ahead, at the far end of the corridor, and she knew what lay beyond. The crypt was bad enough, but the tunnel would be worse. Dark and cold and likely home to more than just spiders. Could she do this?

She hesitated when they reached the doors, but Adena grabbed a handle and pulled one open. It creaked loudly, enough to make them both wince, but a peal of laughter reached them from down the hall and seemed to cover the noise. They stepped inside.

A long cavernous room with a wide central passage and numerous thick pillars stretched before them. Caskets carved out of marble and stone sat on either side of the central aisle, most bearing a life-sized likeness of the deceased Royal on top. Hundreds of candles lined the corridor and each of the recesses between the caskets.

Erynn took a deep breath and started forward, glancing cautiously back and forth at the spaces between the caskets. Holden had thought enough to take his father's key to the tunnel. She just hoped he hadn't also thought enough to post a guard.

"I know you said they kept it lit," Adena whispered, "but I didn't imagine it would be like this. Who comes down here?"

"No one really. Maybe the king sometimes, to visit the queen. I think it's more out of respect for the dead."

"The dwarves built it?"

"Yes, a very long time ago."

"I can see why you hated having to work down here. It would take me all day to light this many candles."

Erynn wanted to tell her that it wasn't the candles she hated, but didn't bother. She was finding it hard to keep a lid on her anxiety as it was and knew that voicing her fears would only make it harder. "Well, hopefully whoever Mirella assigned to do it today isn't still down here."

They passed dozens of caskets before the room came to an end and they turned right through a passageway into another large room, similar to the first. More caskets lay before them, and minutes passed before they finally reached the last one. The room continued on, but there were no more candles. No lights of any kind. Just an endless room stretching on into darkness.

A vase full of fresh red flowers sat at the foot of the casket.

"Queen Sera," Adena said, reading the name etched into the stone.

Erynn didn't want to take candles from the queen's resting place, so she went to another casket across the aisle and selected the largest two she could find. She returned and handed one to Adena.

"Think they'll last the whole way?" Adena asked, a trace of concern in her voice.

Erynn was already trying hard not to imagine what might happen if they didn't. "I sure hope so."

"Where's the tunnel?"

Erynn motioned to the stretch of darkness that lay before them. "I think it's at the end of this room."

"Think? You've never seen it?"

"This isn't exactly a place I like to spend my time," Erynn snapped. She wanted out of the crypt. Now. And yet she was about to enter a space that was going to be much, much smaller. "I read about it. The book said it was at the end of the second crypt."

"Then let's go find out," Adena said, and she started forward into the darkness.

Erynn took a deep breath, hitched up her pack, and followed after her, keeping her candle raised so she could see the ground ahead.

They moved as quickly as they could and after several minutes finally came to the end of the crypt — which was marked by a short stone wall, about four feet high, with a narrow passage in the center. From there, the floor sloped downward about thirty feet to the far wall. In the center of the wall was a black iron gate.

Erynn swallowed and looked away, checking both sides of the narrow passage behind the short wall to make sure no one was hiding in the shadows.

Adena started down the slope.

Erynn hesitated a moment, but then followed her and fished out the key. Her fingers were trembling so she slipped the chain off and handed the key to Adena. "You better do it. With my luck I'd lose it."

Adena seemed to notice the nervous edge to her voice and the slight shake in her hand, but said nothing and simply handed Erynn her candle. She put her pack down, inserted the key in the lock, and tried turning it a few times, but it wouldn't budge. "You're sure it's the right one?"

"I'm sure," Erynn said, glancing back at the narrow passage in the short wall and searching the darkness for any signs they were being followed. "It's probably not been used in a hundred years, that's all."

Adena tried again, fiddling with the key, and finally it clicked right and the lock popped open. She lifted it off, pulled the gate open, and grabbed her pack. Then she stepped into the tunnel and turned to wait for Erynn.

Erynn hesitated again, staring at the dark gaping hole that now lay before her. Her throat was so tight that she could barely breathe, but she knew she had no other choice. She had to get out of the castle and the tunnel was the only chance she had left. So she gripped the candles tight and stepped inside.

Adena locked the gate behind them and slipped the chain around her neck. Then she took her candle back from Erynn. "You alright?"

"No," Erynn said. "But let's get this over with."

The tunnel wasn't wide enough to walk side-by-side, so Adena took the lead, raising her candle high enough to see the ground ahead of her.

Debris lay everywhere. Mostly loose rock and old discarded torches, but also the occasional piece of armor or bit of weaponry. Even a few arrows. Adena stopped to pick up an old dagger at one point, but the blade promptly fell off and she tossed the rest of it back on the ground.

Erynn stepped over yet another old torch and wondered about the person who'd carried it. Had the fire burned out and left him alone in the dark? And if it did, did he ever find his way out? The thought of stumbling across bones in the tunnel — skulls gazing up at her with empty eyes — made her heart beat even faster.

Something moved on the ground ahead, scurrying away from them with series of tiny squeaks, and they both gasped and stopped.

"Rats," Adena said with disgust.

Erynn shuddered and squeezed her eyes closed, her mind

now rapidly filling with images of being trapped down there in the darkness of the tunnel and eaten alive. Their bones picked clean.

A second later, Adena started forward again, muttering something to herself.

Erynn followed, not wanting to be left behind. Panic was setting in now, her breath coming fast, and it was getting even harder and harder to stay calm. She told herself to focus on the floor and not the walls around her. To focus on her breathing and not the squeak and the scurry of the rats. To focus on just getting through this tunnel one step at a time — and that she wasn't going to die. She also tried to think about what might be going on up in the great hall. She hoped Holden was frantic, and that his plan with the Galians was now in jeopardy with her missing, but that he still hadn't figured out where she went. Mirella had likely alerted him and the guards by now, but hopefully they were still searching the keep. And even checking the stables. Every once in a while she peered back into the darkness of the tunnel behind them, looking for glimpses of light that would signal pursuit. But she saw nothing.

Then Adena stopped as several more rats scurried away down the tunnel and Erynn accidentally walked into her. Her candle brushed her friend's pack and the flame flickered and almost went out.

"Careful," Adena whispered. "This place is bad enough with the light. It'll be a hundred times worse in the dark."

"I know," Erynn said, waiting for her heart to start again. "I just want to get out of here."

"So do I, but if we go any faster, we're only going to get ourselves in trouble."

Erynn stood there, waiting, and finally Adena started walking again. This time Erynn stayed focused on what was ahead of them and didn't look back.

Soon the floor started sloping downwards.

"We're going down," Adena said, obviously not expecting this.

"Yes," Erynn said. "Down to the lake. That's where the tunnel comes out."

"All the way down?"

"Yes, where did you think we came out?"

"I don't know. The woods behind the castle somewhere."

Erynn thought she caught a touch of fear in her friend's voice, but said nothing and they continued on in silence.

A few minutes later, Adena turned her head. "What happens when we get to the lake?"

"I don't know. I haven't exactly done this before."

"It didn't say in that book?"

Erynn tried to remember, but other than the drawing of the key and the details of where to find the tunnel, her mind was blank. "I don't think so."

Adena was quiet a moment. "I can't swim, Erynn."

This time Erynn did hear fear in her friend's voice. She wanted to tell her they would be fine, that they should be able to find some way around the lake without having to swim, but she really had no idea what to expect and right now was just trying to concentrate on getting through the tunnel. "I'm sure we'll manage."

"I hope you're right."

The floor continued downward and after a time they picked up their pace. Rats still scurried away from them along the rough stone floor, loudly squeaking their displeasure, but they were almost too focused on getting out of the tunnel to care.

Then Adena lowered her candle. "I think I see something ahead. A light."

Erynn peered over her shoulder. She could see a tiny pinprick of light in the darkness ahead, and with every step they took, it seemed to grow larger and larger.

"It looks like a window," Adena said a few minutes later.

Soon a waft of cool, fresh air, reached them and they started walking faster — and then almost running.

It was a window. Paneless, about two feet square, and located in the middle of the wall at the end of the tunnel. Vines grew thick around the outside and beyond were tree tops and glimpses of snow-capped mountains.

Erynn pushed back the vines and stood up on her toes to peer outside. She took several deep breaths of the cool air, and just the feel of it coursing through her helped calm her down. When she stepped back to let Adena have a turn at the window, she noticed her friend staring off to their left, her candle raised.

The tunnel turned sharply at the outer wall, dropping almost straight down into darkness. Steep stairs had been cut into the rock and a similar sized window set in the outer wall every few steps. The windows let in some light to reveal the stairs, but many were almost completely overgrown with vines.

Erynn wondered how far it was to the bottom.

"This must take us down to the lake," Adena said.

"I guess," Erynn replied.

Adena seemed uneasy, but finally she raised her candle and started down the stairs. "I sure wouldn't want to do this without a torch or something."

Erynn took one last look back along the tunnel before heading down the stairs after her. She stepped carefully, one stair at a time, and used her free hand in places where the stone had broken loose. The descent seemed to take forever, but eventually the bottom came into view — a small open space ending at a high wall and another black iron gate.

Adena reached the gate first and had the key out by the time Erynn arrived. And this time she was the one trembling. "I hope it's the same lock. I'd really hate to go back."

"Wouldn't make sense if it wasn't," Erynn said, peering through the gate to the passage on the other side. "They had two keys in case the king and queen were separated. Not for two locks." The passage turned a few feet from the gate, so she couldn't see very far, but she could definitely see light ahead. Sunlight. Which thankfully meant they wouldn't need the candles for much longer. And she could smell something, too — something she knew right away was responsible for the shake in her friend's hand. The smell of lake water.

Adena inserted the key and this time the lock popped opened after a couple of tries, sending a layer of fine dust to the ground. She lifted it and pulled the gate open, waiting for Erynn to walk through with the candles before grabbing her pack and following after her.

As Erynn stood in the passageway, waiting for her friend to lock the gate behind them, she felt a wave of relief wash over her. She had survived the tunnel and escaped the castle.

Now she just needed to get out of Alyria.

CHAPTER 15

The passage beyond the gate wound to the right and opened into a large cave. Except for a narrow ledge, which ran along the left wall and disappeared behind two massive rocks at the mouth of the cave, the entire space was filled with lake water. Halfway along the ledge, sticking up out of the water and secured by only the tiniest thread of rope, was the wooden hull of an old rowboat — the rest of the boat submerged.

Adena went pale. "What if we need that to get across the lake?"

Erynn set her candle down and went to the boat. A large hole in the floorboards was just barely visible in the murky water. A hole that didn't look like it had arrived there by accident. "Hopefully we don't."

"I guess it's been a while since they sent anyone down here to check on it."

Erynn turned to the rocks at the mouth of the cave, eager to get out of the darkness and into the sun. "Let's go see what's outside. See if there is another way out of here."

The ledge narrowed as it passed around the rocks, but it lead them outside and from there wound sharply left and disappeared into the trees and bushes along the edge of the lake. High above, the outer walls of Caraden Castle rose up from the dark and jagged cliffs on which it sat. To the south, past the high rock and trees, lay the numerous distant cottages that marked the outskirts of the village. To the north, the lake continued on for miles along the edge of the mountains, and on the far side, an open field stretched west at least a hundred yards to the trees.

"Looks like there might be a path around the lake," Adena said, sounding a little relieved.

Erynn heard her, but her eyes were still on that field on the far side. "We need to get to those trees. They'll give us some cover as we head south."

"You don't want to go through the village? Like we originally planned?"

Erynn shook her head. "It's too open between here and the village. If Holden has figured out how we escaped, we might just run into him on our way there. I think we should cut across the wood to the road down to Farglen and follow it to South Crossing. Maybe stop and buy horses in Farglen. Food, too."

"Cut across the wood? Do you think that's safe?"

"What do you mean?"

"What about the elves?"

Erynn realized she hadn't thought about the elves, and for a moment it threw her off and she wondered if going through the forest was the right choice. Like every child growing up in Valentia, she had heard the stories of people going missing in the deep forests where the elves were either known or rumored to live, or being attacked for merely stepping into their lands — as well as all the stories of man's battles with them long-ago. Before the uneasy silence of the last several hundred years. She had never seen an elf before and had

151

hoped she might on their trip to Galia two years earlier, passing as close as they did to the forests surrounding the mountains of Hale, but she had had both her father and Jared with her at that time, and Jared was good with a sword. Now it was just her and Adena, and they didn't have any weapons at all. As she gazed back across the lake, she wondered if cutting across the forest was the best choice. But then she remembered, too, how her father had felt about all the stories and the things he had told her about the elves, and she knew she had to trust in him and brush those fears aside.

"I don't think there are any elves this close to Caraden," she said. "At least not any more. And if there are, there aren't many. We're too far north."

Adena didn't exactly look convinced. "My uncle disappeared in the Bryan Forest. Everyone thinks the elves got him."

Erynn remembered Jared saying something about his uncle on their way to Galia. She also remembered that it set her father off on a rather long lecture about the elves and how he didn't believe half of the things that were said about them. Or the dwarves for that matter, even though he did admit that much less was known about them these days as they tended to stay deep within the mountains and were no longer being rounded up and used as slaves as they had in the past. Or if it was still happening, it certainly wasn't something people talked about.

"The Bryan Forest is farther south of here," she said. "And besides, my father saw some elves there once. They were sitting up in the trees along the edge of the Ring Road. He said they watched him pass by, but that was about it. He used to say if we just left them alone — and the dwarves — they'd probably leave us alone, too." She paused. "He was actually on his way to Highcastle that time."

"But he didn't go in the forest? And it's still possible there might be elves?"

Erynn didn't want to argue. They didn't have the time. "We don't have another choice, Adena. We can't go south from here. And right now I'd rather risk running into elves than running into Lord Caden." She turned away from the lake, hitched up her pack, and started down the path.

Adena continued scanning the trees, then turned and followed after her. "I guess they might not expect us to go that way. To head west instead of trying to make for North Falls. But what about the guards on the wall? What if they see us cross the field?"

That was the part Erynn was most worried about. If the guards did see them cross and alerted Marik, it wouldn't take riders long to catch up. They could wait until dark, when the guards were less likely to see them, but if Holden had figured out how they escaped, he would probably order Marik down the tunnel after them — and send riders around to the lake. They couldn't afford to wait. "We just better hope they don't."

Adena said nothing more and they continued walking, making their way along the path and around the edge of the lake as quickly as they could. But it wasn't an easy journey. The trees and brush grew thick in places, making it difficult to even find the path, and in others large rocks jutted up in their way and they had to climb over them. Twice they found the path flooded and had to slip off their shoes and wade across — which Adena did not enjoy at all and slowed them down considerably. Splintered arrows lay everywhere along the open spaces, as well as bits of armor and clothing and old swords — and even worse, the weathered bones of numerous long dead invaders.

At the sight of one skull, gazing up at her from it's resting place between two rocks, Erynn paused to glance up at the castle walls, wondering what it must have been like to be stuck down here, trying to reach the cave in a heavy rain full of arrows. She also wondered how many soldiers were up on the wall right now, gazing out across the lake. Or even down at the water's edge.

"Think they've seen us?" Adena asked, pausing next to her for a breath.

"If they have, we'll soon find out."

"Maybe Marik hasn't alerted the men on the wall yet. Maybe he's still looking for you inside the castle."

Erynn doubted it. Holden's deal with the Galians was too important. "He'll make sure his men know. I don't think he'd risk it."

"Then we'll have to run fast," Adena said, and she moved past Erynn to take the lead for a while.

Erynn glanced over at the lake, wondering if they even stood a chance. But then she returned her attention to the path and continued walking. They had come this far already. She was just going to hope their journey was not over yet.

As they rounded the far side of the lake, the path grew wider and more open and they were able to walk faster. Soon Erynn noticed that strange rushing sound in her ears again, followed shortly after by a dull ache spreading out across her brow. She wished they had something to eat, assuming once more that this was some symptom of her being both hungry and exhausted, but as much as she tried to ignore the noise and the ache and just press on, they both grew worse.

When they finally reached the field, they sat down in the bushes by the side of the lake for a rest — trying to gather as much energy as they could for their sprint to the trees.

"Are you ready?" Adena asked.

Erynn wasn't, but she nodded anyway and pulled herself

up into a crouch, clutching her pack tightly to her chest so it wouldn't slow her down. She was just about to spring out into the field, when a terrifying scream ripped through the air.

Krystalix was flying high along the castle walls above them, his golden scales sparkling in the morning sun. He banked slightly to follow the walls east, and as he did turned his head and gazed right down the cliffs to the path near the lake.

Adena gasped. "He saw us!"

Erynn ducked back down. Krystalix raised his head and screamed again. Then he was gone — out of sight over the castle walls.

"What do we do now?" Adena asked.

Erynn barely heard her, too busy searching the sky for his return. The rushing in her ears was growing louder, the ache in her head pounding. She wanted nothing more than to run, to get across the field to the trees, but was suddenly terrified of running out into the open. She remembered what the dragon did to Lord Caden's men that day. How he had snatched them from their saddles and ripped them apart right in front of her. But then, slowly, other memories came back, too. The entries she had read in the history book on Krystalix. The dark-haired woman by the river, with her hand on his nose. The king's words in the pantry. And then she knew why the dragon was there. "He's come to help us."

Adena looked at her like she was crazy. "Help? How?"

Erynn knew she was right. She could feel it. "I'm a Daughter of Maegan, remember? He's been trying to drive the Galians out of Alyria ever since they arrived. The king thinks it's because of me. That Krystalix somehow knows why they're here and is trying to help me. Lord Caden even said so in his letter. Naedra warned him the dragon might attack."

"You think he'll attack them if they try to come after us?"

Krystalix screamed, but this time he sounded farther away,

on the far side of the castle.

"Maybe," Erynn said. She glanced back across the field. A voice inside her was screaming at her to run. To get to the trees as fast as she could. And that she didn't have much time. "Or maybe he's trying to draw their attention. So they don't see us cross."

Adena raised a brow. "That would definitely help."

Erynn raised herself up again, clutching her pack. "We need to go. Now."

Adena signaled she was ready, and together they sprinted out from the bushes and raced across the field as fast as their legs would carry them. It was early yet, the grass still damp with dew and a little slippery; worn in places and taller in others. Erynn stumbled once, her pack slipping down her arm, but she quickly righted herself and kept going. Then the sack of coins started slamming against her hip, making an annoying noise, but she just ignored it and ran faster.

By the time they reached the trees, she was out of breath and her throat raw. She pulled up, Adena close behind, and glanced back at the castle. Krystalix was flying low over the outer ward, smoke rising from what appeared to be the stables behind the keep. Movement could just barely be seen on the outer walls, but it was impossible to tell if any of the guards had seen them cross the field.

"I think you were right," Adena said. "He was trying to distract them."

"We better not wait around to find out if he succeeded," Erynn said. She took one last look at the castle that had been her home for the last two years, and the dragon flying overhead. Then she picked up her pack and turned away — heading deeper into the forest.

CHAPTER 16

They moved quickly, trying to put as much distance as they could between themselves and the castle. Erynn wondered if Krystalix had broken off his attack now that they were across the field. If he hadn't, she couldn't tell. The forest was quiet around them, the only sounds she could hear the steady labor of their breath and the crunch of dried leaves and twigs beneath their feet.

They hadn't been in the forest long when Erynn noticed that she was feeling better. The rushing sound and the ache across her brow had once again vanished almost as abruptly as they had arrived. It still didn't make any sense, especially since her hunger and exhaustion had only grown worse, but she didn't give it any more thought. All that mattered was that both ailments were gone.

Up ahead, Adena was gazing around at the trees, and up at the branches above — something she'd been doing off and on ever since they entered the wood.

"Still worried about elves?" Erynn asked.

Adena returned her attention to the path. "I guess."

"I never saw any on our trip to Galia and we were in the woods a lot."

For a while Adena said nothing, but she continued to glance around at the trees. "You said your father went by the Bryan Forest on his way to Highcastle. When he saw those elves. Will we have to go by it to get there, too?"

"I think so. The Ring Road runs by it. But we won't have to go into it."

"I guess it would be marked on the map? A forest that size?"

"What map?" Erynn asked. And then something Adena had said in the study came back to her and she stopped. Something about the king's map. "You didn't …"

Adena shrugged and lightly patted her pack. "I figured we might need it. More than the king does anyway."

Erynn couldn't believe it. "You stole his map? The one in the cabinet? Do you have any idea how much he loves that thing? What Holden would do to us if he found out?"

"Lower your voice," Adena said, casting an even more nervous glance around. "Or we will have the elves on us."

Erynn didn't care. She raised her hands to her face, imaging the king's reaction when he went to his cabinet and found his precious map gone. He'd probably want Holden to find her, just so he could get it back. "You shouldn't have done that, Adena."

"Erynn, Queen Naedra wants to kill you. If the map can help us get to Highcastle and find this Paddon guy, then I think it's worth taking. Besides, the king should have done something. At least warned you the minute the Galians arrived. I think he owes you a bit more than an apology and a few gold coins."

"But that map means a lot to him, Adena. With Gareth gone he —"

Adena threw her arms up. "Who cares? Why are you always protecting him?"

Erynn lowered her hands. "I'm not."

"You are, Erynn. Ever since the Galians arrived. You couldn't tell him the truth about the falconry because you were worried what might happen to him, and you couldn't tell him about Gareth, either. Maybe if you had, he would have said something sooner. Maybe you would be in Highcastle by now."

Erynn crossed her arms over her chest. "So this is all my fault?"

"No, I'm not saying that. Just that you think about him more than you think of yourself."

"And what do you think will happen to you if they catch us? When they find the map in your pack? That you'll just go back to working in the stables?"

Adena sighed and ran a hand through her hair. "I was just trying to help us, Erynn. Have you been to Highcastle? Do you know how to get there?"

"It's the biggest town in southern Brye, Adena. I'm sure we'd find it sooner or later."

For a moment Adena just stared at her. Then she hiked up her pack on her shoulder and brushed past her, not saying a word.

Erynn rubbed her forehead. This wasn't about the king, or about not telling him the truth. It was about stealing something that didn't belong to them. Why couldn't Adena see that?

Neither of them said anything further, and just focused on their path through the trees and moving as quickly as they could. And as the morning wore on, that path took them further and further down into a valley where eventually the trees thinned and the warm light of the sun reached them through the leaves.

Erynn couldn't stop thinking about the king as she walked,

and how he would now forever think of her as a thief, but the more the day wore on and the more miles they traveled, the more bothered she also grew at the continued silence between her and Adena. She was angry at her friend for taking the map, but knew they were going to need each other's help if they were to get out of Alyria.

"The Bryan Forest is on the map," she said finally. "But I'm pretty sure most of it is north of where we're going. We won't have to go through it."

Adena glanced over at her, but a few seconds passed before she spoke. "The farther north the better, if you ask me."

Erynn kicked at a stone lying on the path, trying hard not to be mad. "I always think of Queen Sasha when I hear about the Bryan Forest."

"Naedra's older sister?"

Erynn nodded. "She managed to escape the castle in Tallon after the Galians invaded but died not long after. A Bryan knight was executed over her death, but some think it was the elves in the Bryan Forest who killed her. It's said she was pregnant and that they might have stolen her baby to raise as their own. Or killed it, too."

"That's horrible," Adena said, but then a moment later she laughed. "You don't suppose that's you? The lost princess of Tallon?"

"That was a few years before I was born. I don't think I look nineteen."

"Do you know how many Daughters there are in Valentia? Besides you and Naedra, I mean?"

"Sasha was the only other Daughter my father ever mentioned. I asked the king once, but he said he didn't know."

"Or maybe he didn't want to tell you."

"Maybe."

Erynn gazed up at the cloudless sky, wondering if she might eventually see some sign of Krystalix. But all she saw was a couple small birds dart by overhead.

"Have you thought about what it might be like to meet your mother?" Adena asked.

Erynn was silent, thinking back again on that one warm summer day many years ago. "I think maybe I have. Met her I mean."

"What? When?"

Erynn told her about the woman on the dapple-grey horse she had seen as a child.

"You never told me that story before," Adena said.

"It never came up. It was just some woman I met in the woods once, and I had no idea my real mother was even alive anyway. But now that I think about it, my parents did seem upset when I told them about her, and we did move to Caraden not long after."

"Maybe they suspected who she was?"

"Maybe."

It was well past mid-day when they came to a narrow river winding its way south along the valley floor. Although it didn't appear more than a couple of feet deep, it moved swiftly, and they followed it downstream until they found a calmer area with enough large rocks they could cross. On the other side, they found a row of bushes bursting with ripe blackberries and stopped to feast. Then they returned to the river to drink and wash the juice from their hands.

"I wish we could have grabbed something from the kitchen," Adena said as she sat back along the edge of the river. "Even some bread. I'm still hungry."

"We can buy food in Farglen," Erynn said. She cupped her hands and took another long sip of the cool fresh water.

They rested there for a few minutes before Adena finally sighed and pulled herself to her feet. "I guess we should get going. Do you think we should follow the river south? Or keep heading west?"

Erynn gazed downstream, and over to the trees on the far side of the valley. "I think we should keep heading west. The road from Caraden crosses this river south of here, but it's really open along that stretch and its probably best we don't go too close. The road on the other side of this valley would be better. Maybe we can get there before dark."

Adena headed back to the blackberry bushes to grab her things.

Erynn was reluctant to leave. She was exhausted and wanted nothing more than to rest there in the sun for a while longer, but she knew they needed to keep going. So she pushed herself up with a slight groan and brushed the dirt and grass from her cloak. She had just turned to follow after Adena when she heard a noise. A noise that sounded very much like a distant screech.

Erynn spun around, her eyes scanning the eastern sky. "Did you hear that?"

"Hear what?" Adena replied, grabbing a few more blackberries.

"I thought I heard something."

They both stood still. Listening. But all Erynn could hear was the babble of the river against the rocks, the chatter of some birds nearby, and the drone of a dragonfly overhead.

"Think it was Krystalix?" Adena asked.

"Maybe." Erynn scanned the tree line, but all she could see was blue sky and a few wisps of cloud. Still, she felt uneasy. She grabbed her pack. "We better go."

They continued west in silence, too focused on finding a good path across the valley and listening to sounds behind them to talk. Eventually they came to the edge of the valley and headed back into the trees, soon discovering that this side was much steeper than the other and the further west they traveled the steeper the valley wall became.

Erynn paused to take a breath some time later, wondering if continuing west had been the right decision after all. Or if they should have followed the river and taken their chances with the open road. The climb was growing even more difficult, especially considering how tired they already were, but she knew there was no time to change their mind and go back. The light was already changing and soon it would be dark.

She turned back to the hill and continued to climb, but hadn't gone more than a few feet when she heard a sound that stopped her cold.

Somewhere across the valley behind them, dogs were barking.

Several feet above, Adena stopped and glanced back. "You don't suppose Holden gave up and decided to go hunting?"

Erynn started to climb. "Only if we're the game."

They scrambled up the hill as quickly as they could, propelled by a new sense of urgency. But with every step they took, every rock they scaled, and every fallen tree they navigated, it seemed the valley wall grew steeper — steeper and more difficult to climb. At one point, a sheer cliff-face rose up almost twenty feet above them and they had to work their way south until they found a better place to climb. Several more rock faces, although not as high, forced them even farther south.

"I think we're getting close," Adena said some time later, pausing to take a breath and glance up the hill.

Erynn grabbed a nearby branch and looked up. She could see more light ahead, about thirty feet above. The hill appeared to level. Below her, the barking was louder now. She gazed back down, searching the trees for movement, but saw nothing. She knew the dogs were getting closer, and could tell by the excitement of their barks that they knew it, too.

"At least their horses won't get up this," Adena muttered, starting to climb again. "Maybe that'll slow them down."

Erynn continued climbing. She knew her friend was right. The hillside wasn't just steep, it was covered in loose rock and strewn with fallen logs and branches. Too dangerous for horses. But it wouldn't stop the dogs and she didn't even want to think about what might happen if they caught up to them. She slipped on a log but pulled herself up and kept moving.

By the time they reached the top of the ridge, they were both covered in dirt. Their clothes were littered with bits of leaves, moss and twigs, their hair twisted and tangled, and their hands and arms covered in scratches. But they didn't stop, and kept on running until finally they broke through a line of brush and found themselves on a wide and well-worn dirt road. The road ran north as far as the eye could see, and south about a quarter mile before disappearing around a bend in the trees.

Erynn bent over to try and catch her breath.

Behind them, the barking had grown labored.

"They're climbing the hill," Adena said, almost out of breath herself. "Now what?"

"Head south," Erynn said, stumbling forward down the road. "Maybe we can get to that bend before they see us."

"They're dogs, Erynn. They don't need to see us."

Erynn just ran, not seeing what else they could do. She could barely feel her legs, her lower back was stiff and sore, and she had a burning stitch in her right side and a fire in her lungs and throat. But she refused to give up and continued on down that road as fast as she could, the heavy coins in her pack slamming noisily against her hip.

Halfway to the bend, she heard the sound of horses.

She glanced back, amazed the men following them could have climbed the hill so fast, but she saw nothing. The road was clear. Confused, she turned back and nearly ran into Adena, who had stopped in the middle of the road and was staring at something ahead of them. Erynn gasped.

Six riders had just come around the bend and were now galloping toward them — and out front rode Quinn.

Erynn froze, unable to believe her eyes. What was he doing here?

Then the barking changed — growing louder.

Six large black dogs had emerged from the trees. The same dogs she had seen with Holden and Lord Caden only two days earlier. They quickly caught sight of their prey and leapt down the road toward them, their paws tearing up the dirt and sending chunks flying into the air.

Erynn couldn't move. They were trapped!

Adena grabbed her arm and yanked her back toward the trees.

Quinn was shouting to his men, but Erynn couldn't make out the words. All she knew was he was headed in her direction — and fast. And so were the dogs.

"Don't let them catch you, Erynn."

Tears burned Erynn's eyes as she raced after Adena, dodging low branches and leaping over rocks and tree roots. She had tried so hard. Come all this way. And now it was over. Even if they could outrun the dogs or somehow throw them off their trail, how would they get away from Quinn? He would catch her and take her back to the castle. Or wait for Marik and whoever else was hunting them to show up. And then Lord Caden would take her to Galia. She looked up at the trees. Where was Krystalix? Didn't he know she was in danger?

It didn't take long. Quinn and his men reached the trees around the same time as the dogs, but were closer to the girls and intercepted them first. After splitting up and spreading their horses out around them, the men quickly closed in, cutting off access to the ridge so they couldn't escape down the hill.

Erynn grabbed Adena's arm and pulled her back as one of the horses came dangerously close. They whirled around, trying to find a break in the circle that they could slip through, but each time they tried, one of the men promptly rode forward and cut them off. And soon it was no more use trying.

The dogs raced towards them through the trees and brush, their barks deafening.

"Quickly," Quinn said, riding closer. "Why does Marik hunt you?"

Erynn glanced at Adena, but neither of them said a word.

He pulled out his sword and pointed it at Erynn. "I won't ask you again."

"I – I don't know," Erynn said. "We're on our way to Farglen to visit a friend."

"Awful long walk," said a blonde-haired man that Erynn knew was named Briggs Colson.

The dogs reached the horses and tried to get through them to their prey.

"Hold those beasts back!" Quinn shouted to his men. The horses shifted, uneasy, and some stomped their feet and snapped at the dogs. But the men kept the dogs back. Quinn returned his attention to Erynn. "You still haven't given me the truth. Marik's been watching you lately. Why?"

Erynn was amazed he had even noticed, but still refused to say anything.

"Did you steal something?" Briggs asked.

"I didn't steal anything!" Erynn snapped.

"I'm losing my patience," Quinn said. "Let the dogs through."

"Because she knows what Holden's really up to with the Galians!" Adena blurted out.

Quinn held up his hand, signaling to his men to still hold the dogs back.

Erynn shot Adena a look, not sure if it was a good idea to tell Quinn anything.

"It's not like this can get any worse!" Adena said.

The dogs were still barking and circling the horses, trying to get at their prey.

"Quinn?" Briggs said, looking concerned.

Quinn's eyes shifted from Erynn to the dogs, then he set his jaw and slid his sword back in its sheath. "Fate brings them to us, Briggs. I say we act now and take our chances." He turned to the others and motioned with a quick jerk of his head toward the dogs. "Take them. Quickly. We'll meet up later at the old wood."

Before Erynn could even register what he'd said, one of the men slid down from his horse and grabbed her from behind. She struggled, but soon found herself roughly hoisted in the air and set down in the saddle in front of Quinn. He wrapped an arm around her waist.

"Hang on," he growled.

And then his horse leapt forward, galloping off through the trees.

CHAPTER 17

Quinn didn't return to the road, instead heading south along the ridge. Erynn tried to glance back, to see what was happening with Adena, but he was holding her tight around the waist and she could barely move. The barking behind them intensified, as if the dogs had just realized their prey was getting away, and amid the noise she could hear her friend struggling. Then came the loud "thwack" of a blade and the barking changed. A dog whined and went quiet. And then another "thwack."

Quinn urged his horse on, riding hard, and soon Erynn couldn't hear anything but the pounding of hooves on the forest floor. Then another horse came up fast behind them and she saw Adena, sitting in the saddle in front of Briggs and looking anything but pleased. She saw no sign of the other men — or even any of the dogs.

The light was fading quickly. Quinn continued south, and soon the ground beneath them sloped downward and the ridge grew less steep. Then he turned east and headed down into the valley.

Erynn still had her pack, wedged under her arm, but as they headed down the hill it slipped loose and the sack of coins bounced noisily against her thigh. She tried to pull it up, but he had pinned her arms with his and she was still limited in how much she could move.

"Is that your life savings or did you steal it?" Quinn said.

"I didn't steal it," Erynn snapped.

"Sounds like a lot for someone who works in the kitchen."

"Maybe my father left it for me."

"Or maybe you stole it from the king the night I caught you in his study."

Erynn didn't bother to respond. She didn't see the point. She couldn't exactly tell him the truth about the coins and once he searched Adena's pack and found the map he wasn't likely to believe her anyway.

They emerged from the trees onto the valley floor and continued east.

Erynn glanced up at the darkening sky, wondering if Krystalix would come to her aid. He had before — in Galia, and earlier at the lake. But she saw no sign of the golden dragon anywhere.

Soon a road appeared, cutting east across the valley towards the trees. Back to Caraden. Erynn expected Quinn to take it, but instead he rode over it and continued on, heading in a southeast direction. Then they came to the same river she and Adena had crossed earlier, miles to the north. He followed it south a while and eventually guided his horse across and on through the trees and up the hill to the edge of the forest. Here he stopped, to wait for Briggs to catch up. It was dark, but several miles to the north, the flickering torch-lights marking the outer towers of Caraden Castle could be seen high up on the cliffs.

Erynn was so tired and sore from the ride and her long journey from the castle that she could barely sit upright, but as soon as Briggs arrived, Quinn continued on, riding through fields of wheat and over numerous low hills before finally coming to a stop in a clearing near the edge of another wood.

Erynn was relieved the ride was over, and too exhausted to even think about running, but Quinn didn't appear to be taking any chances. He pulled her down from the saddle and marched her over to an old fire pit in the center of the clearing. Three old logs sat around the pit, the area littered with the bones of several small animals.

"Sit," he said, motioning to one of the logs.

Briggs was having some trouble with Adena, but he finally managed to drag her over to the pit and forced her to sit next to Erynn. Then he reached for their packs.

"They killed the dogs," Adena said to Erynn. "Sliced their heads clean off."

"I know," Erynn said, her eyes still on Quinn. "I heard." The mercenary didn't look particularly worried, given what his men had done, and she found that puzzling. Marik wasn't likely to have been too far behind the dogs, delayed only by the steepness of the hill, and if he found out who killed them he'd likely have their heads. Unless Quinn thought he could make money off her somehow? But she didn't get the sense he knew who she really was.

Briggs searched Erynn's pack, laughing as he pulled out the sack of coins. "Must be 50 coin here. Looks like we do have a couple of thieves on our hands."

"I didn't steal it," Erynn said, annoyed that they kept calling her a thief.

"Then where'd you get it?"

Erynn sighed and rubbed at her forehead. "The king gave it to me."

"Gave it to you?" Briggs laughed. "Now why would he do a thing like that?"

"I don't know, maybe I really am his daughter. I'm sure

you've heard the rumors."

Briggs cradled the sack of coins and continued rifling through her pack.

"Anything else?" Quinn asked.

"Three letter tubes," Briggs said. "One still bearing the king's seal." He handed the tubes to Quinn.

Quinn opened the one with the king's seal. The same one she'd shown him in the hall outside the study. He shook out the letter and read it, his face remaining its usual blank self until he reached the bottom. Then one brow raised. "*Silas Caden killed Davy Taylor.*" He looked up. "Is that true?"

"Of course it's true," Erynn snapped. "Why else would I write it?"

"Your addition?"

"Yes."

Briggs seemed confused. "I thought your father was killed by thieves?"

"He was killed by a thief!" Erynn shouted. "Lord Caden stole the king's horses and killed my father. And one day I'll make him pay for it."

Briggs laughed. "Someone's gotta tell that to Marik."

Quinn didn't seem amused. "Why didn't you give this to Faris?"

"Because I didn't see the point. He doesn't take orders from the king anymore."

Briggs frowned. "What makes you say that?"

Erynn sighed. "Because I saw him give one of the king's letters to Marik, that's why. Everything goes through Holden now. That's why he's got guards in the falconry. Holden probably isn't even sending any of his father's letters. Or giving him the ones that come in. Even from Gareth."

Briggs looked at Quinn, but the mercenary was still focused on Erynn. Then he slipped the letter back in the tube and opened another.

Erynn knew which one it was. Tears came to her eyes and she gazed down at her feet, blinking hard and praying he wouldn't read it out loud.

"A letter from Gareth," Quinn said with a slight snort. "How thoughtful of our fine prince to write."

Erynn waited for him to say something more, to make some comment about her father, but he stuffed the letter back in the tube and opened the last one.

"Task accomplished. Did not find book. Returning to castle. S." He glanced up. "What's this?"

"Ask Lord Caden," Erynn replied. "I found it after he killed my father. Krystalix ate the rest of the falcon it was attached to."

Quinn remained still, staring at her. Then he returned the letter to the tube and handed them all back to Briggs. He motioned towards Adena's pack. "That one next."

Erynn felt her friend tense as Briggs stuffed both the letter tubes and the sack full of coins back in her pack and reached for Adena's.

"Why have you brought us here?" Adena demanded. "And why did you kill Marik's dogs?"

"We'll ask the questions," Quinn said.

Briggs grinned as he pulled the map from her pack. "And what might this be?"

Adena scowled. "None of your business."

"I'm making it my business," Quinn said, taking the map from Briggs and turning it over a few times in his hands. "And I'm guessing it's a map. And a pretty valuable one at that." He handed it back.

"Did the king give this to you, too?" Briggs asked as he slid it back in Adena's pack and set it down on the ground.

Erynn stared at Quinn. "What do you want?"

Quinn smiled. "Answers. That's what I want. And real answers this time. Like the real reason Marik's hunting you. What it is you know about the Galians?"

"Marik will kill you when he finds out what you did," Adena said. "You really care that much?"

Quinn shrugged. "I like to know what's going on. In my line of work it helps keep you alive." He stepped closer, his face serious. "I know the Galians aren't here for a friendly visit and right now I don't have a lot of time. Tell me what you know now or neither of you are leaving this wood."

Briggs shook his head. "They don't know anything, Quinn. They've obviously stolen these things." He motioned to Erynn. "She has access to the king's study."

Adena turned to Erynn. "Might as well tell them what you heard. Like I said, it's not like this can get any worse."

Erynn wasn't so sure. She didn't like the look on Quinn's face at all. He might just kill them once he had what he wanted, considering what they knew about the dogs. But she didn't know what else to do. Telling them who she really was might help keep her alive — if he thought he could ransom her somehow — but she didn't want to do that unless she absolutely had to. "You were right the other night. I was hiding and I did hear something."

Briggs glanced at Quinn, but the mercenary hadn't moved, his eyes still on Erynn.

"Tell me," he said.

"The Galians are going to kill Gareth. Holden's made a deal with them."

"That's why Marik's after you?" Briggs said with a laugh. "The Galians have been trying to kill Gareth for four years. And it's not exactly a secret that Holden's hoping they succeed."

"They're going to do it at a banquet in Sarda," Erynn said,

173

glaring at him. "Twenty-five days from now." Just saying the words made her feel worse — a reminder that the days were ticking away and she still hadn't done a thing to warn him.

"How?" Quinn asked.

"I don't know how."

Briggs still didn't seem convinced. "Doesn't make sense, Quinn. We're talking about a couple of girls. Why send the dogs?"

"Because we could warn him," Adena said, sounding a little insulted. "If Gareth found out, Naedra's plan would be ruined."

"And how are you going to do that? You got a falcon? I didn't see one in your pack."

Adena shrugged. "We could find another way."

"Really?" Briggs laughed. "You going to deliver the message yourself? Sarda's an awfully long walk. Even with a horse, you'd be awfully pressed to get there in twenty-five days."

Adena rose to her feet. "I'm not scared."

Briggs leaned forward and pointed a finger at her chest. "You should be. You might have saved Lord Caden's horse from that fire, but the road can be a pretty dangerous place. Especially for a couple of girls."

"I know what the road's like," Erynn snapped.

"Then maybe you want to explain that to your friend."

Adena was about to say something, but Quinn raised a hand.

"Enough!" he said. He glared at Adena and motioned towards the log. "Sit." Erynn thought she might refuse, but he didn't take his eyes off her and after a few moments her friend finally sat back down. He turned to Erynn. "Now. Did you tell the king about this little plan?"

Erynn shook her head. "I didn't see the point."

The men remained quiet for a while, watching them. Erynn hoped they were finished with their questions and would just get whatever it was they were going to do with them over with, but then horses approached from the west.

Quinn and Briggs both tensed and reached for their swords, but seconds later the rest of their men rode into the clearing and they relaxed. Quinn left Briggs watching the girls and went to talk to them. Minutes later, two of the four men slid down from their horses, one producing some rope from his saddle bags, while another rode off through the trees, heading south. As the fourth man waited on his horse, Quinn walked back to Briggs and whispered something in his ear, while the other two went to the girls and proceeded to tie their hands behind their backs.

Quinn and Briggs turned and went to their horses.

Erynn realized they were leaving and tried to stand up, pulling against the man still binding her hands. "Wait. You're leaving us here?"

Quinn gathered up his reins and guided his horse closer. "I'm going to find out if your story matches the one I get from Holden."

Erynn didn't like the sound of that. If he talked to Holden, he might find out who she really was. "But I told you why he's after us. They're going to —"

"Marik was watching you long before I caught you outside the study," Quinn said, leaning forward in his saddle. "Which tells me there's something else going on here. Something you're still not telling me. Perhaps it has something to do with why the Galians are really here, or why Krystalix suddenly seems to have gone crazy, but neither of you are going anywhere until I find out what it is."

It was dark now, but Erynn thought she caught a certain look in his eyes — like maybe he had some notion of the truth but still wasn't sure. He seemed to be waiting, giving her a chance to change her mind and tell him everything, but she wasn't even sure Holden would tell him the truth. So she remained quiet.

He straightened in his saddle, nodded once at the two men he'd obviously ordered to stay behind and guard them, and rode off with Briggs and the other man through the trees.

CHAPTER 18

When Quinn returned with Briggs the next morning, Erynn could tell right away they had learned the truth. She rose slowly to her feet — still stiff and sore from her journey the day before, as well as a long and rather uncomfortable night's sleep on the cold ground next to the fire pit, and hampered by the fact her hands were still bound behind her. Adena pulled herself up next to her.

"Untie them," Quinn said the second he rode into the clearing.

The two men who had watched them all night came over and untied their ropes, but they remained close behind them — as if afraid they might bolt.

"Didn't exactly tell us the truth, did you?" Briggs said. He walked over and plunked a roll of bread in each of their hands, his gaze lingering on Erynn. "Daughter of Maegan."

Erynn hated his tone, but was almost too hungry to care. The men left behind to watch them had given them each a couple stale biscuits and some water overnight — untying their hands for a few minutes one at a time so they could eat — but it hadn't done much to curb her hunger and she was still starving. As she tore into the roll, Briggs started pacing back and forth in front of them.

"Lord Caden was sent here to arrest you," he said. "That's why Marik's after you. Not because of some plot to kill Gareth. If any of that's true."

"I'm not lying," Erynn said through a mouthful of bread. "I just didn't tell you I was Holden's part of the deal."

"The deal?" Quinn said as he walked over. "You mean where Holden gives you to Naedra and in return she kills Gareth?"

He didn't seem particularly surprised that Naedra was after her, which was something Erynn found a little surprising herself. "I did hear them talking about it. They just didn't mention my name. I didn't even know who I was until the king told me the night of the banquet."

"And that's when he gave you the coins? And the key to the tunnel?"

Erynn glanced at Adena. Holden had figured out how they'd escaped. "The king gave me the coins, but not the key. I found that in his cabinet." She smiled a little, almost wishing she could have seen the look on Holden's face when he found out. "Holden took the king's tunnel key the night I heard them in the study. I guess he forgot his mother had one, too."

A trace of a smile appeared on Quinn's face. "And is that also where you acquired the map?"

"I stole the map," Adena said, with a sideways glance at Erynn. "I thought we might need it."

Quinn remained quiet a moment, staring at Erynn like he was still trying to decide whether or not he believed her. Then he shook his head. "I always knew something wasn't right about you. The way the king brought you to the castle after your father died. The way he chose you to write his letters. Then there were the rumors about him really being your father, but I always had trouble with that because he just didn't seem the type. But this? This makes sense. He was in Tallon during the war. He would have met Queen Sasha. And possibly others in the Order of the Cael. If you were a couple of years older I'd say maybe you were her lost child — and worth a very high price — but unfortunately you're not. Still, Wryden could have met another Daughter when he was in Tallon. Did he tell you who your parents are?"

Erynn stuffed another piece of roll in her mouth, curious how Quinn knew so much about the Daughters of Maegan. "He doesn't know. A friend of his brought me here and apparently he didn't say."

"Then how'd the Galians find out you were here?" Briggs asked.

"He doesn't know that, either. He just gave me those coins and told me to leave Alyria. To go find his friend and get the answers from him."

"What's the friend's name?" Quinn asked.

Adena had finished her roll and now she stepped forward, her arms crossed over chest. "Why do you care?"

Quinn didn't look amused. "Because now that I have your little friend here, I'm trying to figure out what I want to do with her. And you."

"You can't give her to the Galians. They'll kill her."

This time Quinn smiled. "Well, firstly, I can do what I like. And second, your friend's far too valuable to just hand over to the Galians without us getting something. A reward, let's say. Maybe the Order would even pay for her."

Erynn wondered if he was serious. If he did ransom her to the Order, she wouldn't have to worry about Paddon. He might just deliver her to her mother. She waited for him to say something more, or to even ask again who it was that had brought her to Alyria, but he no longer seemed interested and turned to the other men.

"Best get your things together," he said. "Cole should be here soon and we'll want to clear out."

"Yes, we've got one mighty upset Galian Lord ready to tear up half of Alyria to find this one," Briggs said, nodding toward Erynn. "Not to mention Marik tracking us as we speak."

The other men immediately began gathering up their bedrolls and packs.

"What are you going to do with us?" Adena asked.

"Lock you up for a while," Quinn said. "At least until this place cools down and I can figure out a plan."

Erynn was glad that he wasn't taking them back to the castle, or handing her over to the Galians, but she didn't like the idea of being locked up at all. She had just ripped off another chunk of roll and was going to ask him about delivering her to the Order, when a rider approached from the south.

The men tensed, but it was just another man from their group, the one who had left the clearing on his own the night before. Quinn walked over to him as he dismounted, leaving Briggs and the other two men with the girls.

Erynn finished off her roll as she watched them talk, wondering where Quinn was planning to take them. Minutes later, a wagon pulled by two light-colored horses approached from the same direction. The driver was a middle-aged man with a bald head and a reddish beard. A younger man of about sixteen, and looking very much like his son, sat next to him on the bench.

Erynn's mouth dropped open. The driver was the same man she had seen talking to Gareth and her father in the back of that shop in Caraden! Right before Gareth left for Ridan. The man's beard had been shorter then, and a little darker, but she knew without a doubt it was him. For several moments she was so stunned that all she could do was just stand there and stare. But then she frowned. What would a friend of her father's — let alone a friend of Gareth's — be doing here in the woods, meeting with Quinn?

The bald man set the brake on the wagon, climbed down from his seat, and glanced around. His eyes passed briefly over Erynn — and then quickly returned. He blinked a couple of times, as if he thought she looked familiar, and then recognition passed across his face. Recognition and fear.

And right then Erynn knew the answer. "You're not working for Holden. You're working for Gareth." At first she didn't realize she'd spoken the thought out loud, but then a silence descended over the clearing.

One of the horses hitched to the bald man's wagon snorted and shook his head.

"Working for Gareth?" Adena said. "Erynn, what are you talking about?"

"I saw him talking to Gareth and my father," Erynn said, nodding to the man she now assumed was Cole. "In a shop in the village. Just before Gareth left for Ridan. They killed the dogs so they could find out what we knew. And that's why he wanted to know what I heard in the study." She looked at Quinn. "He's spying on Holden."

Adena looked speechless, and for several moments, no one in the clearing moved or made a sound. Then Quinn let out a breath and slowly reached up to rub the back of his neck.

"Seems I should have just let them catch you," he said, shooting Cole a very displeased look.

Cole raised his hands, shaking his head. "Mason didn't tell me you had Davy's daughter. Only a couple of servant girls from the castle."

"And I wasn't aware the two of you had already met," said the man who had arrived just before the wagon.

Erynn's mind was reeling, trying to understand what this all meant. Was her father spying for Gareth, too? And if he was, how could she not have known?

Briggs and the other men were staring at Erynn, not looking very happy at all. Even the younger man still sitting up on the wagon seat appeared rather shocked.

"Marik will kill us if he finds out, Quinn," Briggs said. "You know that."

Quinn didn't seem like he needed reminding. "Obviously this complicates things a bit."

"A bit?" Briggs said with a laugh. "You know what'll happen if he gets his hands on them. What he'll do to get the answers he wants."

Quinn rubbed a hand down over his face. "I say we just stick to the plan. Lock them up until things cool down." One of the men had grabbed the girls' packs and he took them and tossed them into the back of the wagon.

"Should be fine once we hit the road," Cole said with a bit of a shrug. "Can't track us in that much traffic."

Briggs snorted. "You don't know Marik. He doesn't need the dogs."

"Then what do you suggest, Briggs?" Quinn snapped. "Do to them what we did to the dogs? We knew this job would be risky. We just need to be more careful."

Briggs stared at Quinn. Then he turned to the other men and motioned with his head to the girls. "Get them in the wagon."

As the men stepped forward, Cole came around and opened the tailgate. Six large bales of hay sat in the back of the wagon, plus a number of heavy horse blankets and a few large bags filled with what Erynn could only guess was grain.

"But we're on the same side," she said, shaking off one of the men as he tried to grab her arm. "Can't you help us get out of Alyria? Or to the Order?"

"If Holden hasn't sent word to the bridges to watch for you, he will soon," Quinn said. "And Marik's expecting us to meet up with him later and I know he'll ask questions if anyone's missing. That man notices things more than anyone I've ever met. Not to mention he's got spies everywhere."

"Then let us go," Adena said, scowling at one of the men as he grabbed for her elbow. "We can find a way out of Alyria on our own."

"You two wouldn't stand a chance," Briggs said. "The bridges are guarded and the Delorin too wide and swift. Even if you could find a boat."

"And I'm not exactly keen on you getting caught," Quinn added. "Not now."

"But we wouldn't say anything," Erynn said. "We want Gareth back just as much as you do. We've been trying to warn him!"

Briggs stepped closer to Erynn, pointing his finger at her. "Marik will make you talk, little girl. He'll want to know who killed his dogs and he will make you answer."

Erynn swallowed, remembering the way Marik had questioned her in the kitchen. So calm and friendly. What would he be like when he was angry? Still, she refused to let Briggs scare her. If she could survive Galia, she could survive Marik. She stood up taller and looked him right in the eye. "I'd tell him we were captured by some men on the road. Maybe those thieves you've been looking for. They didn't tie us up well and we escaped." She looked at Adena, who nodded in agreement.

"We did think they were in the area," the man named Mason said.

Briggs didn't look convinced. "He won't buy it."

Quinn just pointed to the wagon. "In."

Mason grabbed Erynn's elbow and this time she couldn't wrench it away. He dragged her to the back of the wagon and motioned for her to climb inside, but she resisted. "What about Gareth? If you're working for him you must be communicating with him. Can you warn him?"

A somewhat uncomfortable look came over the men's faces and they all exchanged glances.

"Our falconer's dead," Briggs said. "Marik killed him a few months ago."

"Him and his wife," one of the other men added.

Erynn's mouth dropped open. "Your falconer was Sheldon Birch's son? I looked for Sheldon when I went to the village two days ago. I thought maybe he could help us warn Gareth."

"He's gone into hiding," Briggs said. "Left town after Caelin died and now no one can find him."

"Town?" Erynn said. "You know where he lived?"

"Blackwood."

Erynn knew Blackwood was a small town in the southwest corner of Alyria. Her father had gone there twice in the years after Gareth left, but had never taken her. Was that why he went? To see Sheldon? Or to give Caelin information to send to Gareth? "That's why Sheldon came to town so often. He wasn't just there to sell his daggers at the market. He was delivering messages for you."

Quinn hadn't said a word, but she could tell by his face she was right.

"Do you know if he has any falcons?" she asked. "Could he send a message to Gareth?"

"Marik took all of his falcons after he killed them," Briggs said. "We haven't been able to reach Gareth since."

"We don't that know for sure," Cole piped up. "Sheldon left to come see me that morning, right before Marik showed up. He told me Caelin had just sent a letter."

Erynn realized what this meant. "Then that falcon might have come back. At some point Gareth would have sent it back. Right?"

"Doesn't do us much good if we don't know where Sheldon is," Quinn said. "If it even went to him."

"But it is possible, isn't it?" Erynn asked. Sheldon had told her how smart the falcons were. How loyal they were to their handlers and the lengths they might go to find them. She looked around at the men, and even up at Cole's son, but none seemed in a rush to answer.

"Sheldon always said those falcons were well trained," Cole said. "Trained to find Gareth no matter where he was and to find Caelin when they came back, too. And other than him, I can't imagine anyone else who knew those falcons better than old Sheldon."

"Well, it's of no use to us now," Quinn said. "Marik has far too many spies down there to go asking questions." His eyes shifted to Adena. "Thanks, I suspect, to your father, Holden's figured out that Gareth has a contact at the castle. Someone feeding him information. And now Caelin and his wife are dead and Marik's on the hunt for Sheldon."

Adena's mouth had dropped open. "My father? How do you know it was my father?"

"Because he's working for the Galians," Briggs said. "Gareth told us so in his letters."

Adena was about to respond, suddenly looking very angry, but Quinn held up a hand. "We haven't got time to discuss Keegan Fields. Or warning Gareth about that banquet. Or finding Sheldon and a falcon he may or may not have. I want you both in that wagon. Now."

At first Adena refused, but then one of the men made a grab for her elbow and she shook him off and climbed up into the wagon.

Mason was pulling on Erynn's arm, trying to get her into the wagon, too, but she still had a question. "What about sending someone to Sarda?"

"In twenty-five days?" Quinn said. He shook his head. "Briggs is right. Even with the best horse, that's not much time. And like I said, Marik notices things. He'd notice one of us missing and would also probably hear about it if any of us crossed the river."

"What about Cole?" Erynn asked waving a hand at the wagon driver. "I mean, you are working for Gareth. You can't just let the Galians kill him."

Something flashed behind Quinn's eyes, but he remained calm and simply pointed once more towards the wagon. "I need Cole to watch you. Now get in the wagon or I'll pick you up and throw you in there myself."

CHAPTER 19

The men ordered the girls to lie face down on either side of the wagon, between the bales of hay and outside walls, and stretch their arms out over their heads. Then they bound their wrists once more, securing them to corner posts under the seat so they couldn't even think of jumping out of the wagon, and stepped back to let Cole and his son — who Erynn learned was named Jaynus — cover them with heavy blankets and arrange the sacks of grain at their feet.

Smothered in a darkness reeking of hay, horse, and mildew, and blocked from even talking to Adena by a thick wall between them, Erynn found the only comfort was a few wide cracks in the floorboards. She inched over, until her nose was right on top of one, and pressed her forehead down, drinking in the fresh air.

The men talked briefly, away from the wagon where she couldn't hear, and then Cole and Jaynus climbed back up to their seat and the wagon lurched forward, turned in a circle, and headed out of the clearing the way it came. For a long while the path was rough, each bump slamming Erynn down on the floorboards and jarring her bones, tiny splinters pricking her face and arms, but eventually it grew smoother and the wagon picked up speed. Soon other horses passed by, and wagons, and she realized they were on a road.

It was hot and musty under the blankets and the hay made her nose tickle, but Erynn tried to stay focused on the sliver of dirt passing by below. She wondered where Cole was taking them, and whether they might have a chance to escape when he moved them from the wagon, but she figured he'd probably take them out one at a time so there was likely not much chance of that. She also thought about Sheldon, wishing Quinn and his men knew where he was, or were more fired up about finding him. She had a feeling he did have that falcon and that it was the only chance they had to warn Gareth in time. And even though she tried hard not to, she also thought about Briggs and whether he was right when he said they didn't stand a chance of getting out of Alyria themselves. And whether it might be better to let Cole lock them up and keep them fed and warm and hope that Quinn could get them to Brye when it was safe. The only thing that worried her was would it ever be safe?

Above her head, the seat creaked, as if someone had turned to check the cargo in the back of the wagon. This had happened every few minutes since they left the clearing and she assumed it was Jaynus. But this time she heard him gasp.

"Look! Father!" he cried. "It's the dragon!"

Under the blankets, Erynn tensed. Krystalix? After the long ride with Quinn and then the long night tied up in the woods, she had pretty much given up hope that he might come to her rescue.

The seat creaked again — a little louder.

"Where?" Cole asked.

"Back there, above the trees. Or he was a second ago."

Cole muttered something and the seat creaked again. He slapped the reins, shouting at the horses. The wagon picked up speed, and for what seemed like forever to Erynn, neither he nor his son said another word.

"What do you think it means?" Jaynus asked finally.

"That Marik might be a lot closer to finding that clearing than Quinn thought," Cole said, tension in his voice. "And that it's good we got out of there when we did."

Erynn lay still, waiting for dragon's scream, or some other sign he meant to help her. Would he attack Cole and his son? She didn't want to see either of them hurt, but she didn't exactly want to be locked up either — despite her fear that Briggs might be right. She hated being stuck under the stuffy blankets and not knowing what was going on and was tempted to wrestle them back so Krystalix could see her, but a wagon had passed by only a short time ago and she knew she couldn't chance someone else seeing her. A girl tied up in the back of a wagon was sure to be remembered — and reported.

Minutes passed but she heard nothing more, only the occasional creak of the seat. Whatever Krystalix was doing out beyond the trees, it didn't appear to be coming to her rescue. Erynn closed her eyes and pressed her head against the boards, and it wasn't long after she heard another sound — distant at first but quickly growing stronger. The sound of a half-dozen or more horses thundering down the road behind them.

The wagon slowed and moved left to the side of the road. Tufts of grass and weed appeared amongst the dirt through the crack below. The horses caught up to them in no time, but did not pass. Instead, they maintained an even pace behind the wagon and then at least two or three rode up alongside.

"You there!" came a man's voice. "Stop the wagon!"

The voice wasn't one she recognized, but Erynn was still struck cold with fear. She could tell by his tone and the sound of the horses, the clinking of bits and spurs, that they were soldiers from the castle. And she could think of only one reason why they might want to stop the wagon.

Cole called to the horses, easing them back, and soon the wagon came to a stop.

Erynn was too scared to breathe, terrified the slightest movement might be noticed. Or that the blankets and sacks of grain by her feet had shifted during the journey and exposed her to view. The horses next to the wagon were so close she could hear them munching on their bits right above her, and practically feel the exhale of their breaths through the blankets. The rest of the soldiers remained behind them.

"Morning," Cole said, a slight trace of tension in his voice. "What can I do for you fine men?"

"Where are you coming from?" the man who had requested they stop asked. He sounded young, perhaps only a few years older than Erynn herself.

"Caraden. Just went to visit my brother and pick up some grain and a few supplies."

"We're looking for two girls. Around sixteen. Possibly in the company of some men."

"Perhaps not willingly," said another man, sounding older, near the side of the wagon.

"Yes," said the first. "Perhaps not willingly. Have you seen anyone like that?"

"Saw plenty of girls that age in town," Cole said, obviously trying to sound confused. "But I don't recall seeing any on the road, although truthfully I really haven't paid much attention."

"Did these girls do something wrong?" Jaynus asked.

"You could say that," the man said, with what sounded like slight amusement. "They're wanted for the murder of King Wryden."

It was like someone had stabbed her in the chest with an ice cold blade. Erynn let out a gasp, before she could catch herself. The king was dead? But how could that be?

One of the horses next to the wagon snickered and shook his head, as if he had heard her down there under the blankets.

"I – I hadn't heard he died," Cole said. "When did this happen?"

"He was found a few hours ago. The girls were both servants in the castle. One of them his scribe. Someone he trusted."

Erynn bit her lip hard, fighting back tears and a sudden urge to sit up and tell whoever this man was that he was lying. That she would never hurt the king. And that she couldn't have! She wasn't even there! Holden was just desperate to find her and was obviously using this as an excuse to do it. He was going to turn everyone in Alyria against her so no one would help her escape. So anyone who saw her would report her on sight. She didn't even want to think about what some of those people — especially those who had loved the king — might do if they found her. If Briggs wasn't right about their chances before, he definitely was now.

"That's horrible," Cole said. "Well, I sure hope you catch them."

"We will," the young man said, sounding quite confident. "After all, there isn't anywhere they can go. The bridges are watched and Holden's declared that anyone found helping them will be put to death. It's only a matter of time really."

Cole was silent a moment. "You – You think they're in the area?"

"They were last seen west of Caraden, but we believe it's possible they've been picked up. We're just out spreading the word. Obviously the more people who know we're after them, the faster we'll find them."

"If I see anything, I'll report it immediately," Cole said.

"And I'll be sure to tell anyone else I see, too."

"What are you looking at, kid?" came that second older voice by the side of the wagon.

"Krystalix," Jaynus said. "He's there again. Just over those trees."

Saddle leather creaked all around and for several seconds it was quiet.

Erynn listened, hoping the dragon would attack this time. Hoping he would tear to shreds every last one of these men who worked for Holden. Holden had killed his father, she was absolutely sure of it. He had killed him for helping her escape.

"It's just the Galians," the first man said, as if he'd seen the dragon a million times before. "They're waiting for word from Marik. Krystalix must be pestering them again."

"Glad we're not assigned to them," a man behind the wagon said. "He's already killed four of their men."

"We will be if we don't get to Chapley before dark," said the second man.

The leader of the group reminded Cole to report any sightings of the girls right away, and then they departed, galloping off down the road.

One of Cole's horses snorted and stomped a hoof, but the two men seated up on the bench remained still.

"Does this mean Holden is now King?" Jaynus asked finally. "Because Gareth isn't here?"

"I don't know," Cole said, his voice quiet. "But I do know things have changed in Alyria. And not for the better."

He slapped the reins and the wagon lurched forward, slowly moving back onto the road.

CHAPTER 20

Trapped under the heavy blankets in the heat, Erynn thought she might die. The tears flowed for a while, dampening the floorboards, but eventually they stopped. Then her nose grew stuffy and it became even more difficult to breathe. Several times she came close to pushing the blankets back so she could get some air, no longer caring if she was seen, but somehow she hung on and finally they left the main road and headed east on another riddled with rocks and small holes. They passed over a hill and along what sounded like fields of grazing sheep before the wagon slowed and Jaynus leapt down and ran ahead. The light under the wagon dimmed and then it stopped. Somewhere nearby a pig snorted.

Cole climbed down and went around to Erynn's side of the wagon. He pulled back the blankets and in seconds had produced a dagger and cut the ropes from her hands.

Erynn sat up slowly, rubbing her sore wrists and wincing at the light. She hadn't expected him to free her so soon, assuming he'd take her to wherever it was he planned to lock her up before removing the ropes. As her eyes adjusted, she saw the wagon was parked in the middle of a large barn, the sliding doors still open and the afternoon sun blazing bright

outside. Four horses gazed at her from stalls on either side of
the aisle, several pigs in a pen near the doors. Jaynus stood
near the tailgate, watching her, as his father walked around the
wagon.

"Run up to the house and tell your mother to pack some
food," Cole said, as he pulled back the blankets covering
Adena. "Enough for a few days if she can. And keep an eye
on the road. If you see anyone coming — anyone at all — I
want you to come tell me right away."

"Yes, father," Jaynus said, and he turned and jogged out of
the barn.

"Don't worry about trying to escape," Cole said when he
was gone. "I'm letting you both go." He cut through Adena's
ropes and the second she was free she grabbed her pack and
hopped over the side of the wagon, backing away from him as
if she feared this might be some kind of trick.

Erynn just blinked. He was letting them go?

"Why?" Adena asked. "I thought Quinn wanted us locked
up until things cooled down?"

Cole slid the dagger back in a sheath on his belt, not
looking particularly pleased with his decision — or Adena's
reminder. "Well, that was before I found out the king was
dead and Holden's blaming you for it." He reached back into
the wagon, under the seat, and pulled out a sack, handing it to
Adena. "There's some apples in there. It's not much, but I'm
sure you girls are starving. Jaynus will bring something more.
Hopefully enough to last you a few days."

Erynn grabbed her pack and climbed over the side of the
wagon. Learning about the king hadn't left her with much of
an appetite at all, but she had had a difficult time sleeping the
night before and knew she needed to eat something.

"We were lucky today," Cole said, as Adena handed her
one of the apples. "I thought for sure those soldiers were

going to search the wagon. Tomorrow we might not be so lucky. If Marik finds that clearing, which I'm sure he will, he'll know you left in a wagon. And if he spreads the word and those men remember my face ..." He paused and rubbed a hand over his bald head, looking quite pale. "When your father asked me to hold letters for Sheldon, and to meet with Quinn, I agreed because he was a friend and because I believed in Gareth. And because I didn't think there was much harm in it. But then Holden went and passed that stupid law, making falconry illegal, and Caelin and Kendra were killed. Now the king's dead and Galians are running around Alyria. It's getting out of hand."

"I understand," Erynn said between bites of apple. "Believe me, the last thing I want is anyone else getting killed because of me." Just the thought of the king brought tears to her eyes again, but she forced them back down.

"We don't know that's what happened," Adena said. She had wandered over to the open doors and was peering carefully outside as she munched on her apple. "The king was old. And you've said yourself he hasn't been well lately."

"You didn't hear Holden, Adena. He killed him for interfering with his plans. For helping me escape. I'm sure of it. Quinn thought the king gave me the tunnel key. Holden must have thought that, too."

"It's still not your fault. You didn't ask for this. To have Queen Naedra after you, or to be who you are."

Erynn didn't agree, but she didn't want to argue, either. She wiped her eyes and sat down on a bench outside one of the stalls. It was like she was stuck in some kind of bad dream. Just a few hours ago she was running from the Galians and trying to get used to being a Daughter of Maegan. Now she really was a fugitive — wanted for the murder of the king. And soon Gareth would be dead and Holden would officially be the next King of Alyria — if he wasn't calling himself that already. And she had known it was going to happen. In a way, Gareth's death would be her fault, too.

"What about Quinn?" Adena asked. "He wasn't exactly keen on us running around on our own."

"He won't be pleased," Cole said. "But he'll know Wryden's death and the warrant for you changes things. And that I can't risk Marik finding you here. Of course, you two need to be careful. Get out of Alyria as soon as you can and don't get caught. The longer you're here, the greater the risk Marik will catch up to you. He's smart, that man. More so than he's given credit for. And if you do get caught, you better tell him that story you told Quinn. And make him believe it. If you don't we could all end up dead."

"We will," Adena said.

Erynn wished she had her friend's confidence, but just the thought of facing Marik made her feel sick — and terrified to head back out on their own. Part of her wanted to crawl up in one of Cole's empty stalls, right there in the barn, and hide. To wait until things had cooled down. What if they did get caught? She could still see Marik's face as he stood next to her at the wash basin, studying hers for some sign the king had warned her. Looking for the truth. Would he believe her?

Cole lowered the tailgate and began folding the blankets he had used to cover them, but he seemed bothered. "I wish there was more I could do to help. Even take you to Brye myself. For your father at least, Erynn. He was a good friend. A good man. He didn't deserve what happened to him and I know Lord Caden will get what's coming to him one day."

Erynn finished the last of her apple and fed the core to the horse in the stall behind her, realizing Quinn must have filled Cole in about her father and Lord Caden before they left the clearing. Then she leaned back against the wall and sighed. "I

196

still can't believe my father was spying on Holden. And that I had no idea."

"Not Holden so much," Cole replied. "More the king. Your father had access to him that Quinn didn't have. Had his trust. He tried to keep Gareth informed on what his father was up to. What he was thinking on certain things. Stuff like that."

Erynn knew her father went up to the castle every day, but didn't realize he had spent so much time with the king. "Did he and Quinn bring you the information? And you gave it to Sheldon? Is that how it worked?"

"Davy would come here if he had something important he thought Gareth should know, or else he'd give it to Sheldon when he saw him in town. Sheldon would stop by on his way to and from Caraden, to drop letters off or pick any up, and then he'd take them down to Caelin to send. But he didn't know about Quinn. And neither did Caelin. Only that Gareth had someone else in Caraden, besides your father, feeding him information. Your father and I were the only ones that knew. I'd meet up with Quinn in that old wood every few weeks to exchange information. Occasionally your father would meet us there, too."

"What is Quinn doing for Holden, exactly?" Adena asked. "I've never really understood why he even has him around."

"Helping him build an army. Among the other odd jobs Marik likes to throw his way."

Adena frowned. "I thought he already had an army."

"Yes, but Holden knows a lot of those men are still loyal to Gareth. Especially if he comes home. Marik's trying to weed them out, but they know they'll never get rid of everyone. What they need are more men. Men who will fight for money, not loyalty. Quinn knows people like that."

Erynn still found it all so confusing. "The king didn't trust

Quinn at all. And until today, I didn't think Gareth — or my father — did, either."

"Well, Quinn will be the one to tell you about that. Although I must admit it came as a surprise to me, too. I thought he'd picked his road. I don't know what Gareth said to him." He paused, scratching at his chin. "I don't suppose he asked about your trip to Galia?"

"No," Erynn said, surprised. "Why would he ask about that?"

Cole hesitated, as if he wasn't quite sure he should have brought it up. "He never did figure out who your father went there to meet. I thought he might have asked you."

"You mean who my father bought the horses from?"

"Buying horses was the excuse that got the three of you across the bridge without drawing attention."

"I don't understand."

Cole took a deep breath. "Your father went to Galia to buy horses a few months before Gareth left. He told us when he got back that he'd met someone while he was there. Someone who had access to Naedra and who he thought might be able to help with some information, but at the time wasn't willing to talk. Something changed before your father made that last trip, but he wouldn't say what. Only that he wanted to go talk to this person again. So he persuaded the king he needed some fresh breeding stock and off the three of you went."

Erynn stared at him, stunned. The trip to Galia wasn't about horses? She closed her eyes, thinking back on everything that had happened up until the time they left Cold Lake. Everything her father had said or done. Everyone he might have spoken to. Searching for some sort of proof that Cole was right. Something she hadn't noticed at the time. But she couldn't remember anything. Could it be true?

"Erynn?" Cole asked.

She opened her eyes.

"Do you remember your father meeting with anyone?" he asked. "Other than the man he bought the horses from? Or even mentioning names? It could be important."

Erynn shook her head, feeling almost numb now. Not a single person or name stood out. She couldn't even remember the name or face of the man they'd bought the horses from. "I don't remember."

"Maybe Jared would know," Adena said. "If we could find him."

"My father wouldn't tell Jared something like that and not tell me, too," Erynn said, a little angrier than she had intended.

Cole sighed. "Well, there's not much we can do about that now anyway, even if we did know. We have no way to tell Gareth, or even arrange for him to get the information." He reached for the last two blankets and quickly folded them. Then he set the blankets on another bench and started to unhitch the horses.

"Did Gareth know?" Erynn asked.

Cole paused. "Gareth?"

"Did he know my father went to Galia again? The real reason?"

Cole was quiet. Then he nodded. "Quinn did mention it in one of his letters."

Erynn rested her head against the wall. Now she knew why Gareth had sent her that letter. The one telling her how sorry he was to hear the news. Perhaps he felt responsible for what happened.

Jaynus returned a short time later, carrying two small bundles of food. The girls took them and slipped them in their packs while Jaynus took over tending to the horses and

Cole walked them to the back door. Outside was an open pasture scattered with more sheep and some trees on the far side.

"You'll need to watch out for Thornhill," Cole said. "It's about twenty-files miles south of here and you'll want to avoid the towns as much as you can. The news about the king will spread quickly and people will be watching for you."

Erynn simply nodded, feeling somewhat awkward standing there at the door with Cole. She supposed she should thank him for letting them go, but had to admit she was almost reluctant to leave. She was still worried about Marik, and what else they might face on the road now that there was a warrant out for their arrest. And she also wanted to know what else Cole knew about her father. What else he might have been up to in those years before he died and had never told her. And that brought her back to Gareth. "Do you think Quinn will change his mind about looking for Sheldon?"

Cole shook his head. "Like he said, it's dangerous now. Marik's looking for Sheldon himself, and if he hears Quinn is, too, he might just figure out what's going on."

Erynn glanced out the door at the trees on the far side of the pasture. "I just hate to think we might go right by him and not even know it."

"Well, I doubt he's up here anywhere. Not this far north. Sheldon has more friends in the south now. More people he trusts. And he knows the terrain better. My guess is he hasn't gone all that far from Blackwood. He also has his granddaughter to take care of now. If he needs help, he'll have it down there."

"Then surely one of those friends must know where he is?"

"Wade Parsons is the only person I can think of who might. He runs the Blackwood Inn, where Sheldon's been living ever since his wife died, and is probably his closest friend down there — or at least that's what I've gathered from talking to Sheldon. Wade even let Caelin move that falconry of his to the inn after Holden passed that stupid law."

"They had their falconry at the inn?" Adena asked. "Wasn't that dangerous?"

"Yes, which is why they eventually ended up moving it. Only a few weeks before Caelin was killed actually. Truth be told, I think they underestimated how serious Holden was about that law, and figured Gareth would be back soon enough and eliminate it. But it worked well for a while, hidden as it was up in the attic. The place is surrounded by trees. Enough to help hide the birds."

"Maybe that's how Marik found out what they were doing," Adena said. "Someone did see the falcons."

"We wondered about that, but if it was, Wade would probably have been killed, too. Or at least questioned. And he wasn't. Quinn's tried to find out, but Marik's never said much. Still, he doesn't get the sense Marik knows about that falconry." He paused, now looking a little uncomfortable. "Of course, you mustn't tell anyone I told you about that. Wade still could be killed if Marik found out. Whether he has falcons hidden up in that attic or not."

Adena hitched her pack up on her shoulder. "Well, I think his secret's safe. Not much chance of us going to Blackwood. We're going to have enough trouble just getting out of Alyria."

CHAPTER 21

They headed out across the back pasture of Cole's farm, running for the trees until they were nearly out of breath, and avoiding open fields to prevent being seen. Cole's wife had packed them some biscuits and apples, and even a few fresh carrots and tiny tomatoes from the garden, but they ate little, too focused on getting out of the area in case Marik was able to track the wagon — and not sure how long the food would have to last. Erynn still had the sack of gold coins in her pack, but the money was almost useless to them now. As long as they were wanted for the murder of the king, they couldn't risk going into one of the towns to buy food or horses, let alone approach any cottages they might pass along the way.

It was late in the day when they came to the main road south from Caraden, the sun already starting to dip down in the sky. The road was fairly busy, people passing by in wagons and on horseback, and they followed it for a while — keeping safely out of sight — until they found a place where the trees came close on either side. As they sat down in the bush for a rest, and to wait for the road to clear, a man rode by on a bay mare, and then a short while later a wagon appeared, headed north and driven by a man with two teen boys and a box full of hay.

Erynn glanced up at the wisps of cloud overhead, just as she had several other times over the course of the day, even though she had seen no sign of Krystalix.

"Wondering where your friend is?" Adena asked.

Erynn felt strange hearing her call him that. "One thing's for sure. If he's still following the Galians, then at least we know they're not in the area."

"If he's still following them," Adena said. "I still don't understand why he didn't come when Quinn caught us. If he is trying to help you."

Erynn didn't understand that herself, but didn't see any point in debating it further. They were free and that was all that mattered. She returned her attention to the road, where another wagon was disappearing down a hill to the south. The rest of the road was clear.

"Ready?" Adena asked, pulling herself up into a crouch.

Erynn nodded, but before she could gather up her pack and dart out to the road, she heard horses.

"Wait!" she said, grabbing Adena's arm and quickly pulling her back down.

Seconds later, five soldiers rode around the bend to the north, from the direction of Caraden, and thundered down the road toward them.

Erynn recognized the dark-haired man riding out in the front of the group. She had seen him around the stables, and talking to Marik, but didn't know his name. Most of the others she had also seen around the stables. She cringed as they rode by, ducking down into the bush as much as she could to avoid being seen.

"They're searching for us," Adena whispered when they were gone. "I saw them scanning the roadside."

Erynn had seen that, too. "Go. Now. In case they come back."

Moving together, they darted out to the road and then across to the other side, scrambling down a short bank and into the trees. From there they headed inland, ignoring the aches in their legs and feet, and continuing on until it was dark and they could go no more. Then they rested near the edge of a creek for the night.

Erynn woke early the next morning and reached into her pack for one of the apples. She had just finished munching on it when Adena pulled out the king's map.

"Can we look at this?" her friend asked. "I didn't mention it yesterday because we were in a rush, and I knew you were still upset about the king, but I'd like to get a better idea of where we are. And where we're headed if we can."

For a moment Erynn hesitated, the sight of the map tearing at her heart as she thought once again of the king, but then she reached out and took it from Adena's hand. "It's not as detailed as you think. Valentia is a big place."

She slipped the ribbon off, wiped her slightly sticky fingers on her cloak, and spread the map out on the grass in front of them — hearing Adena's breath catch at the sight of it. Erynn immediately thought the map seemed different somehow, no longer the same one she used to stare at from across the king's desk in the study. But in a way she suddenly felt glad they had it — glad they did and not Holden. She could picture him at his father's desk, sitting in his chair and reading the old letters from Gareth in the top drawer. Trying on his crown. And it made her angry. So angry that she wished once again that she could do something to stop him. To make sure Gareth came home.

And then she realized what it was about the map that seemed different to her this time. Up until a few days ago she had always looked upon Brye as the place she was born. Her first home. Now, staring at the map, she knew that story was a lie and that she had no idea where she was born. Any one of the eleven kingdoms could be her first home — even Alyria, she supposed. Paddon may have lived in Highcastle his whole life, but that didn't mean she had started out there.

"Is this the road we were on yesterday?" Adena asked, pointing to the road that ran south from Caraden before forking into the two smaller roads leading out of Alyria. "The same one we crossed last night?"

"Yes, and we're probably getting pretty close to Thornhill, which is right where that road forks. We'll need to be careful."

"Do you think we should follow the road down to South Crossing? Or just head for the river from here?" Adena didn't look very excited at the thought of her second choice, although she did seem resigned to the fact that crossing the Delorin at some point other than a bridge was likely their only chance now. The bridges were sure to be watched.

"Probably best to make for the river," Erynn said. She pointed to a town about halfway between North Falls and South Crossing. Right on the edge of the river. "Renford's a big place. We might be able to find a boat near there."

Adena didn't look so sure. "I thought the Delorin was easier to cross the farther south you went?"

"It is. But they might not suspect us to go there. And we might never find a boat near South Crossing with everyone watching for us."

Adena was quiet, and Erynn could tell she was worried, so she figured it was probably good to change the subject. She pointed to a large cluster of trees near the west coast of Alyria. "Blackwood's over here, on the eastern edge of this forest."

"Definitely nowhere near where we're going," Adena said, gazing at it briefly before her eyes drifted back across Alyria.

"Maybe Quinn will change his mind about finding Sheldon when he learns about the king. Especially if he thinks Holden is responsible."

"I doubt it. He might even think it's more risky. Now that Holden can do whatever he wants and doesn't have to worry about his father interfering."

"Well, maybe we can find a falcon when we get to Brye. At least they're not illegal there."

But Erynn had already thought about that. "I don't think we'll have time."

Adena looked up, frowning. "Why not?"

"Because I think it's going to take us longer to get across the river than you think. It's a long walk to South Crossing, Adena. If we do have to go all that way. Over three hundred miles from Caraden. And even if we do get across, you can be sure Holden will send word to King Agar about us, if he hasn't already. The Bryans will be looking for us, too. Going into towns and asking about falconers there will be just as dangerous as buying food or horses here. It would be easier — and probably faster — if we knew where Sheldon was. You heard Cole. Caelin's falcons know Gareth. They're trained to find him."

"But there isn't anything we can do about that now. Blackwood's too far away and we need to get out of Alyria before Marik catches up to us."

Erynn gazed back down at the map and sighed. "I know. I just wish it wasn't."

"Besides, we don't even know if Sheldon does have that falcon," Adena said, seeming a little concerned that Erynn was still dwelling on this. "Even if we could find him." She paused. "You told Quinn what they're planning. Now it's up to him to warn Gareth. He is supposed to be working for him, remember?"

"Supposed to be," Erynn said. She tried to shift her attention back to the Delorin River — and how they were going to get across — but found her eyes kept returning to Blackwood. She did wish it wasn't so far. She'd go there herself and find Sheldon. Marik's spies or not.

"What's this?" Adena asked, pointing to a symbol near the center of Alyria — a circle with the letter "M" inside.

"It supposedly marks the site of an old temple. One built to honor Maegan."

"A temple?" Adena frowned. "I've never heard of that."

"There are three of them," Erynn said, pointing briefly at the other two symbols in Brye and Cardel and remembering how the king had always seemed so reluctant to answer her questions about them. At least now she knew why.

"Have you ever seen one?"

"I didn't even know they existed until I saw the map. My father never mentioned them."

"Never?" Adena looked a little surprised.

Erynn shook her head.

"Do you think he knew about them? About the one here?"

"I can't see how he didn't. He traveled all over Alyria."

Adena thought about this for a few moments. "Maybe he was worried you'd want to go there. And that if you did maybe you'd somehow figure out the truth."

Erynn didn't see how she could, but didn't really feel like talking about that now. "Maybe."

"Would you like to see one? I mean, if we had time? The one in Brye is not that far from Highcastle and we are going in that direction."

"It's pretty close to the Bryan Forest. I thought you didn't want to go near there?"

Adena appeared to have forgotten about that. "It's not inside the forest."

Erynn shrugged. "I guess."

"You don't sound very excited. I would have thought you'd be interested in finding out more about the Daughters of Maegan. Now that you know you are one."

"We wouldn't exactly be in this mess if I wasn't."

Adena smiled. "Yes, you'd still be in the kitchen, peeling potatoes and listening to Mirella, and I'd be out in the stables, knee deep in manure."

"Well, at least that wouldn't get us killed, Adena." Erynn reached into her pack and broke a chunk off one of her biscuits. She knew she shouldn't — that she needed to make the food last — but the apple hadn't filled her up much and she was still hungry. "I just want to find the Order and my real parents. Figure out some way to get Marik and Lord Caden off my trail."

Adena watched her as she quickly downed the biscuit, and then she pulled the map closer, shifting her attention east this time. A furrow appeared in her brow. "The Ethlon castle is in Ortelion, right?"

"Gareth's letters never said your father was there, Adena. Just that he left."

"But Jared heard those men talking, didn't he? They said my father was living at the castle and that's where he was planning to go, right?"

As Erynn swallowed down the dry biscuit, she thought back to that last night in Cold Lake. How she had sat on the small cot in their room at the inn and watched her father argue with Jared, trying to convince him that Ethlon was too dangerous. Eventually he gave up and went downstairs and Jared started packing his things. She had just sat there, watching him. Not wanting him to leave but not knowing how to tell him. He was only three years older than she was, but it had always seemed like so much more. "That's what he said."

"I wish I knew what else Gareth might have written about in those letters. The ones Briggs mentioned. If he'd said anything about Jared."

Erynn pulled herself up and brushed the biscuit crumbs from her hands and the dirt and grass from her cloak. "We should go."

Adena nodded, but she continued to stare at the map — and Ortelion — for several more seconds, as if trying to commit it to memory. Then she carefully rolled the map back up, slipped the ribbon on, and handed it to Erynn. "I suppose you should carry it."

Erynn didn't say a word. Just took the map and slipped it in her pack. Then, when Adena was ready, they left their resting place and resumed their journey south, following the creek and snacking on berries they found along the way. Neither of them said much. Erynn was still thinking about Brye and whether it might be possible to find a falconer in time, and she had a feeling Adena was still thinking about Ethlon. Then, later that afternoon, she saw cows grazing in a field about a mile away and started to wonder if maybe they were drifting too far east. And not long after she caught a whiff of smoke and stopped.

"I think we should cross the creek," she said. "Maybe head west for a while."

"You don't think we should follow it?" Adena asked. "It's pretty warm out and we don't have any way to carry water."

"I think we're going too far east. Too close to Thornhill. I can smell smoke."

Adena sniffed at the air. "I don't smell it."

Erynn wasn't surprised. "Well, I do. There must be a cottage up ahead somewhere."

Adena turned back to the creek, raising a hand to shield

her eyes from the sun. "It looks tricky here. Too deep. Let's try going a little farther. See if we can find a better spot."

Erynn wanted to cross the creek now, growing even more worried about that smoke and that it meant there were people nearby who might see them, but the water did seem to have grown both deeper and faster and there weren't enough rocks to cross. So when Adena started walking again, continuing in the same direction along the path, she simply followed along behind.

Soon the terrain along the edge of the creek grew rocky and steep, as if they were traveling along the top of a ridge, and eventually they reached the end of the path. About twenty yards east, the ridge dropped sharply to the trees, and up ahead the creek continued on for a while before disappearing swiftly out of sight over the edge of what appeared to be a short falls.

Adena glanced around, not seeming particularly pleased with their situation and perhaps wishing they had crossed earlier. Then she pointed to a gap in the rocks along the edge of the ridge. "Maybe there's a way down over there."

Erynn followed her over to the gap. The drop was only about thirty feet, and it certainly looked possible they could climb down, but the face of the ridge was steep and it wasn't going to be easy. Still, they didn't seem to have any other choice but to go down, so when Adena dropped to her knees and started down the hill, Erynn waited until she was out of the way before climbing down after her.

"How long do you think it would take to get to Ortelion from Highcastle?" Adena asked as they descended. "Weeks do you think? By horse, I mean?"

Erynn swatted at a fly that had buzzed too close to her face. She was trying to stay focused on where she was going and on what she was doing, a little annoyed at herself for not insisting on crossing the creek earlier — even if they did get wet — and the last thing she needed was to be thinking about Ethlon. "It's dangerous there, Adena. Way more than Brye. Or here." She thought she might have heard a horse snort nearby, but brushed it off as creek water rushing down over the rocks. A second later she slipped on a patch of loose dirt on one of the rocks, but managed to catch herself. She wiped the sweat and grime on her hand against her cloak and continued her descent.

"I know," Adena said, reaching the bottom and pausing to wait for Erynn. "It just doesn't seem as far from Highcastle as it does from here. Once we get there anyway."

Erynn reached the bottom and wiped her hands again. "I think we should just concentrate on getting across the river." She walked past Adena around the edge of the ridge, heading back toward creek and hoping there would be a place calm enough to cross.

But when she finally came around the bend and saw the falls, she froze.

Five horses stood saddled and waiting near the pool at the bottom, their riders not far away. One was crouched by the pool, having a drink of water. Three more were standing nearby. The fifth, a dark-haired man, was sitting on a rock a few feet from where she stood, chewing on what appeared to be a strip of dried meat.

They were soldiers — the same five soldiers they had seen galloping down the road from Caraden the day before. And they had walked right into them.

The men near the creek turned in surprise, obviously not hearing the girls over the rush of the falls, and the one with the dark-hair smiled.

"How about that," he said. "If it ain't the two girls we've been looking for."

CHAPTER 22

The second Erynn stepped out of Cole's barn she had worried they might get caught before they reached Brye. But she hadn't expected it to happen so fast. So distracted by the steep climb down the rocks and Adena's talk about Ethlon, she didn't pay any attention to where she was going and didn't even think that those five soldiers they had seen on the road the day before might still be in the area. Or that they might seek rest and water at the very same creek she and Adena had been following all morning.

"Don't let them catch you, Erynn."

Erynn heard her father's voice and started to run, turning and darting into the trees at the base of the ridge. But the soldiers were after her in seconds and before long she was caught and dragged rather roughly back to the falls. Adena gave them more of a chase — and a struggle — but the soldiers were too strong and before long she was standing there next to her and not looking at all pleased.

Erynn hung her head. Her journey was over. She had failed.

She expected the soldiers to take them north to the castle, but while one of the men headed north to advise Marik of their capture, the others bound them at the wrist and marched them east into Thornhill, only a few miles away. The dark-haired soldier made a comment about Krystalix and how he didn't want the dragon interfering with his collection of the reward Holden was offering for catching his father's killers, but as far as Erynn could tell, he had no idea who she really was or why the dragon was even acting so strangely in the first place.

The walk into town seemed to take forever, and Erynn again saw no sign of Krystalix, even though she continued to watch for him and to hope he might come help them this time. When they finally arrived, the soldiers didn't know where to take them, but eventually they settled on a blacksmith's shop on the far side of town and forced the girls on down the road. People everywhere stopped to stare as they passed by, confusion on their faces, followed by anger and hate as they realized who the girls were. Several even followed the group down the road, taunting.

"Killers!" one woman yelled.

"String them up!" came another cry.

Erynn trembled and kept her eyes on the road. She had done nothing wrong, but still these people wanted her dead. She didn't even want to think about what might have happened if the townspeople had found them first.

Three men streaked in sweat and soot were hard at work in the blacksmith's shop when the soldiers pushed the girls through the open doors and demanded they drop what they were doing and assist them in shackling their captives to the back wall. One of the workers retrieved two pairs of irons from a pile of junk in the corner and assisted in locking them up — close enough to the forge to feel the heat, but too far away to reach any of the tools and weapons strewn along the rough stone ledge next to it. The girls were then forced to sit amidst their chains on the dirt floor, waiting, while the soldiers stood guard and the men in the shop returned to their work.

Erynn felt miserable. Captured twice in as many days, they had now gone from ropes to chains and this time escape seemed impossible. Other than the open double doors at the front of the shop, which the soldiers had closed halfway to prevent anyone in the growing crowd outside from trying to get in, there was only one other way out — a large wooden door along the back wall. And it was barricaded by a heavy beam.

Marik arrived just as the sun was setting, entering the shop with Quinn. Two of the shop workers were still present and he immediately ordered them to leave.

"Erynn," Marik said, walking across the shop toward them. "How good it is to see you again. I've sent word to Lord Caden that you've been found. I'm sure he won't be long behind me." He appeared rather pleased, but Quinn seemed tense, his hand not straying far from the hilt of his sword.

Erynn stood, chains rattling, but tried hard to keep her eyes on Marik and not look at the mercenary.

"You're not taking us back to the castle?" Adena asked, rising to stand next to her.

"The Galians will take Erynn from here. You I'll be taking to the castle, where I look forward to seeing justice served."

"Justice?" Adena said with a laugh. "You know we didn't kill the king. We weren't even there."

"We can discuss our dear departed king later," Marik replied. "First we have other business to attend to."

Erynn swallowed. She knew exactly what business he was talking about: the dogs.

The dark-haired soldier stepped forward, still present with his three other men in the shop. "We found some letter tubes in their packs. And a sack of gold and what looks like a map." He pointed to a table on the far side of the shop, where one of the men had set their packs and pulled out the items inside.

"Must have stolen them from the king," said another one of the soldiers, glaring at the girls.

Marik motioned for the four of them to leave. Then he walked over to the table and picked up the sack of coins. "I assume His Grace gave you the gold at the same time he warned you about the Galians and gave you the key to the tunnel?"

"He gave me the gold," Erynn said. "But he told me to leave by the gate. I found the key in his cabinet."

"So that's why you were in the study. You weren't looking for parchment." He put the coins down and turned to the map, spreading it out on the table. "I was just about to head into the tunnel when I heard you two were seen running across the field. Saved me from what I'm sure would have been a rather long and unpleasant walk." He studied the map a few moments longer. "I've seen this in the king's study. Did His Grace give this to you, too?"

Erynn hesitated, not sure if there was much point in lying about it now.

Marik looked up. "I didn't take you for a thief, Miss Taylor."

"I took it," Adena said. "I didn't tell her until after we left."

Marik smiled. "Keegan's daughter. Now that makes more sense." He studied the map a moment longer, and then he walked back toward them and held out his hand. "I assume you still have the key? Neither of you will be needing it anymore."

Erynn motioned for Adena to give him the key. The last thing she wanted was Marik searching her and finding the one the king gave her.

Adena pulled it out from under her dress and slipped it over her head, handing it to him rather reluctantly. He slipped it in a pocket and walked back to the table, turning his attention to the letter tubes.

Erynn couldn't tell which one he had grabbed first, but watched his face, waiting for a reaction. A second later she saw a smirk.

"That Gareth," he said. "Always the gentleman." He set the letter down and reached for another. This time his brow raised, and he walked back over to Erynn and held the letter up so she could see it. "Is this true? Lord Caden killed your father?"

Erynn didn't even blink. "And stole the king's horses."

Marik seemed surprised — and even slightly amused — but he continued to hold her gaze. "I'll have to have a word with him about that. I'm sure those horses cost us a fine sum."

Erynn didn't respond. The last thing she cared about was what the king paid for those horses.

"Must have been a shock to see him at the castle. And to find out he'd come for you."

Erynn knew he was waiting for a response, but still didn't say a word.

"You'd like to see him dead, wouldn't you? I know I would if he killed my father the way he killed yours. And I'd do it myself, too."

"Then maybe you should let me go so I can," Erynn replied.

Marik smiled. "Part of me really wishes I could, Erynn, but I'm afraid I do have my orders." He gazed back down at the letter. "Was that extra note the king's idea? Or yours?"

"Mine."

He chuckled. "So that's why you wouldn't give Faris the letter. And why you were looking for Sheldon Birch in the market. Faris told me you'd figured out what was going on in the falconry. You were trying to find another way to send this, weren't you? Maybe hoping that if Gareth came back he'd see to it that Lord Caden was arrested and hung for your father's death?"

Erynn felt tears come to her eyes, but blinked them back. Hard. She cleared her throat. "So?"

"So falconry's illegal, Erynn. You do know it's a crime punishable by death?"

Erynn didn't see any point in denying it. "It was the only thing I could think of."

"I admire your resolve, but you would have been disappointed. Gareth's not coming back. And if I find Birch, I promise you he won't be messing with falcons ever again."

Across the room, Erynn sensed a change in Quinn — a shift of his feet, a straightening of his back, even a tightening of his jaw — but she kept her eyes on Marik. Had Holden told the him about the banquet in Sarda?

Finally Marik turned and wandered back to the table.

This time Erynn's eyes went to Quinn. The mercenary nodded his head once, and so briefly that if anyone else had still been in the shop they might have missed it, but she caught the message: make Marik believe you.

Marik tossed the letter on the table and grabbed the last tube, seeming impatient as he shook out the folded parchment inside. *Task accomplished. Did not find book. Returning to castle. S."* He looked up. "What is this?"

"You'll have to ask Lord Caden," Erynn replied. "He tried sending it the day he killed my father."

"Tried?"

"Krystalix ate his falcon."

Marik held her gaze a moment longer. Then he slipped the letter in his pocket and walked across the shop to the forge. A long poker-like piece of iron lay partly buried in the hot charcoal, abandoned by the men working in the shop when he arrived. He grabbed a nearby pair of tongs and slid the poker deeper into the heat.

Across the room, Quinn shifted his feet again, his hand moving even closer to the hilt of his sword.

"So you stole the key and escaped through the tunnel to the lake," Marik said. "And then Krystalix returned and torched another one of our stables, keeping us busy while you two ran across the field." He pulled the poker out, the tip red hot. "Have I got that right?"

Erynn swallowed. "Yes."

Marik returned the poker to the forge. "Then what happened?"

"We ran."

Anger flashed briefly in Marik's eyes. "Yes, I know that, Erynn. What I want to know is what happened after you ran."

Erynn hesitated. She could feel the tension coming from Quinn without even looking at him. "We – We ran into some men and they caught us. They seemed to think that maybe they could ransom us."

"What men?" Marik asked, not raising his eyes from the forge. "Who were they?"

"I've never seen them before."

"Well, what did they look like? You're a smart girl, Erynn. And very observant. Were they short? Fat? Ugly? What were they wearing?"

"They put sacks over our heads," Adena said. "We didn't really get a good look."

Marik pulled the poker back out — the tip glowing even hotter. "And these men killed my dogs?"

"We didn't see that," Erynn said, unable to take her eyes off the poker. "But that sounded like what they were doing."

"And where are these men now?"

"I – I don't know. We escaped a couple days ago."

"They were talking about Farglen," Adena added. "About some business they had there."

A very slight look of understanding passed over the Army Commander's face. He turned his head, toward Quinn, but kept his eyes on the poker. "Think they're the same men you were tracking?"

Quinn cleared his throat. "We last heard they were in that area."

Marik's eyes shifted to the girls, watching them, before finally returning to the forge. He slid the poker back into the heat. "I saw Brock in the village on the morning of the banquet. He had Dillon with him. I was going to have a word, but was otherwise engaged."

The mere hint of a smile appeared on Quinn's face and he seemed to relax a little. "Wouldn't put it past either of those fools to try something like that."

"You didn't hear anything about either of them being in town?"

"Haven't spent much time in town lately."

Erynn didn't know who they were talking about, but Marik did seem to be buying their story and right now that was all that mattered. She vaguely recalled the two men she had seen in the market — the ones with the dark cloaks and swords that had appeared so out of place. Was that who they were referring to?

"I told Brock I'd kill him if I caught him thieving again," Marik said. "I'm disappointed he didn't listen."

Quinn shrugged. "You know his type. They never listen."

Marik smiled. "You used to be his type, my friend."

"And some days I still don't listen."

Marik released the poker and set the tongs back down on the ledge. "As soon as our Galian friends are gone, I want you to find Brock and bring him to me. Dillon, too."

"It would be my pleasure."

Marik walked back toward Erynn. "Now. About the king."

The relief Erynn had felt at successfully escaping the matter of the dogs faded quickly at the mention of the king. "Did you kill him, or was it Holden?"

"Why Erynn, accusations like that can get you in a lot of trouble," Marik replied. "I wasn't even there. I was out looking for you. I must say though, that it was very wise of you to put your little plan in motion before you left. Very wise, indeed."

Erynn frowned. "What plan? What are you talking about?"

"You know exactly what I'm talking about. We all saw you with those herbs in the market."

"What herbs?" Erynn said. And then it hit her — hard — and a warm and prickly sensation coursed through her as she remembered the herbalist's mother and the small package with the nutty smell she'd placed in the palm of her hand.

Marik was watching her, a slight grin on his face.

"I – I bought him tea," she stammered. "I've bought it for him several times. It helps him sleep!"

"Oh, it helped him sleep all right. He just never woke up."

Erynn stepped forward, pulling at the chains. "You're lying! I didn't take those herbs! I told her I didn't want them!"

"We have witnesses that say you did, including that old woman and her son. We even found bits of it in your cot and scattered by the king's bed."

Erynn couldn't believe this was happening. If she could have reached out and grabbed the red-hot poker from the fire she would have done it, burns and all, and run him right through. "If I wanted to kill someone, it would be Lord Caden!"

Just then what sounded like a dozen horses pulled up in front of the shop.

Quinn leaned forward to peek out the doors. "His Lordship."

Marik smiled. "What perfect timing."

Seconds later Lord Caden limped through the gap in the doors. He paused to glance at Erynn and Adena, and the shackles, before nodding at one of his men outside to close the doors behind him.

Erynn glared at Marik, still so angry she was shaking, but he just turned and walked calmly back toward the Galian.

"You don't think this would be easier at the inn?" Lord Caden asked. "And a little more pleasant?"

"They're shackled," Marik replied. "The rear door's barricaded, and I have two dozen men setting up camp out front. I'm sure it will be fine."

Lord Caden didn't look convinced. "I'll add some of my men to yours then, just to be sure."

Marik shrugged. "Suit yourself."

Lord Caden moved past him toward the back of the shop. "A pleasure to see you again, Erynn. I've already sent word to Queen Naedra that you've been found. I know she's looking forward to meeting you finally."

Erynn knew she should be terrified, but the news about the herbs still had her seething. Seething so much she almost didn't care what happened. "I don't understand why she sent you here. Why she's so afraid of me."

Lord Caden smiled. "That's a question you'll have to ask her. I'm simply here to make sure you're delivered safely."

"Has she found my mother? I heard she's been hunting her, too."

"Tara has been elusive, but I'm sure we'll find her soon. After all, it should be much easier now that we have you."

Tara. Erynn felt her anger fade at the mention of her mother's name. She repeated it over and over in her mind, but the name wasn't one she recalled hearing before. Was this the woman on the dapple-grey horse she had seen as a child? She knew one thing for sure: she didn't like the idea of being used as bait.

Lord Caden turned to Adena. "And what are we going to do with you?"

"You could let me go," Adena replied. "I did save your horse."

"Yes, you did. But I think we'll hang on to you just the same. In case your father gets out of line."

"Holden wants her," Marik said. "He needs to hang someone for his father's death. Besides, I doubt either of her parents would care what you did with her."

"You don't know anything about my parents," Adena snapped.

Marik smiled. "I know enough."

Lord Caden started back toward Marik. "Very well. We'll leave as soon as I hear from Naedra. Hopefully in a few days."

"I thought you were in a hurry?"

"I am. But I have lost a few more men than I expected."

"Sending for more won't help," Quinn said.

Lord Caden and Marik both turned to the mercenary, as if they had forgotten he was even there.

"What makes you think I'm doing that?" Lord Caden asked.

Quinn gestured towards Erynn. "I know Krystalix is trying to protect her. That's why he's been after you ever since you arrived. Why he attacked the castle. He won't let you leave Alyria with her, no matter how many men you have."

Erynn wished that were true, but right now she wasn't so sure. If Krystalix was trying to protect her, where was he? She hadn't seen him since they left the castle and surely he could have saved her at the creek?

"Krystalix won't be a problem," Lord Caden said. "He's old, and I don't think he's as invincible as everyone thinks. I do have some experience with dragons."

"Yes, we can see that," Marik said, with a nod at the other man's scars. "And Erynn was just telling us about your previous encounter with him in Galia. I wasn't aware the three of you had met before."

The slightest look of unease passed across Lord Caden's face, but then it was gone. "That was such a long time ago, Erynn. I'd already forgotten."

Erynn stepped forward, clenching her fists and pulling at the chains. Wishing again that she could grab that poker. "I haven't."

Marik pulled the letter she had found in Galia from his pocket and handed it to Lord Caden. "She had this in her pack, still in the tube."

Lord Caden scanned the letter, but didn't seem overly shocked. "My falconer tried to send it when Krystalix attacked. I guess that old dragon didn't get as much of that bird as I thought. Which only goes to prove my point."

"What's this book you were looking for?" Marik asked.

The Galian didn't appear particularly pleased at being questioned. He folded the letter and slipped it in his pocket. "Just something Naedra's been interested in for a while. Nothing that would be of any concern to Alyria."

"Was that why you killed my father?" Erynn asked. "Because you were angry you didn't find it? That you failed?"

"I killed your father because I wanted his horses," Lord Caden replied. "No more than that." He glanced at Marik.

"Horses that Holden will be more than compensated for by this alliance, I assure you."

Marik gave a single nod. "I'm sure he will."

Erynn could tell there was something going on between Marik and Lord Caden. Some sort of friction. But she didn't care. "You could have just taken the horses." She almost didn't get the words out, her voice breaking at the end.

Lord Caden sighed, seeming annoyed they were still on the same subject. "I could have, Erynn. But I didn't."

Erynn glared at him, hating this man more than ever and wishing more than ever that there was some way she could get out of this. That she had another chance to make him pay. She wanted him dead.

Marik smiled. "I think you better watch your back going home, my friend. She looks like she could run you through right now."

Lord Caden laughed. "She's in shackles. And no more of a threat than her father."

CHAPTER 23

Lord Caden said nothing more about Erynn's father and minutes later all three men had left the shop and the girls were alone. Quinn had seemed reluctant to go, as if he had something he wanted to say to the girls, but there was clearly nothing he could say that wouldn't draw attention and he simply followed Marik outside.

When they were gone, Erynn sank to the floor and lowered her head to her hands. How could she have let this happen? How could she have been so foolish to get caught?

"Maybe we should have poisoned his soup," Adena muttered, kicking her chains out of the way and sitting down next to her. "Marik's, too."

Erynn thought about the old woman in the market and her warning that she would one day regret not taking those poison herbs. She wondered what might have happened if she had.

"Think Quinn will help?" Adena asked.

Erynn almost laughed. "With a couple dozen men outside?"

"What about Krystalix?"

"If he wanted to help us, you'd think he would have done it at the creek."

"Well, they'll have to move us some time. Maybe we'll have a chance then."

Erynn held out her arms and gave her chains a rattle. "Doubtful. And they're not moving us together, remember?"

Adena leaned back against the wall. "Well, there has to be something we can do."

Erynn wanted to tell her it was pointless, that she couldn't see any way out of this, but she couldn't bring herself to say it. She had dragged Adena into this mess and now her friend would hang for the king's death. Just the thought was almost too much to bear. She wished now that she had left the castle on her own. That she hadn't stopped to say good-bye.

"I wonder who this Brock is," Adena said. "Boy is he going to be in for a surprise."

Erynn thought again of the two men she'd seen at the market, but didn't have the strength to mention them. "I just hope Marik doesn't run into him any time soon. Or Dillon."

"Or he kills them before he can ask any questions."

Erynn doubted that would happen. Marik would want Brock and Dillon to know exactly why they were going to die. "At least he bought our story."

"Do you think he knows about the banquet?"

Erynn remembered the look on Marik's face when he told her Gareth wasn't coming home. "I don't think so. I think he knows the Galians have a plan, but not the details. Just like Holden said."

"Think we should tell him?"

Erynn shook her head. "I don't see how it would help. And who knows, maybe it would be better to know something he doesn't."

"I don't think he likes Lord Caden much."

"I don't think he likes anyone telling him what to do. Anyone besides Holden."

Adena was quiet for a few moments. "If they do separate us, you'll have to watch for a way to escape. Maybe you could find a weapon or something."

Erynn sighed. Lord Caden was right. She was in shackles. And not much of a threat. She didn't know how Queen Naedra ever got it in her mind that she would one day destroy her, but she knew beyond a shadow of a doubt that she was wrong. "I just wish we could find Sheldon and that falcon. Ruin their plans. All of them."

Marik's men returned to check on them periodically, bringing them food and water and ensuring that they hadn't somehow found a way out of their chains, but otherwise they were left alone. Two candles had been left on nearby tables and provided just enough light to see each other in the growing dark. Marik returned once, later in the evening, but he said little and they didn't see any sign of Lord Caden. And eventually, as the night wore on, more ale from the local inn flowed to the soldiers in the street, and their checks grew less and less frequent.

Erynn rested her head back against the wall, chains nestled in her lap, and listened to the laughter and talk outside. The soldiers had shut both of the shop doors, but she could hear them clearly. Most of the talk was about the king and how Alyria was going to change now that he was gone and Holden was in charge, but she heard no mention of the Galians and suspected that was because Lord Caden's men were nearby. She might not be able to see or hear them, but she knew they were there — ensuring she didn't escape.

Two more Alyrian soldiers came in a short time later, and when they left she finally closed her eyes. Some time later — she wasn't sure how long — she found herself awakened by an odd fluttering sound. Adena was sound asleep next to her, her head resting on her shoulder. Erynn glanced around the shop, but didn't see any source of the noise. Then one of the candles flickered and she assumed she must have been imagining things. Or at least she hoped she was. An image flashed in her mind of rats scurrying away from them in the castle tunnel, but she banished the thought from her mind and closed her eyes. She wasn't going to think about that. Not while she was stuck there in chains.

A second later she sensed something move inside the shop. Her eyes flew open.

A figure dressed in a long brown cloak stood in the shadows by the front doors; the hood drawn.

Erynn flinched — waking Adena, who raised her head and looked around.

"What?" she asked. Then she noticed the same figure and immediately sat up.

At first Erynn thought it was one of Marik's men, come to check on them, but then the figure stepped toward the side wall — and further into the light of one of the candles — and she realized it was an older man. He was thin in build, and slightly stooped in the shoulders, most of his face hidden in the shadows of his hood. He carefully lifted a ring of keys from a hook on the wall, and then turned and walked toward them.

Erynn opened her mouth to ask who he was, but he quickly raised a finger to his lips.

"Let me free you," he whispered. "But we must be quiet or they will hear."

Erynn's breath caught. She knew that voice! But from where? She tried for a glimpse of his face as he came closer and bent towards her, but the shop was too dark and his hood too deep. The keys clinked together as he searched for the right one, and then he motioned for her to raise her hands and seconds later the shackles slipped from her wrists. She caught them and scrambled to her feet. Moments later, Adena was standing next to her.

"How did you get past those men?" her friend asked, keeping her voice low.

The old man's bones seemed to creak as he lifted himself back up. "No questions. We must hurry."

Erynn again tried to remember where she'd heard that voice, but her mind was blank. She went for her pack. Marik had taken the gold, the map, and all of the letters and tubes, but she thankfully still had her quill and ink pot, along with the small black stone she had taken from her father's grave and the bundle of food from Cole's wife. She held the stone in her hand for a second, more relieved that she still had it than she had expected, and squeezing it tight as she remembered her conversation with Lord Caden. Then she slipped it away and returned to the back of the shop.

Adena was already there with her pack, watching as the old man somehow lifted the heavy beam barricading the rear door and set it down gently against the wall. Her eyes went to the swords and tools strewn along the ledge next to the forge.

"Are there guards out back?" she asked.

"There should be," the old man replied. "But right now they are taking part in the celebration of your capture out front. You can be sure they will pay for it in the morning."

He opened the door. It creaked, but the sound seemed to pass unnoticed amidst the laughter and talk outside.

Behind the shop was a yard littered with more tools, scraps of iron, an old and battered bellows, and an overturned tub partially buried in the dirt. A shed sat to the left side, the door hanging ajar, and a well in the center of the yard. Beyond was a wall of dark trees.

The old man stepped outside, and as he turned and motioned toward the trees, the light of the moon revealed his face.

Erynn gasped. It was Soren! The old man who had rescued her from the caves in Galia! He seemed older than she remembered, like he'd aged ten years instead of only two, but she knew beyond a doubt it was him. "I – I know you. You were there. In Galia."

The old man smiled, but simply motioned again to the trees. "Quickly, Erynn. We must go."

Adena's eyes were wide, obviously as confused and surprised as Erynn that he could be there now, helping them, but she just shrugged, hitched up her pack, and followed him across the yard. Erynn ran after her.

The forest was dark and close and quiet, the light of the moon barely penetrating the leaves. Erynn stayed close to Adena, barely able to see more than a few feet in any direction, but Soren seemed to know exactly where he was going and never once faltered. He walked quickly, even faster than she had imagined for a man his age, and almost faster than they could keep up, but he refused to answer any of their questions about who he was or where he was taking them, and simply repeated that there wasn't any time.

Erynn wondered if he was with the Order of the Cael and had been sent to keep an eye on her. Perhaps watching over her and following her all this time. Or maybe some other friend of her mother's. The king had said her mother would come for her when the time was right. Maybe it was still too dangerous for her to come herself and she had sent Soren instead.

They walked throughout the night, never once stopping, and it was still dark when they finally came to the edge of the wood. Below them lay a shallow valley, bordered on both sides by a series of low hills and a line of trees far to the south.

Soren drew back his hood and turned to face them. "This

is as far as I can go. To the west, beyond those hills, you will find the road south. Should you decide to follow it, you must be careful. Keep out of sight."

Adena blinked. "You're leaving?"

"I must retrace our steps. Try to draw Marik away from you if I can. Hopefully give you more time."

"Who are you?" Erynn asked. "And how did you know we were here?"

Soren smiled. "A friend, Erynn. One who doesn't want to see you delivered to Naedra."

"You know who I am? What I am?"

"I have known about you for some time. I feared Naedra would one day find out about you, too. And that she would come for you."

"You knew when you found me in Galia?" Erynn asked, her voice betraying the hurt she felt at learning this. That yet another person she had thought was a friend had known who she was all along and said nothing.

"I did, but it was clear you had not yet learned the truth and it was certainly not my place to tell you. You also had more than enough to deal with at the time."

"Are you with the Order? Or a friend of my mother's?"

Soren shook his head. "No, but the sooner you leave Alyria and find the Order of the Cael, the sooner they can help protect you. It is dangerous for you here, especially with the reward Holden has put out for your arrest. He is a desperate man, and now everyone will be looking for you."

Erynn was confused, but then she had another thought. "Are you Paddon? The king's friend?"

Soren again shook his head. "No."

"But I don't understand. Were you following us in Galia? Is that how you found me?"

Soren smiled. "I know you have many questions, Erynn,

but you must trust me. Now is not the time. Soon those men will notice you gone, if they have not already, and will advise Marik. And you can be sure he will not wait until morning to come after you. You must be swift now, and careful."

"More careful than we were today," Adena muttered. She stepped out into the cool night air, away from the trees, and paused to wait for Erynn.

But Erynn couldn't move. She didn't want to go anywhere until she had some answers. She wanted to know who Soren was and how he had found them. And something else had crossed her mind, too, now that she'd had a chance to recover from their flight out of the blacksmith's shop and their race through the woods. Something that just a few short hours ago she had wished more than anything else she could do. But it meant going another way entirely. West.

"We have to go, Erynn," Adena said. "You know he's right. It's too dangerous now."

Erynn could hear it in her voice. Her friend knew what she was thinking. She could also hear the fear. A few hours ago, Adena was facing the noose for killing the king. For helping her escape. Now she had a second chance. And she knew if Marik caught up to them again, she might not get another.

"We will meet again, Erynn," Soren said. "And at that time I promise to give you the answers you seek. I also have a favor to ask of you. Something very important. But for now, you must go." He glanced back into the trees, as if he'd heard something, but all Erynn could hear was the gentle rustle of leaves. Then a grave look came over his face and he motioned down the hill. "Go now! Quickly!"

Erynn knew she had no choice. She stepped out from the trees and started down the hill after Adena. She glanced back once, just a few seconds later, but the old man was gone.

CHAPTER 24

Erynn followed Adena down the hill and then west across the valley until they reached the road. It was still dark, and would be for a few more hours, and since the road was quiet and much easier to travel, they decided to follow it south for a while, running as often as they could and then heading inland again just after sunrise when the first wagon approached.

They stopped mid-morning for a rest, but were too worried about Marik to even think about sleep and were soon moving again. Dark clouds gathered as the day wore on, the air growing cooler than normal, and by late afternoon, as they climbed yet another hill and gazed out over open fields that met up with a large wood in the distance, the clouds were heavy and threatening.

When the rain came, light at first, they were still a couple of miles from the trees. They pulled up their hoods, shifted to holding their packs in front of them, under their cloaks, to help keep their extra clothes dry, and started to run. Lightning flashed in the sky, thunder shook the ground, and soon the rain fell heavier. By the time they reached the trees, it was getting dark and Erynn was soaked almost through to the skin, her hair plastered to her face and her teeth chattering. But still they kept moving, trying to take advantage of what light they still had left to push their way deeper into the woods.

"I — I'm freezing," Erynn said after they'd been walking for a while. She had wrapped her arms around her pack in front of her, snug across her chest, but was still wet and hadn't been able to shake the cold. The trees provided some shelter from the wind and the rain, but large drops still splashed down all around them.

Adena paused on the trail ahead and waited for her to catch up. "Maybe we should stop. See if we can build a fire."

Erynn wanted nothing more than to sit in front of a warm fire, but they had already been caught twice since leaving the castle and she wasn't about to let it happen again. She couldn't. "Marik might see the smoke. And besides, the wood's probably all wet."

"We might get sick if we don't. And it's getting dark anyway. I'm sure it'll be fine."

Erynn still didn't like the idea. "I think we should keep going as long as we have light. We need to keep ahead of them." She continued on, moving past Adena to take the lead. Her friend looked like she might protest, but said nothing more and soon fell in behind her.

Erynn tried not to think about warm fires as she walked. Or about how cold and wet and miserable she felt. She even tried not to think about whether her current predicament was some sort of punishment for the fact she wasn't headed west towards Blackwood right now. She tried to think instead about Soren — who he was, where he was, and whether or not he'd actually thrown Marik off their trail. Marik was bound to be furious that they'd escaped and she did not want to cross paths with him again. She'd go on all night if she had to. She just wished it wasn't so cold.

A large raindrop splashed down through the leaves and landed on her nose. As she reached up to wipe it away, her foot slipped off the edge of a loose rock and she fell.

Hard.

"You alright?" Adena asked.

"Fine," Erynn muttered, pushing herself up from the dirt and twigs and bits of rock on the path. Her hands stung, but she ignored them and pulled her legs under her to stand, hoping the fall hadn't shattered the small pot of ink in her pack. The second she put weight on her left foot, a throbbing pain radiated up her leg. Not intense, but enough to catch her breath. She reached out and leaned her weight against a tree, and a few seconds later tried again. She could put weight on her foot, but it wasn't comfortable at all. She cursed to herself. The last thing she needed right now was an injury.

"I think we should rest here," Adena said, sounding concerned.

Erynn shook her head. "Marik might not be far behind us, Adena."

"Maybe Soren led him off."

"And maybe he didn't." Erynn brushed a few more twigs and leaves from her cloak, then took a deep breath, readjusted her grip on her pack, and limped forward. "I've probably just twisted it a bit. Let's keep going."

Adena was quiet a moment. "Are you sure?"

"Yes."

Erynn kept her eyes on the ground, watching where she stepped and cursing herself again for being so careless, but every time she put weight on her left foot, she felt the same throbbing pain. She tried to ignore it, and to keep walking, but after only a few minutes, she stopped and leaned up against another tree. "I can't. Maybe it is time to rest."

Adena dropped her pack. "You're shaking, Erynn. We need to start a fire."

Erynn wiped another splash of rain from her brow. "We can't, Adena. They'll see."

"We have to, Erynn. You rest here and I'll go find some wood."

Erynn was about to repeat that they couldn't risk it, but before she could say a word, Adena turned and disappeared through the trees. She heard her friend muttering something to herself as she walked, heard the snap of twigs under her feet, but soon her voice faded and all she could hear was the patter of rain.

Erynn glanced around. The forest was quiet, save for the splash of rain. Almost too quiet. And getting darker by the minute. She dropped her pack, leaned the rest of her weight against the tree, and sank slowly to the ground — pulling her knees up tight to her chest and wrapping her arms around them to try and keep warm.

She couldn't believe she'd gone and injured her foot. First she'd been careless enough to walk right into a bunch of soldiers, and now this. Slipping off a stupid rock! She lowered her head on her knees and hoped that if she concentrated hard enough maybe she could stop shivering. But it didn't work. Then seconds later she smelled something — the slightest whiff of smoke — and had just turned her attention to that when something moved in the bushes a few yards away.

Erynn raised her head. "Adena?"

She listened hard, but heard no response — and soon realized with some alarm that the noise had come from the direction opposite the one Adena had gone. Was it a bear? Or some other animal skulking through the woods? One looking for a meal? She sat up and was about to call for her friend when a man stepped out from behind one of the trees in front of her.

Except it wasn't a man at all.

Erynn flinched. She had never seen an elf before.

He stood about her height, quite slender, with pale white skin, green eyes, and slightly pointed ears. His white-blonde hair was tied back from his face, hanging down almost to his waist, and he was dressed in light animal skins with a darker-colored pouch strapped across his chest and a quiver full of arrows on his back. He carried a bow in his left hand.

Erynn didn't move. Another drop of rain landed on her forehead and trickled down the side of her face, but she didn't wipe it away.

He stood still for several moments, watching her, and then he stepped further into the small clearing between the trees and pointed at her foot. "You have injured yourself, Daughter of Maegan."

At first, Erynn was so captivated by his voice, so soft and clear amongst the patter of rain, that she didn't even realize what he'd said. Then she frowned, her surprise at his words cutting through her fear. "You know who I am?"

"You carry the blood of the dragon. We can sense it."

Erynn's mouth dropped open. The blood of the dragon?

He kneeled down and motioned for her to extend her sore foot. "Let me help you."

But Erynn couldn't move — too shaken by what he had just said. Was it true? Her mind flashed back to something the king had said in the pantry. Something about not understanding the relationship between Daughters and dragons, but knowing there was one. And then she remembered the two women she had read about in the history book on Krystalix — the one who supposedly lived in the mountains and the one seen with him by the river. And she somehow knew in her heart that it was. The blood of the dragons did flow in her veins. That was why the Daughters were able to communicate with the dragons and why she had had so many dreams about them over the years. They were somehow part of a mixed race!

Slowly, she extended her foot.

"You did not know?" he asked as he gently removed her shoe.

Erynn shook her head.

He opened the pouch at his waist and pulled out several large leaves, each folded twice. He set them down next to him and reached back into the pouch and carefully scooped out what appeared to be a handful of a thick, dark mud, mixed with tiny bits of ground up leaves. He started to apply the mud in a thick layer around her ankle and foot and immediately she felt a cool tingling sensation and the slight throbbing she had felt ever since she fell started to lessen.

"What is that?" she asked.

"It will reduce the swelling and help your foot heal faster. It is not broken."

Erynn breathed a small sigh of relief at that and realized she was probably very lucky that he had chosen to help her. She had heard stories about the elves and their gifts of healing — gifts they were not generally known to share with men. At least not now. "I – I slipped on a rock."

"You were not paying attention to the path."

Another raindrop landed on Erynn's forehead, and this time she wiped it away. "My name's Erynn."

"And I am Cathus." He finished with the mud and now reached for the leaves, wrapping them one-by-one over top of the mud all around her foot and ankle, until every inch was layered several times over, except for her toes.

Erynn glanced around as he worked, wondering if there

were any more elves nearby. Elves that were watching him apply the strange mud and leaves to her foot. "How many of you are there?"

At first Cathus didn't respond. "Elves are taught not to talk of such things with the race of men. Too often such information has been used to destroy us."

"Oh, I didn't mean ..." Erynn started, not wanting to offend or anger him even though she didn't get the sense that she had. "I mean, I understand. Right now someone wants to destroy me."

"It is a dangerous time in Valentia. Especially for Daughters of Maegan."

Erynn was a little surprised, wondering how an elf could know such things — especially when she'd never heard much about them venturing outside their forest homes. "I wish I had known that before. I only found out I am one a few days ago and don't seem to be having much luck."

Cathus pulled a long strand of woven grass from another pocket and wound it around the leaves, tying them securely in place. "The blood of the dragon is stronger than that of man." He glanced up and met her eyes. "Are you listening to what it tells you?"

Erynn stared at him, at first not sure what he meant. Then she looked away, back down at her foot. "I – I don't know. I mean, I —"

Twigs snapped nearby and Adena appeared through the trees, her arms loaded with branches. "I found some wood, but most of it's —"

She saw the elf and jumped in surprise, dropping the branches at her feet.

Cathus rose. "You will need no fire." He raised his arm and pointed off between two nearby trees. "Head south one hundred yards and you will find warmth and shelter from the rain." He glanced at Erynn. "And perhaps a better view of the path." Then he turned to leave.

"What – What about my foot?" Erynn asked, frowning at her new green boot.

Cathus paused. "Leave it on until morning. Then you must rest your foot three more days."

"Three days?" Erynn said. "Are you saying I can't walk for three days?" She had hoped whatever it was in the strange mud would heal it long before that.

"If you try, you will only awaken the injury and it will take much longer to heal." He smiled. "I wish you luck, Daughter of Maegan." Then he was gone.

Erynn just sat there, staring at the gap in the trees.

"He knows who you are?" Adena asked, still looking rather dazed.

All Erynn could do was nod.

Adena laughed. "I can't believe I just saw an elf."

Erynn sighed and rubbed her forehead. She was still shocked herself — and at the news about who and what she really was — but what was even more disturbing to her now was what he had just told her. Three days. What were they going to do for three days? A shiver rippled through her, reminding her of the cold, and she clenched her teeth and slowly pulled herself up on her good leg with the help of the tree. "I guess we should do what he says. Head south. Can you help me?"

Adena was still gazing off in the direction Cathus had disappeared, but finally she slung both of their packs over her shoulder and stepped closer. Erynn wrapped an arm around her other shoulder and slowly they set off south, through the gap in the trees and in the direction Cathus had pointed.

Erynn glanced around as they walked, and up into the darkness of the high branches above, wondering if he was watching. She had a strong feeling he was — and that he wasn't the only one. Other elves were watching her, too.

He had said one hundred yards, and it was a journey that to Erynn and her sore foot seemed to take forever. All along the way she continued to smell smoke, the smell growing stronger with every step, and finally, when they reached the edge of the forest, she discovered the source: in front of them lay an open field, with a barn and small cottage on the far side. A wisp of smoke was rising from the cottage chimney, and a warm, yellow glow visible through a crack in the curtains.

Erynn was tempted to walk right up to the door and beg whoever lived there to let them inside for a while, just long enough to warm themselves by the fire. But she knew it was too dangerous. By now most of Alyria likely knew about the warrant for their arrest and would be watching for them. They would have to settle for the barn.

As they started across the field, stepping out into the full force of the rain once more, Adena chuckled. "Maybe those elves aren't so bad after all."

CHAPTER 25

Erynn kept an eye on the cottage as they made their way across the field and when they finally reached the barn they slipped in the side door. Several goats were roaming around loose inside and they ran away, bleating in alarm. Erynn cringed, hoping no one in the cottage had heard their cries over the rain.

The barn was almost pitch black and as they carefully felt their way around Erynn was able to determine that four horses, two or three cows, and what sounded like a dozen pigs also resided there with the goats. They found a stall used for storage at the far end of the center corridor and slipped out of their wet cloaks and dresses and hung them over the door. Then they changed into the extra clothes they each had stuffed in their packs, which were slightly damp in places from the rain but at least drier than what they already had, and curled up on the floor to rest.

Erynn's hair was still wet, but it was warm in the barn and she was already feeling better. Even her foot didn't seem as sore, although she had taken care not to put any weight on it since they left the clearing in the wood. She had no idea what they were going to do for the next three days, but didn't want to think about that now. All she wanted to do was sleep. She didn't even have the energy to tell Adena about her conversation with Cathus and what she had learned about the Daughters of Maegan, even though she hadn't stopped thinking about it since he left.

She had just closed her eyes when a dog started barking.

Adena scrambled to her feet. "Someone must have seen us."

Erynn felt her heart sink, unable to believe this was happening. Just when she had finally thought she might get some warmth and rest. "The curtains were drawn. I watched them the whole time."

"Then they must have heard the goats."

The barking was close by, and getting louder, the dog whining between barks as if it was being restrained. Whoever was with him, they were definitely headed toward the barn.

Erynn sat up. "Maybe they're just coming to check the animals?"

Adena thrust a cloak at her in the dark and she grabbed it and carefully pulled herself up on her good foot.

"I think there's a loft," Adena said, handing her one of the packs next. "Maybe we could hide."

Erynn heard her slide back the stall door. "It won't matter with a dog. Besides, I don't even know where the ladder is to get up there. Do you?"

Adena sighed. "No."

"What about the front doors?"

"I think there's a lock on them."

Now Erynn really couldn't believe this was happening. "So we're trapped?"

Adena didn't answer. Someone was talking to the dog outside, the voice growing louder even though the words were lost in the rain.

Erynn felt disoriented in the dark. A wave of panic rising inside. She wished she had listened to Adena. Wished they had stopped and built that fire when they had a chance. And that she hadn't listened to Cathus. He obviously knew about this barn when he told them to come this way. Didn't he know that whoever lived here also had a dog? The king had warned her not to trust anyone and already she had failed. The elf had seemed to understand she was in danger, but how could he possibly know about the warrant? The only hope they had was that whoever was now headed to the barn hadn't heard of the two girls wanted for the murder of the king.

The side door opened and the barking grew louder. The goats ran bleating from the door once more, and this time the horses, cows, and pigs all added their voices to the protest. Then the dog whined and a light swung about in the darkness over the stall door.

Erynn and Adena both ducked down out of sight.

"I know someone's in here," a woman's voice rang out. "Show yourself or I'll set my dog on you."

Erynn hadn't expected a woman, although she supposed it didn't really matter. All it would take was one person to notify Marik.

"What do we do?" Adena whispered.

Erynn sighed. "I don't think we have a choice."

"Did you hear me?" the woman said, louder this time. "I'll set my dog loose. He'll find you."

Erynn handed Adena her pack. Then they both straightened up and she wrapped an arm around her friend's shoulder and stepped with her out of the stall.

The dog barked louder and the light swung toward them.

A middle-aged woman with curly red hair was standing in the center of the barn. She was dressed in a dark cloak and was holding a lantern with a candle in one hand and the collar

244

of a large brown dog in the other. She looked stunned as the girls walked toward her and raised the lantern up higher for a better look.

"Two girls in my barn?" she said.

"We got caught in the rain," Adena replied. "We were just looking for a dry place to sleep."

"Thought we had thieves in here again. They stole two of my best pigs last week."

"We're not thieves," Erynn said, a little angrier than she had intended. "We just needed a place to wait out the rain."

"Come closer so I can see you better."

Adena helped Erynn forward. The dog strained toward them, still barking.

"Oh do be quiet, Voltan!" the woman said to the dog. "It's just a couple of girls." The dog stopped barking, but continued to whine. "What's wrong with your foot?"

Erynn studied the woman's face, looking for some sign that she was aware of the warrant and had connected it to the two girls in front of her. But she saw none. "I twisted it."

"What's that you've got on it?"

Erynn hesitated, not sure if she should tell her the truth. Elves were not known to help people suffering minor injuries in the forests, and she had a feeling the only reason he had helped her was because of who she was — although even that still left her confused. But she couldn't think of any other way to explain her strange green boot. "An elf helped me. In the wood out back. He put something on it."

"An elf?" the woman said, clearly surprised. "In our woods?"

Erynn just nodded her head.

The woman's eyes narrowed. "Where are you girls from?"

"Farglen," Erynn said before Adena could respond. "We're on our way to Renford and got a little lost in the rain."

"On your own?"

"We've got no family left in Farglen," Adena said. "And we thought maybe we'd find better work there."

The woman remained silent for a short time, eyeing them carefully, but then her face relaxed. "Well, you certainly don't look like thieves. What you look like is a couple of cats that fell in a well. I suppose you best come inside. We haven't much, but at least the fire will warm you up. And it just so happens we have some leftover stew."

Erynn almost didn't know what to say. She was so relieved at the thought of sitting in front of a warm fire, and eating a hot meal, that any fears she had about what this woman knew or what trouble she might bring suddenly melted away. They thanked her, and slipped into their wet cloaks again, then followed her and Voltan across the yard.

The cottage was small, but as cozy and warm inside as Erynn had imagined, and the smell of pork and spices coming from a cauldron over the fire made her mouth water. An old woman with white-gray hair and wearing a green dress was dozing on a couch by the fire, but she raised her head the second the door closed.

"What was it, Callie?" she asked, concern in her voice. "Is everything all right?"

"Just a couple of girls, Amara," the other woman replied as she showed them where to hang their cloaks. "Got caught in the rain on their way to Renford and decided to seek shelter in our barn. They looked miserable so I invited them in. One's twisted her foot, but it sounds like one of your friends out in the woods put something on it."

"One of the elves?" the old woman asked, sitting up straighter and turning even more toward the door.

"Was a shock to us, too," Adena said with a bit of a laugh. "Neither of us had seen one before."

Erynn was curious what Callie had meant by "one of your friends," but not sure it was wise to say much about their encounter with Cathus and hoped they wouldn't ask too many questions.

"Don't normally hear of that sort of thing," Callie said. "Do you, Amara?"

"No," the old woman said. "The elves do tend to keep to themselves." A bit of a frown had formed on her face, but then it cleared and she smiled. "Well, come on in girls. There's plenty of room by the fire. I'm Amara and you've met my niece, Callie. What are your names?"

Erynn was about to say her name, but caught herself just in time. "I'm Loren. And this is my —"

"Cousin," Adena said. "Serena."

A slightly unsettled look flitted across Amara's face. "Loren, did you say?"

"Yes," Erynn replied. As Adena helped her around the couch to the fire, the old woman's head slowly turned to follow them, and she reached up one hand and touched her throat. Erynn noticed that both of her eyes were almost completely white and realized she must be blind.

"You sound so young," Amara said. Her voice seemed to crack slightly and she paused to clear her throat. "How old are you girls?"

"I'm seventeen, and she's sixteen," Adena said as she sat down next to Erynn by the fire.

"Something wrong, Amara?" Callie asked.

The old woman seemed to have gone pale, but she simply waved her hand. "Just surprised is all. Don't normally hear of girls their age traveling such a long way on their own. Or elves coming out to help someone like that, either. Which one of you has the sore foot?"

"I do," Erynn said. "Loren."

"What did he put on it?"

"A mud of some kind. And he wrapped it in some leaves. He said to leave it on until morning and then rest it for three more days. I guess he must have seen me fall."

"Not much happens in those woods that they don't see," Amara said. "Did he tell you his name?"

"Cathus," Erynn replied. She thought something in the old woman's voice sounded strange, even distracted, but Callie was ladling stew into a couple of bowls she had fetched from a shelf near the hearth and she didn't give it any more thought.

Callie handed Erynn one of the bowls. Then she turned toward her aunt as she reached for the second bowl. "Didn't you once say Cathus was their leader?"

"Yes, that he is," Amara replied. "Not just any elf of the wood. I used to go out walking back there — before my sight left me anyway. Got to know a few of them over the years. Even met him, too. I'm sure whatever he put on your foot will help. Probably help it heal much faster than it would have alone."

"It actually feels better already," Erynn said, still relishing the warmth of the hot bowl in her hands, but distracted from digging in by this news about Cathus. Was that why he guided them to their barn? Because he knew Amara and her niece would likely take them in? Help them?

"Well, you're more than welcome to stay as long as you need," Callie said, handing the second bowl of stew to Adena. "It's only the two of us here now, and it's not often we get company."

"That would be nice, thank you," Erynn said. She felt relieved at the thought of having a warm place to stay for the next three days — and plenty of hot meals — but was still nervous at the thought of Marik finding them. And she remembered what that soldier on the road had told Cole — about what Holden would do to those found helping them. "I wish I had been more careful."

"Not your fault you hurt yourself," Amara said. "These sorts of things happen sometimes. I often think it's a sign. Telling us to slow down. Or that maybe we're not on the right path."

Erynn paused, her first spoonful of stew halfway to her mouth. Struck by how similar Amara's words were to those of the elf. She glanced at Adena, but her friend was busy eating and she remembered she still hadn't had told her everything Cathus had said. She hesitated, not sure if she should respond, but then the smell and heat of the stew caught her attention again and she forgot about the comment and dug in — not surprised to find the stew tasted even better than it smelled.

Amara turned to Callie as her niece sat down next to her on the couch. "Could you take them to Renford in the wagon? When her foot heals?"

"I could when I get back from Chapley," Callie said. "We still need to sell a few of those pigs."

"You're going into Chapley?" Erynn asked through a mouthful of stew.

"I was planning to go tomorrow, Callie replied. "But if this rain keeps up I might push that back. I'd rather wait it out than risk getting stuck in the mud."

Erynn glanced at Adena, not liking the sound of that. So far, it didn't seem like either woman had heard about the warrant, or at least hadn't made the connection to the two girls now sitting in front of them, but that would change if Callie went into town.

"Couldn't Nolan take the pigs in?" Amara asked.

Callie snickered. "He could, but he wouldn't get us a fair price. Besides, I think he's already gone into town."

"It's alright," Erynn said, knowing they couldn't accept the offer anyway. "We actually don't mind the walk. Just need to wait for my foot to heal."

"How close are we to Chapley?" Adena asked.

"About ten miles," Callie replied.

"So you haven't been there recently?"

Erynn shot Adena a warning look. If the women did know about the warrant but just hadn't made the connection, it probably wasn't good to remind them. Her friend cast her a look back that said she understood — and that she knew what was doing.

"Not in a few weeks," Callie said.

"So you haven't heard about the Galians?" Adena asked.

Erynn again shot Adena a look, but this time her friend's eyes stayed on Callie.

"Yes, we heard about that from Nolan," Callie said. "One of our neighbors. He goes into town more often than we do and likes to check in on us now and then."

"I still can't believe it," Amara said, looking rather outraged. "Galians in Alyria! And without Gareth here?" She shook her head. "I can only imagine what the king must have been thinking when he saw them."

Erynn gazed down at her stew, almost glad the old woman couldn't see her face.

"It might not be that bad," Callie said. "Maybe it is just a short visit. Like they said."

"They're Galians, Callie," Amara said, anger in her voice now. "There's more to it than that. I guarantee it. And I'm sure Wryden knows it, too."

Erynn glanced at Adena again, wondering if she planned to tell the women the rest — about what had happened to the king — but this time her friend simply raised a brow, as if to say she was now leaving that up to Erynn. At first, Erynn wasn't sure they should, but after giving it some more thought, she supposed it couldn't hurt. It was clear the women didn't know about the warrant. "We heard the king died a few days ago."

"Died?" both women said at once, turning to Erynn with their eyes wide.

"That's dreadful," Callie said. "What happened? Was it his age?"

"I don't know," Erynn replied, keeping her eyes on her stew and trying to act like she wasn't really interested. "We only heard about it the other day."

"It was the Galians," Amara said, tears appearing in her eyes. "It had to be. I knew something wasn't right when I heard they'd come here."

Erynn stared at her, finding something about her reaction somewhat unexpected.

Callie seemed to notice. "My aunt knew King Wryden once. Many years ago now. During the Tallon War."

"I didn't know him, Callie," Amara said, sounding a little embarrassed at the comment. "I was a servant. Simply in the room a few times when he was there."

"You were in Tallon during the war?" Erynn asked.

"I was born there," Amara said. "And worked at the castle for many years. My father was a cook in the kitchen. My mother a maid."

Erynn could hardly contain her surprise. "You served Queen Sasha?"

Amara smiled. "I was one of her maids for several years. And one of the last to see her alive."

Erynn almost dropped her spoon. A million questions had suddenly formed in her mind, but she suspected it wouldn't be wise to appear too eager.

"Do you know how she died?" she asked, trying again to

pretend she was only casually interested. "I heard she was betrayed by a Bryan knight —"

"That is a lie!" Amara said, her voice so full of anger that for a moment Erynn and Adena both froze. "I knew that young man and I can tell you he never would have done such a thing."

"You can't know that for sure, Amara," Callie said. "You were separated."

"I knew Branen, Callie! Radel needed to destroy him. Sasha's death just gave him the excuse he needed to finally do it."

"Radel?" Adena asked.

"King Agar's father," Amara explained. "The former King of Brye." Color had risen to her face. "I tell you, I celebrated the day I heard that old fool had passed. Didn't shed a tear."

"Why did King Radel want to destroy the knight?" Erynn asked.

"Because many thought Branen should be the one sitting on the Bryan throne. Not Radel. As long as Branen lived, he was a threat."

"The knight blamed for Sasha's death was of royal blood?" Erynn asked.

"Through his grandmother," Amara replied.

Erynn found Branen's story interesting, but wanted to get back to Queen Sasha. "So if he didn't kill her, what do you think happened?"

"The elves?" Adena asked.

Amara snorted. "No, not the elves. They knew who she was and would never have harmed her." She was quiet for a moment, the anger fading completely, and then sadness came over her face. "I think it was the childbirth." She paused to wipe away a few tears. "You see, King Maslin sent word to Radel some weeks before she died, asking for help in getting her safely out of Tallon. Unfortunately, by the time Branen and his men arrived, the baby was already due. We waited for days, hoping it would come so we could leave, but then the Alyrians were lost in that horrible battle and we couldn't wait any longer. It was very difficult for her. We barely got out of Tallon in time."

"Then what happened?" Adena asked.

"We ran into Galians and I was separated from them. I searched for days. Saw bodies everywhere. Most of Branen's men dead. But I never found Sasha or Branen. My brother had gone to Berridge some months earlier so I decided to go there, but it took me weeks and by the time I arrived, Branen was dead. Executed. He had returned to the castle with her lifeless body and had been blamed for her death."

Erynn was surprised to hear the name Berridge, the town where she and her father had been headed when they ran into Lord Caden. It was certainly a long walk from Tallon.

"There was no sign of her child when he returned?" Adena asked.

"No," Amara said. "But there were lots of rumors. Some said Branen killed it accidentally. Some that it was a girl and he either purposely killed her or sold her off somewhere. And, of course, some blamed the elves — because we had been so close to the Bryan Forest at the time."

"He never said what happened?" Erynn asked.

"If he did, it never got out. I've always wondered what would have happened if I'd gone to the castle instead of my brother's farm. If I could have saved him. I started to. Walked for days. But then I had this terrible dream that the castle was on fire. It scared me so much I decided not to go after all. Or to at least wait until I reached Berridge and could ask my brother to go with me."

"But how could you have done anything?" Callie said.

"You weren't there at the end to know what really happened."

"I knew Branen, Callie. I could have at least said that. And I knew the state Sasha was in. How difficult the travel had been for her."

"They might have killed you, too," Erynn said. "If King Radel really did want Branen dead."

Amara sighed. "Yes, that's what everyone told me. Still doesn't make it any easier."

Erynn gazed down at her stew, not quite as hungry as she was a few minutes ago. She felt bad for upsetting Amara and decided to save the rest of her questions about Sasha for later. "Did you see King Wryden often?"

"Just a few times. The last time was right after we learned about the Alyrians. He was devastated."

Erynn knew that thousands of Alyrian soldiers had been killed in the Tallon War, but had never understood what happened. "Were they really ambushed?"

"Yes, and it was Wryden's fault," Amara replied. "Maslin's too, to be fair. Sasha had warned both of them, but neither of them listened."

"Warned them about what?" Adena asked.

"About the young knight Maslin chose to assist Wryden while he stayed in Tallon. She told them something wasn't right about him and it wasn't until later that they found out he was feeding information to the Galians. They had planned to use those Alyrian soldiers in a final assault against the Galians — one last battle they hoped would win the war — but the Galians sent fresh men to ambush them and every last one of those men was killed."

"The king must have felt awful," Erynn said.

"Oh, he did," Amara said. "But that wasn't the worst. Those Alyrians were led by the only son of his closest friend. He was killed in that ambush, too."

For a moment, Erynn couldn't take her eyes off Amara. Then she gazed back down at her stew. Was this the reason the king grew so obsessed about Gareth? About him coming home? Did he fear he might lose his son the same way his friend had lost his? Perhaps as some sort of punishment for what happened? Her father had once said the king was never the same after the war. Now she knew why.

"What happened to the knight?" Adena asked. "The one that betrayed them?"

"The Galians killed him," Amara said rather matter-of-factly. "Some months later. I don't know why, but it wasn't all that surprising, really. He had obviously proved his loyalty couldn't be trusted."

"Do you remember the name of the king's friend?" Erynn asked. "The one who lost the son?" As far as she knew, Lord Brison was his closest friend, but she had never heard mention of him having another son and wondered if this might explain why Jeth seemed so upset at the castle. Perhaps he knew the story behind how his older brother had died.

Amara thought about this for a few moments, and then she smiled. "Paddon. That was his name, although I don't remember the rest. He came to see Maslin from time to time as an advisor, but was also close to Sasha. In fact, he was one of the few she trusted."

CHAPTER 26

The rain was still falling when Erynn woke the next morning. She was relieved, knowing that it meant Callie would put off her trip into Chapley for another day, and for a while she just lay there on the hard floor in front of the hearth and listened to it drum down on the roof.

Soon Voltan came padding out of one of the back rooms and tried to stick his nose in her face. Erynn pushed him away and he went to Adena, still asleep next to her, and licked her cheek. Her friend woke and groaned in disgust, shoving him back and wiping at her cheek with the back of her hand. He wandered over to the corner and lay down, but continued to watch them closely.

Adena sat up, still wiping her face, and looking rather disgusted. Then she turned to Erynn and saw she was awake. "How's your foot?"

Erynn carefully flexed her foot. The leaves had loosened during the night, and it seemed most of the mud had dried and flaked off and was now either scattered in small piles on the floor under her blanket or still trapped inside the leaves. "It feels better than it did last night, but I don't think I'll be walking any time soon."

"Did you get any sleep?"

Erynn shook her head. "Not much." She had actually spent most of the night thinking — and dreaming — about Queen Sasha's last days and Branen's wrongful execution at the hands of the former King of Brye. Except in her dreams, Branen had looked just like Gareth. And then later, just before she woke, she'd had an unsettling dream where she had slipped and fallen in the woods out behind the barn, but instead of twisting her foot she'd somehow cut herself and couldn't stop the bleeding. Adena had tried to help her, but couldn't, and Cathus had simply stood there and told her there was nothing he could do.

"Me neither," Adena said, rubbing her eyes and glancing around the cottage.

Erynn thought about telling Adena what she had learned in the woods, but then she felt a couple of the leaves slip and more of the dried mud spill onto the floor. She sat up and pulled back her blanket, swiveling around so her foot was over the fireplace. Then she carefully removed the leaves, dried mud raining down on cold embers, and arranged them in a neat stack nearby.

"I hate that we're stuck here," Adena said, her voice dropping to a whisper. "If Marik finds us, Callie and Amara could be in real trouble."

"I know," Erynn said, not really needing to be reminded. She knew if anything happened to Callie and Amara, it would be her fault. Just like the king. And that was the last thing she wanted. But she wasn't just worried about Marik. She was also worried about Nolan. Callie said their neighbor liked to check in on them every now and then and if he was in Chapley, he had likely heard about the warrant. She hoped he wouldn't decide to come by and bring the women the latest news.

Adena was quiet, gazing out the front window through a

crack in the curtains. Erynn wondered if she was thinking the same thing and returned her attention to her foot. She had finished removing all the leaves and now slipped off the thin cord woven out of tall grass, which had also loosened during the night.

"I dreamt about Ethlon last night," her friend said a few moments later, still keeping her voice low so the two women in the back rooms wouldn't hear them. "That we went there. I couldn't find Jared."

Erynn heard the worry in her voice. "It was just a dream, Adena. I'm sure he's fine." She wiped away the bits of mud still clinging to her foot and swiveled back around. Adena was picking at what looked like a piece of Voltan's fur caught on her blanket. Erynn started to sweep up the mess of dried mud on the floor and scoop it into the fireplace with her hands. What she couldn't scoop up she scraped into the cracks between the floorboards.

"I saw you hesitate when we were with Soren," Adena said. "Just before we left him. You wanted to go to Blackwood, didn't you?"

Erynn wasn't expecting the question. "Marik wants to kill you, Adena. I know this isn't just about me anymore."

"But you wanted to, didn't you? That's what you were thinking."

Erynn shrugged. "I guess." She thought about Cathus and Amara and their comments about the path. And that last question of his before he disappeared. *"Are you listening to what it tells you?"*

Adena was quiet again, gazing briefly toward the window. Erynn had cleaned the floor as best she could and now started folding up her blanket.

"Gareth still might come home before the banquet," Adena said. "Holden can't exactly keep it a secret that his father died."

Erynn didn't agree. "He'll stay until after the banquet."

"But why?"

"Because it's important, Adena."

"But he is the king now, isn't he? Doesn't he have to come home?"

Erynn finished folding her blanket and set it on the couch, not sure why her friend was bringing this up now. "He's planning to use the banquet to get Sarda's support for the war. If he gets it, they could win."

Adena sighed. "I really don't get why what's going on in Ridan is so much more important than what's going on here." She shoved her blanket away and went to grab a couple of logs from a pile in the corner. Then she set about building a fire.

Erynn didn't understand why her friend was getting so upset. She grabbed the other blanket and started folding it, too. "It isn't about Ridan. He's trying to stop Naedra. She's after something and he's worried what might happen to the rest of Valentia if she gets it. It might not seem like it, but he is trying to help Alyria."

Adena reached for another log. "Well, why did it have to be him? Why not someone else? The King of Brye has a son, doesn't he?"

Erynn was about to tell her that it actually had something to do with the King of Parigon's eldest son — that she had heard he was a friend of Gareth's and had asked him to come — but then she saw the look on Adena's face and remembered what she had said about her dream. And in a flash it hit her — the whole reason her friend was so angry. "You blame him. That's what this is about. And why you've been so against me doing anything to try and save him. Ever since the Galians arrived."

Adena opened her mouth to say something, but then she closed it and turned back to the fireplace, leaning the log she was still holding in her hand up against the others. "I don't know what you're talking about."

"Yes, you do. You blame Gareth for your parents leaving. For taking your father with him to Ridan and then your mother going to find him. For Jared going off to Ethlon to find both of them. You don't care if he dies or not."

Adena said nothing, just continued building her fire, but Erynn knew she was right. She could tell by the tension in her friend's shoulders and jaw and the fact that she now seemed reluctant to turn around and face her. Then she did turn around, but before she could say a word, Callie walked out of one of the back rooms.

"Good morning ladies," she said. "How was your sleep?"

They hadn't been talking very loud, but Erynn still searched the other woman's face for any sign she'd heard their argument. She saw none and tried her best to smile. "Great. Certainly better than sleeping in the woods." She finished folding Adena's blanket, set it on the couch with hers, and carefully pulled herself up. Callie pushed the couch back into its usual place and then she sat back down.

"Great," Adena said, turning back to the fireplace.

Callie went to the window and glanced outside, looking disappointed at the sight of the grey clouds and rain. She announced that she would put her trip off for another day, then slipped on her cloak and headed out to the barn with Voltan to feed and water the animals. Amara appeared not long after, and while Adena finished building a fire, she filled a bucket with water so Erynn could rinse the rest of the mud from her foot and set about preparing breakfast.

The rain continued throughout the day, but eventually tapered off and stopped by late afternoon. Erynn spent most of her time on the couch, listening with one ear to Amara as she told stories about her life in Tallon, and with the other to the rain and trying to remain alert for any other sounds outside. She learned more about Queen Sasha, but nothing of any real significance to her own situation, and although she had many questions — especially given what she had learned from Cathus — she kept them to a minimum as she was still cautious about appearing too interested in another Daughter of Maegan's life.

Adena was quieter than usual, barely even making eye contact with Erynn and frequently going to the window to gaze out at the road. She helped Amara around the cottage most of the morning, cleaning up after breakfast and then picking fruits and vegetables in the garden out back and carrying them down to the small root cellar beneath the kitchen. And when Amara finally ran out of things she could help her with, she appeared reluctant to stay inside and headed out to the barn to help Callie.

After dinner, Amara told them more about her walk across Brye. Erynn had grown to quite like the old woman, and to enjoy listening to her stories, and she was still amazed that she had traveled all the way to Berridge on her own — especially with a war going on. She even wished she could introduce her to Briggs. It also made her think about her own situation and that maybe getting to Highcastle wasn't as impossible a task as she had originally thought.

"What was Naedra like?" Adena asked at one point, sometime later in the evening. "Back when you lived in Tallon?"

"I never met her," Amara said. "She actually left Tallon a couple of years before Sasha married Maslin and came to live at the castle. But from what I heard, she certainly seemed like a very determined girl. If she set her mind to something, she wouldn't let anything stand in her way. A trait that's carried her far it seems. But then I only heard about her from Sasha and the two of them never did get along — or that's what Sasha told me anyway. And I never saw much of the other two to hear anything different."

"The other two?" Erynn asked. "Naedra and Sasha had other siblings?"

"Yes, there were four Keightley girls. Carys was the second oldest, after Sasha, and I would say probably the wisest of the four. She was always very involved with the Order of the Cael, even from a young age. And close to Paddon, too. Even more so than Sasha. Tara was the youngest. A sweet girl."

Erynn felt her breath catch. Tara? Was that the name she just said? She stared at the old woman, her mouth going dry as she realized with some horror what this meant. And then she glanced over at Adena and could tell her friend had heard it, too.

"Something wrong, Loren?" Callie asked. "You look shocked."

Erynn cleared her throat. "No, I – I'm fine. Just surprised is all. I didn't realize Naedra had any other siblings besides Sasha."

"Neither of them attended many functions at the castle," Amara said. "And with all the attention on Sasha's death and, of course, Naedra's actions in Galia over the last twenty-five years or so, I suppose they were rather forgotten."

Erynn wiped a hand over her face, trying hard to look like what she had just learned didn't bother her at all. But it did. Although she had never really given it much thought, she had sort of expected some possible close relation to Naedra — given that they were both Daughters of Maegan and it didn't seem like there were many of them left. But she had no idea it would be this close. That the woman who was hunting her mother, had ordered Lord Caden to arrest her and take her back to Galia, and who supposedly wanted to kill her was her aunt! She wanted to ask Amara about Tara, to find out everything the old woman knew about her — especially if she knew how her own sister came to be hunting her — but she was still so stunned that she couldn't find the words.

"Do you know how Naedra ended up in Galia?" Adena asked, seeming to sense her trouble.

"I'm not sure exactly," Amara said. "All I know is that she was still only fourteen when she left Tallon and it was about a year later that she met Krone. Sasha never really understood why she left, although she did say that Naedra had visited the temple in Brye not long before. She told me once that the temples were special places, and that she often went to the one in Brye when she felt troubled. Perhaps something happened when Naedra was there." She paused. "I was at the temple when I had that horrible dream about the castle. I had hoped maybe I would find Sasha there."

"I heard there's a temple here," Erynn said. "In Alyria. But I've never seen it."

"I've been to it a couple times, before I lost my sight. It's a beautiful place, but unfortunately neither site has been very well maintained."

"Did Naedra get along well with her other two sisters?" Adena asked. "Or was it just Sasha she had the problems with?"

Amara chuckled. "No, she didn't get along with Carys, either. In fact, probably less so. I heard she had some conflict with the Order — they're a group dedicated to protecting the Daughters — and I think she might have blamed Carys for that. But Tara adored her and I know Sasha was devastated when she left to go live with her in Galia. That was just a few months before Galia invaded."

Erynn's mouth dropped open. Her mother had adored Naedra? So much so that she had even left Tallon to go live with her in Galia? Now she really didn't understand. How could two sisters, who were once so close, possibly end up so far apart?

Amara entertained them with a few more stories, but Erynn barely heard a word. Too distracted now. And then it was time for bed and Adena was pulling back the couch to make room for them to lie down and Callie was fetching the blankets from one of the back rooms.

Adena said little as they curled up next to each other on the floor again and Callie and Amara headed off to their rooms. Erynn had been waiting all day for the chance to talk to her about Gareth and their earlier conversation — and to tell her what she had learned from Cathus — but she again found herself too tired, and now even more confused and depressed by what she had learned about her mother and Naedra to bring it up. And she had the sense Adena wasn't really wanting to talk about it, either. So she simply wished her friend a good night and rolled over onto her side, deciding she would definitely try and talk to her in the morning.

But the next morning she didn't get the chance.

Erynn woke to find the sky clear and the air warm and before she was even up, Callie had appeared and announced she was going to town. She asked Adena to help her load some pigs into the wagon and then she set off after breakfast, leaving a rather disappointed-looking Voltan behind and saying she'd be back by sunset.

Adena helped Amara with the dishes after she left, but was clearly tense and kept casting glances over at Erynn — who was still stuck on the couch, resting her foot. It wasn't until after the cottage was clean and Amara had gone out to the garden behind the cottage that they finally had a chance to talk. But now they had far more important things to discuss than Gareth and dragon's blood.

"What should we do?" Adena whispered. "Callie's bound to hear about us when she gets to town."

Erynn had been thinking about that all morning. She wasn't sure what Callie would do when she realized the two girls she'd left at home with her aunt were the same girls wanted for the king's murder, but she did know one thing: if they fled the cottage now, she was going to reinjure her foot. And she had finally decided that just wasn't something she could risk. She was going to listen to what her dragon's blood was telling her. She shook her head. "I can't leave, Adena. It hasn't been three days yet."

Her friend looked surprised. "We might not have a choice, Erynn. What if she brings Marik back with her?"

"It's a chance I'll have to take," Erynn said, even though she was aware that was a very real possibility and it scared her.

Adena opened her mouth to protest, but she seemed to read something in Erynn's eyes — or else heard it in her voice — because she stopped. She stared at her friend for a few seconds, and when she finally did speak, her voice was quiet. "You've changed your mind, haven't you?"

"If I leave now, I'll hurt my foot again. I'll never get there in time."

Adena closed her eyes, briefly raising her hands to her head before staring at her friend again. "Going to Blackwood is crazy, you know that, right?"

Erynn knew Adena wouldn't be happy with her decision, but she also knew it was the choice she had to make. "I don't want to end up like Amara, Adena. Regretting I didn't at least try. Lord Caden needs to pay for what he did. And so does Holden. And Marik. Warning Gareth about that banquet and getting him back here is the only way I can do that."

"But you don't even know if you can find Sheldon. Or that he has that falcon. And Amara didn't have someone chasing after her. Someone who wants to kill her." She moved closer, glancing over her shoulder at the back door as if she was worried Amara might return any second. "They have a couple more horses in the barn. Why don't we just take them? That way you can ride and we don't have to worry about your foot? We could get to South Crossing faster. And Brye."

"We can't do that. Even if we still had the king's gold to repay them. Besides, I know Sheldon has that falcon. And that we can find him. Don't ask me how, I just do."

"But it's dangerous, Erynn. The longer we stay in Alyria—"

"Lord Caden's going to follow me no matter where I go. Whether I'm here or in Brye. And I doubt he or Marik would expect me to go west right now."

"So we're just supposed to stay here? And hope Callie doesn't bring Marik back with her?"

Erynn knew that was exactly what she was suggesting. She gave a slight shrug. "She has been harboring fugitives. Feeding us hot meals and letting us sleep on her floor. Maybe she'll be too scared of what Marik might do to say a word."

Adena crossed her arms over her chest and sighed, still not looking persuaded.

"I can meet you in Brye," Erynn said. "Or down in South Crossing."

"You want to go alone?" Now Adena almost looked offended.

"I don't want you to get hurt because of me, Adena."

Adena was quiet again. Then finally she shook her head. "I said I wasn't leaving you to do this alone, and I meant it. If you really feel you have to go to Blackwood, then I'm coming with you."

Erynn couldn't believe she'd changed her mind. "You're

serious?"

"Of course I'm serious. But I still think it's a bad idea. And you can't make me like it. Or Gareth, for that matter. We just better hope you're right, and that Callie is too scared to tell anyone."

Just then, the back door opened and Amara stepped inside. She had a small basket full of tomatoes in one hand and was humming something to herself as she slowly made her way across the room.

Adena took one final look at Erynn and went to slip on her shoes. She told Amara she was going out to the barn to take care of Callie's chores, and when she was gone, Erynn sat back down on the couch.

She hoped with all of her heart that she wasn't making a mistake.

It was shortly after lunch, when Adena was helping Amara with the dishes, and Erynn had again returned to the couch, that Voltan suddenly leapt to his feet and ran to the door — barking loudly. A few seconds later, Erynn heard the horses.

She sat up, her heart pounding.

"That can't be Callie already," Amara said, turning toward the door with a slight frown on her face.

Erynn felt a sinking sensation in her gut. "That doesn't sound like a wagon."

Adena dropped what she was doing and ran to the window. A split second later she pulled the curtains shut and whirled around. "It's Marik. They're coming across the field."

CHAPTER 27

V oltan was barking at the door, wanting to be let outside.

"Marik?" Amara said, concern spreading across her face.

"Soldiers from the castle," Adena explained.

"Oh, I've heard of him. Callie's husband had a rather unpleasant encounter with him a few years ago."

Erynn was a little surprised at the sudden anger in the old woman's voice, but the thought disappeared as she hobbled over to the window and peered out through a crack in the curtain. She counted six men, including Marik, galloping across the field from the direction of the trees. Two split off from the others as she watched and headed for the barn. The others continued toward the cottage.

Amara set down the cloth she was using to dry the dishes and walked calmly toward the door. "Stay inside and keep quiet, girls. I'll handle him."

Erynn had a sudden flashback in her mind — of her father walking forward from the wagon to meet Lord Caden. She turned to the door, fear gripping her heart. "Wait, Amara —"

But it was too late. Amara grabbed hold of Voltan's collar and opened the door. A second later they were gone, the door closed shut behind them.

Erynn started after her, but Adena grabbed her arm.

"What are you doing?" she asked.

"We have to warn her," Erynn said. "She has no idea what she's walking into. Why they're even here."

"Erynn, we need to leave. Maybe she'll give us some time."

The words were like a stab to the heart, remembering how her father had once tried to do the very same thing. *"Run,"* he had said, as he stepped forward to meet the fair-haired soldier with the limp and the scars. *"Don't let them catch you, Erynn."*

As Adena went to grab their things, all Erynn could do was turn back to the window. Amara was slowly making her way out to the road that passed between the cottage and barn, still keeping a tight grip on Voltan. There was a very determined nature to the way she was holding herself — as if she wasn't afraid at all and knew exactly what she was doing. But it didn't make Erynn feel any better.

Adena was running around the cottage, muttering something to herself as she gathered up their cloaks and packs and stowed the extra blankets in one of the back rooms.

"Erynn," she said a few seconds later, her voice growing urgent. "I know you wanted to stay, but it's too late. We need to go. Now."

Erynn glanced around the cottage, trying to think. Trying to decide. Even looking for something she could maybe use as a weapon. Then her eyes landed on the trap door almost hidden in the floor near the kitchen table — and she listened to what she was hearing inside: a voice telling her to stay. "Throw everything in the cellar."

"The cellar?" Adena asked. "We can't hide there. What if they search the cottage?"

"Just do it, Adena."

Adena appeared about ready to drop Erynn's things and

high-tail it out the back door on her own, but then she set her jaw and went to the cellar. Seconds later she had lifted the door and tossed all of their things down the stairs.

Erynn caught a glimpse of the cool darkness down below the cottage — a space barely large enough for the two of them to hide — and a shiver ran down her spine. But she refused to let it scare her. If she could survive the caves of Galia, and the tunnel out of Caraden Castle, she could survive that root cellar, too.

The men slowed their horses as they reached the road. Marik looked tired, as if he'd slept in the same clothes for days, and was sporting a light growth of beard on his face. Erynn recognized the other soldiers from around the castle, but saw no sign of Quinn or any of his men.

Marik spurred his horse forward, until he was only a few feet from Amara, but the old woman just drew herself up taller and kept a firm hold on Voltan. The dog had not stopped barking. Erynn thought the noise might drive her insane.

"Who's there and what do you want?" Amara said, her voice so strong she almost growled. "I might be blind but I heard you lot coming a mile away."

Marik looked her over, appearing somewhat amused by her boldness, but at the same time not in the mood for games. "Marik Fayne, from Caraden. We're searching for two girls we believe might have passed this way. About sixteen years old. We tracked them into the woods out behind your barn. Have you heard of anyone like that in the area?"

Erynn watched Amara, barely able to breathe, but if the old woman was at all shocked or rattled by this news, she didn't show it.

"Someone slept in our barn a few nights back. We thought maybe it was the same thieves we had here last week. Stole two of our pigs. When I heard your horses I thought maybe you were them. But they didn't steal anything this time and seem to be long gone now."

Adena returned to the window, peering over Erynn's shoulder so she could see what was going on. "I still think we should leave, Erynn."

"Wait," Erynn said, finding it hard to hear what was going on over the sound of Voltan's barking. "I want to see what he does."

"What he does? Erynn, by then it could be too late."

At the back of her mind, Erynn knew her friend was right. But something inside her was also telling her to stay. To wait. And that she'd never save Gareth if she ran.

Marik eyed the cottage. "Who else lives here with you?"

"Just my niece," Amara said. "Her husband died a couple of years ago."

"Is she here?"

"She went to town."

"To Chapley?"

"Yes," Amara said, starting to sound annoyed at his questions. "She had a few pigs she wanted to sell at the market."

"When did she leave?"

"Sunrise," Amara said. "Did these girls do something wrong?"

Marik seemed surprised. "You aren't aware of the warrant for their arrest?"

"No. I don't go to town much anymore and my niece hasn't been in a couple weeks."

"They're wanted for the murder of the king."

This time, Amara flinched. She raised a slightly shaky hand to her face. "Murder? I hadn't even heard he died. You say two girls did this?"

Marik was about to respond, but then he turned and gazed west down the road. The rest of his soldiers all did the same, and even Amara turned her head. Voltan barked even louder.

Erynn wasn't able to see what they were looking at, but a few seconds later she heard it. A wagon was coming up the road — and fast. Not long after it came into view — two horses galloping towards the cottage, with Callie leaning forward on the wagon seat and looking very, very alarmed.

"That's not good," Adena whispered. "What's she doing back so soon?"

Erynn tensed. "Judging by the look on her face, I'd say she heard about the warrant."

Voltan was still barking. Amara scolded him and he finally sat down and was quiet.

Callie brought the wagon to a stop near the cottage and quickly applied the brake. Then she jumped down and went to her aunt.

"Amara?" she said. "Is everything all right?"

Amara reached for her niece's hand and even from the cottage Erynn could see the squeeze. "These men are from Caraden, dear. They're looking for two girls they think murdered the king. I told them we had guests in our barn the other night, but that they seem to be gone now."

Callie's eyes were wide. They went from her aunt to the cottage — and very briefly to the window — before returning to Marik and the other three soldiers.

"Go along with it, Callie," Adena whispered.

Erynn could hardly watch. She wondered if Adena was right — if they should have just fled as soon as they saw Marik and hoped that Amara could give them some time.

Callie nervously wiped a strand of hair from her face. "I – I saw a couple of girls as I drove into town this morning. It looked like they were trying to cross the Elks River."

Marik raised a brow. "What did they look like?"

"One was fair, the other dark-haired. But I only saw them briefly."

Marik's men exchanged glances, but he hadn't taken his eyes off Callie.

"And when was this?"

"Not long after sunrise. I thought maybe they were the ones who slept in our barn."

Marik studied both of the women carefully, as if he was trying to decide whether or not he believed them. Then his eyes shifted to the empty wagon. "Your aunt says you went into Chapley to sell pigs."

"I did," Callie replied. "A half-dozen."

"Why the rush coming home? Your horses look ready to drop."

For a moment, Callie seemed speechless. "I – I heard in town you were looking for those girls. I thought maybe they were the ones I saw and was concerned for my aunt. I wanted to make sure she was all right."

"If they were crossing the Elks it sounds like they were headed south. Away from here."

"My aunt's blind," Callie said. "And here all alone. I was concerned."

"Not entirely alone," one of the soldiers said with a bit of a chuckle. "Looks like she's got a pretty good dog to watch over her."

Callie glanced down at Voltan, and then briefly back at the cottage — and the window.

Marik narrowed his eyes. "Did you tell anyone in town what you saw?"

Callie hesitated, now looking even more uncomfortable. "No, sir. Honestly, all I could think of was my aunt. Getting back here."

Marik didn't seem pleased, but before he could say another word, the two soldiers who'd gone to search the barn rode toward him across the yard.

"Looks like someone might have slept in one of the empty stalls," one of the men said. "Probably went in there to get out of the rain." He paused and eyed the cottage — and the two women standing out front. "Want us to check inside?"

Marik gazed long and hard at the cottage. And the window.

Erynn felt her heart pounding in her chest. She knew the army commander couldn't see her through the crack in the curtains, but she stepped back anyway. Ready to bolt if he made the slightest motion to his men, but not entirely sure if it would be to the root cellar or out the back door.

An eternity seemed to pass before he finally spoke. "No. If they crossed the Elks this morning, we might still catch up with them by nightfall." He turned back to Callie. "If I had the time, I would leave a couple of my men behind and order them to go through your barn and select a suitable penalty for not reporting what you saw. So consider yourself lucky. And the next time a warrant is issued and you see someone that fits the description, I hope you will make the report."

Callie nodded her head, but she kept her eyes down — as if she was afraid Marik might see the truth in them: that she knew the two girls he was looking for weren't trying to cross the Elks River that morning and were very likely still inside the cottage. "Yes, sir."

Marik stared at both of them for several more seconds. Then he turned his horse west and rode off past the wagon and down the road — the rest of his men following along behind.

CHAPTER 28

For several long moments, neither of the women moved or said a word. Even Voltan was quiet. Then Amara let go of his collar and started back toward the cottage.

Adena went down to the cellar and fetched their things, depositing them next to the couch and closing the trap door by the time the old woman stepped inside.

Erynn felt horrible and hobbled back toward the couch. She opened her mouth to say something, to try to apologize for not telling them about the warrant, but Amara walked right past her, her face blank, and disappeared into her room. Erynn sat down and lowered her head to her hands, not thinking it was possible to feel any worse.

A second later the door opened and Callie stepped inside. She looked pale — and angry. Voltan trotted in behind her and went to lay by the hearth.

"It's not true," Erynn said, looking up. "We had nothing to do with the king's death."

Callie shut the door, not looking convinced. "They're saying you murdered him. I heard in town."

"Holden's just saying that so people will help him find us," Adena said. "So you'll turn us in." She walked back over to the window and peered outside, as if worried Marik might return.

"Why would he lie about something like that?"

Erynn sighed and ran her hands through her hair. She wished she could explain, but had a feeling it was probably better that they knew nothing. "It's a long story. Believe me, we wouldn't even be here if I could walk. The last thing we want to do is to get either of you in trouble."

"In trouble? Do you know what those soldiers would do to us if they found you here? If they knew we were helping you?"

"Yes, I do," Erynn said. "But we'll go. We'll leave now." She stood back up and reached for her cloak and pack. She didn't want to leave — she couldn't — but it was also quite clear they could not stay.

"We have to help them, Callie."

Everyone turned. Amara was standing in the doorway of her room, holding something in her hand — what appeared to be an object of some kind, wrapped up in an old green robe.

Callie looked stunned. "Help them? Aunt Amara, what are you talking about? Didn't you hear those men? They're wanted for murdering the king!"

"Loren is a Daughter of Maegan, Callie. That's why they're looking for her."

Erynn just about dropped her pack. "A Daughter?" She tried to laugh, but could tell it didn't come out very well. "What makes you think that?"

Amara smiled. "My dear, I recognized her in you the second you walked in the door. It was like Sasha herself had walked right in out of the rain and spoken to me again. From beyond the grave. It gave me goosebumps."

Erynn felt goosebumps rise up on her own arms. She sounded just like Sasha?

Callie looked uneasy. "Amara, what are you talking about?"

The old woman stepped further into the room. "I think she's the reason the Galians are here." She turned her head towards Erynn. "Aren't you?"

Erynn glanced over at Adena, desperate for some sort of guidance, but her friend just shrugged. And then she decided there wasn't much point in lying. At least not anymore. She sighed. "You're right. The Galians did come to Alyria for me and that's why Marik's looking for me now. My name's not Loren. It's Erynn. And this is my friend, Adena. We're not from Farglen. We're from Caraden. We used to work at the castle."

Callie's mouth dropped open. "You are a Daughter of Maegan?"

Erynn nodded. "The king told me a couple days after the Galians arrived. Told me to leave Alyria. Paddon brought me here when I was a baby and asked the king to take care of me. He chose a couple to raise me, but they're both dead now." She paused. "My mother's Tara."

"Tara?" Callie said. "Naedra's sister?"

"I think so," Erynn said. "Unless there's another Daughter out there with the same name. I didn't realize Naedra had other sisters until last night — which is why I looked so shocked. Apparently she's been searching for my mother for years."

Callie looked confused. "I – I don't understand."

"Neither do I," Erynn said. "Just that I'm in a lot of danger if they catch me." She glanced over at Amara and saw tears had appeared in the old woman's eyes.

"Your voice is so much like Sasha's," Amara said, a slight tremor in her voice. "When you walked in the door and I first heard you speak I thought for sure you were her lost child.

But then you said your age and I realized you couldn't be, although I was still sure it had to be the same family. Sweet Tara. I can't believe it."

Callie sank down in a chair at the table, still looking stunned.

Amara walked toward Erynn, her milky white eyes shifting down to the bundle in her hands. "I have something I need to give you. I've kept it all these years, not knowing what I was going to do with it. But now I know it's why you're here. How you managed to find your way to our barn. She wants me to give it to you."

Erynn felt a shiver, even though it was quite warm. "You mean Sasha?"

Amara ran a hand lightly over the bundle. "Yes. She gave this to me after we ran into the Galians, thinking it might be safer with me if we were captured. I've never understood why, but she said it was very valuable and that if anything happened to her, I was to make sure it was delivered to the Order — and preferably to Carys. She did not want Naedra to have it. I always meant to find Carys, but the years went by and I never did get around to it. Perhaps I was too scared after what happened to Branen. Then I lost my sight and couldn't. It's been a terrible weight on my mind for years." She held out the bundle to Erynn.

Erynn lowered her pack and reached out to take it. "What is it?"

"A book of some kind, only don't ask me who it once belonged to or what's written in it because I never did learn how to read and I've never shown it to anyone. Not even my husband. Or Callie."

Callie shook her head in disbelief. "I never knew you had that. I wish you had told me in case something happened to you."

"I always meant to, Callie."

Erynn felt strange holding something that had once belonged to the late Queen of Tallon. Something she had claimed was so valuable. She was curious to know what was written in the book and why Sasha had been so concerned about it — and didn't want Naedra to have it — but she was also a little nervous. She was in enough trouble as it was, with Marik and Lord Caden after her. The last thing she wanted to do was lose it. "If the Galians catch me …"

"You can't let them," Amara said, her voice firm.

"It's not as easy as it sounds. They already did once, but we managed to get away. And now my foot …"

"We should go," Adena said, returning to the couch to grab her things. "In case they do come back."

Erynn reached for her pack again and slipped the bundle inside.

"Wait," Amara said, concern on her face. "What about your foot, Erynn? If you leave, you're just going to injure it again. Cathus told you to rest it for three days."

"I don't have a choice," Erynn said. "I don't want either of you to get hurt."

"But where will you go? Surely they'll have soldiers watching for you at the bridges?"

Erynn glanced at Adena. "We're actually not going to Brye just yet."

"Not going to Brye?" Amara said. "But don't you need to leave Alyria? The longer you're here —"

"There's something we need to do first," Adena said. "Someone we need to find."

"If we can," Erynn said, not feeling quite as hopeful as she had before. Not if she had to leave.

"We can," Adena said. "We'll just be careful."

Amara turned to her niece. "We have to help them, Callie.

Can you take them in the wagon?"

Callie looked aghast at the suggestion. "Amara, do you have any idea —"

"She's a Daughter of Maegan," Amara said. "She has to survive."

Callie just shook her head. "It's too dangerous. They need to leave. Sore foot or not. I'm sorry for their trouble, I truly am, but I think we've helped them enough."

For a few seconds it was quiet, and then Adena let out the slightest gasp and a very uncomfortable look spread across her face.

"What?" Erynn asked.

"I just thought of something," Adena said. "Marik's going to be looking for some sign of us down by the Elks River. And when he doesn't find anything, he's going to suspect they lied."

Erynn sank back down on the couch.

Over at the table, Callie went white.

Adena didn't look like she wanted to go on. But she did. "And if he suspects they lied …"

"He'll be back," Erynn said, finishing her friend's thought. "Maybe not today, but tomorrow for sure."

Callie lowered her head to her hands, and Erynn could tell she was well aware of what this meant. Marik would be angry when he came back, and this time he wouldn't be threatening to seize livestock as punishment. He'd have the two women arrested. Or worse. So it wasn't just a matter of Erynn and Adena leaving the cottage and everything going back to normal. Callie and Amara were going to have to leave, too. Or risk facing Marik. She rubbed a hand over her face, realizing it was possible to feel even worse than she had a few minutes ago. These women had been kind enough to take her into their home and feed her, and in two short days she had completely destroyed their lives.

"Then we don't have much choice," Amara said. "We have to leave, and we might as well go together. Won't make much of a difference now anyway."

Adena looked at Erynn. "West is the last direction Marik would expect us to go. Maybe you're right. Maybe we could shake him off our trail."

Erynn didn't know what to say, and could barely bring herself to look at Callie and Amara.

For what seemed like a very, very long time, no one in the cottage said a word. Then Callie took a deep breath, wiped a hand slowly across her mouth, and nodded.

"Where is it you want to go?" she asked.

COLLEEN RUTTAN grew up in North Vancouver, BC, and currently resides with her husband in Chilliwack, BC. She spent several years studying engineering before finally graduating with a degree in physics from the University of British Columbia, and spent seven years as a criminal intelligence analyst for the Royal Canadian Mounted Police. She started developing the ideas for the Cael Stone Series in 2002, but it wasn't until 2012 that she published the first book, The Last Falcon.

For more information about Colleen, including updates on the release of the next exciting book in the Cael Stone Series, visit her website at www.colleenruttan.com. She can also be found on Twitter at @colleenruttan.

Made in the USA
Charleston, SC
29 September 2012